A romantic suspense by Lily White

LILY WHITE
BESTSELLING AUTHOR

If you are interested in reading additional books by Lily White or would like to know when new books are being released, Lily White can be found on:
Facebook, Instagram and
Twitter

Join the Mailing List!
If you are interested in receiving email updates regarding additional books by Lily White or would like to know when new books are announced or being released, join the mailing list via this link.

http://eepurl.com/Onoeb

Join the Facebook Fan Group!
If you are interested in receiving exclusive previews for upcoming novels, or to participate in giveaways, join the fan group for Lily White Books.
FAN GROUP LINK

Follow Lily on BookBub!
https://www.bookbub.com/profile/lily-white

Author Note and Disclaimer:

This book is intended for entertainment purposes solely. This novel discusses sensitive subject matters. Readers who are sensitive to triggers are advised to proceed with caution.

OTHER BOOKS BY LILY WHITE

MASTERS SERIES:

Her Master's Courtesan
(Book 1 of the Masters Series)
(Available on Smashwords and lilywhitebooks.com)

Her Master's Teacher
(Book 2 of the Masters Series)

Her Master's Christmas
(Novella in the Masters Series)

Her Master's Redemption
(Book 3 of the Masters Series)

Her Master's Reckoning
(Book 4 of the Masters Series)

STANDALONE NOVELS:

Target This

Hard Roads

Asylum

Wake to Dream

Four Crows

Crazy Madly Deeply

Rules of Engagement

Wishing Well

The Five

ILLUSIONS DUET

Illusions of Evil
(Book 1 of the Illusions Duet)

Fear the Wicked
(Book 2 of the Illusions Duet)

DARK EXCLUSIVE - Available only on LilyWhiteBooks.com:

The Director

Table of Contents

CHAPTER ONE

She was barely a woman. A girl with soft brown hair, tangled and long. The ends dusted the small of her back when she turned to look at the camera. Nervous, obviously, she wasn't quite sure what to do with her hands. They fluttered over her lap, her fingers moving as if playing a piano before she lifted them to the table. They fluttered there as well. Constantly moving. It was the first thing I noticed about her.

"This tape is roughly four hours long. The investigator wasn't able to get much out of her. I think - well, he thought and I agreed that there's something off about her."

Without taking my eyes off the screen, I thumbed the myriad of reports and photographs in the brown file folder Detective Grenshaw handed me several minutes prior. Evidence bags were strewn across the table, a war room staged for the investigation of a party gone horribly wrong. I hadn't yet reviewed the materials or asked for many details. It was too important to take an unbiased look at my subject first.

"Pretty thing, isn't she? You don't see many girls like that in Clayton Heights."

Grenshaw was your typical television cop. Deep, gritty voice, observant eyes - a man hardened by years spent working murder cases in a small town a half-hour south of Chicago proper. The first feature I noticed about him was a brown suit that looked cheap, something you would find left dusty on a bargain rack

1

in a strip mall thrift store. I wouldn't have been surprised if sleeping in the damn thing had put the wrinkles in his jacket, but I wouldn't hold it against him.

Life for homicide detectives wasn't easy when gun violence was on the rise and more than forty percent of your cases sat unsolved. Clayton Heights. I knew of the neighborhood's existence only because it was one of those areas you never visited on purpose, and if you ever found yourself there after taking a wrong turn, you never stopped for red lights. *Just keep driving. A ticket is better than being carjacked or mugged.*

I agreed with his assessment of the woman on the screen. She was far too delicate to be living in such a dangerous place. Her features were small, eyes uncertain. If anything, she screamed *Victim.* "How do you think she survived living in such a place?"

"Your guess is as good as mine, but if I had to guess based on her toxicology reports-"

Lifting a hand, "No, don't tell me. I want to watch this first interview blind. It'll be better for me to put my finger on what you and the other investigator consider as 'off' about her."

His leather belt creaked beneath a gut that had seen far too many late night pizzas, sugar loaded coffees and cellophane wrapped pastries while sitting hunched over a desk. I didn't envy him for his career choice. Staring at death day in and day out tended to wear on a person's quality of life.

"Like I said: the tape's about four hours long. I was there when it was recorded, so it's no use to me to watch it again. I'll let you do your thing, and you can get with me in my office before heading to Ms. Day's house. Sound good?"

2

Without looking at him, I waved him off, my interest stolen by the girl's behavior when the investigators finally entered the room. Frightened more than defensive, she tapped the fingers of her right hand over a mark just beneath the inside of her left elbow. A habit more than intentional, that touch. Squinting my eyes, I couldn't quite make out the mark. Noting it on a yellow pad, I relaxed in my seat, crossed a leg over a knee and clicked the end of my pen.

"Ms. Day," the investigator started, his suit jacket off, shirtsleeves rolled up to the elbows, collar unbuttoned. The time stamp on the tape read two thirty five in the morning. Given the late hour, I wasn't surprised he appeared casual. "My name is Leonard Drake, and you've already met my partner, Timothy Grenshaw. We'd like to ask you a few questions regarding the party where your four friends were killed."

One blink, long lashes fluttering much like her hands. Her lashes were a dark brown fan over her pale, almost translucent, skin. She had a smudge of red bruising around the orbital of her eye and over her cheekbone. It would turn a darker color as the days marched forward.

One blink, and one blink only, after the verbal reminder that four of her friends were now dead.

It was as if she didn't understand, either shock or guilt rendering the interview unbelievable. *Give me something, Ms. Day. How were all your friends brutalized, and yet you lived to tell the tale?*

"What would you like to know?"

My brows lifted with surprise at the sound of her voice, deep and husky, the kind of voice you would expect from a woman working a sex line. But this girl

3

wasn't a desperate single mother balancing an infant on her hip while telling the caller to *give it to her good*. No, Rainey Day's voice was all natural, full lips parting on words spoken with a hint of fear splashed over a toxic mixture of nervousness and concern. I'd expected something higher pitched, more desperate to be noticed.

I wasn't paying much attention to the questions being asked nor the answers she gave. We would go over the material again when I interviewed her in person, my thoughts unpolluted by the information being pulled from her now.

What stole my attention was her mannerism when faced by two bullheaded officers in a room full of mirrors. Not once did she glance at her own reflection. I noted it. Most people can't help but look at themselves from time to time. It meant she was comfortable in her skin, unworried about whether a hair was out of place or if makeup was smeared across her cheek. Not that she was wearing makeup. This interview was conducted after she'd been released from the hospital.

Pausing the tape, I opened the folder on the table and pushed the reports aside to review the scene photographs. They were what you would expect to see when hearing four people were bludgeoned to death. Blood splatter on walls. Pools of it on the floor.

One person was found on the couch, the girl's face crushed in while her body was mostly left untouched. Another body on the opposite side of the living room was a heavyset male with what my grandmother would have called *bruiser shoulders*, guessing him to be of old Irish stock. He had to weigh at least seventy pounds more than Ms. Day. The back of his head took the most damage, skull crushed in, brain matter exposed. How would a girl her size have subdued him?

Pushing play on the video, I watched her movement. She had pain on her left side, obvious from the way she winced when leaning in that direction. A bandage covered the forearm of her right arm, another one on her shin. Her bottom lip was swollen from a split on the right hand side, another bruise blooming along her jawline. She didn't escape injury from what I could see.

Glancing at the police report, I read that she was found unconscious and bound to a bed in a first floor bedroom, bleeding from a gash on the back of her head. That explained the significant matting I noted in her hair.

The last photograph was of two people found in an upstairs bedroom, naked. The male was found with his head crushed in on the bed, the female found slumped against a wall, her face, like the girl downstairs, had been the area that took the most damage.

Interesting. I turned the tape off. What was 'off' about the girl being interviewed was a lack of common sense or intelligence. She was slow in her affect; seemingly dim-witted I would guess, but somehow keenly aware of her surroundings.

What I found most fascinating was that she didn't seem to care about the demise of her friends, but again, that could be explained away as shock from having lived through an attack.

Speaking to her in her own environment was the best approach. She would be more relaxed, would have had more time to digest her recollection of the event.

I gathered the materials together, popped the video from the disc player and walked to Grenshaw's office to report.

"Well," he yanked his legs from atop his desk, his wooden chair screeching over old springs. He pulled off wire-rimmed glasses that were too small for his face and tossed them where his legs had been. "What did you think of our girl?"

"Off is an accurate description, but murderer *off*, I'm not sure." I was in a hurry to get to her house for our first meeting and chose to lean a shoulder against his doorframe rather than walk in to take a seat. "How would a girl as small as her overpower four people? Especially two men. The one downstairs-"

"Michael Higgins," he filled me in.

"Michael then, how would she have taken him down without alerting the other people? He must have yelled."

Nostrils flared, Grenshaw sucked in a deep breath, shaking his head. "I have no fucking clue." He rubbed at the bridge of his nose, his movements exhausted. "I'm not sure that she had anything to do with it. We're only interested in excluding her entirely. Finding out exactly what she knows. She gave us nothing in that interview."

"Which could be a result of shock."

His brows shot up. "Very well could be. That's why you've been called in to talk with her."

Nodding, I checked my watch. "I have twenty minutes to get to her house."

"Keep me updated."

"Will do."

Waving as I walked off, I was more than ready to sit down and have a long talk with Ms. Rainey Day, an admittedly beautiful girl who'd not only survived five years in Clayton Heights, but also the scene of a rampage style murder.

. . .

Driving through Clayton Heights, I slowed my speed, paying special attention to the kids running barefoot down the streets, their clothes dirty, their skin shimmering with sweat. It was a hazy summer day, the sun beaming down when the clouds broke just right. Dreary and hot, the kind of heat that forced people outside to sit on their stoops because their window unit air conditioning couldn't keep up.

The street was a mix of run down stores and run down houses, chain link fences surrounding the latter, while the former had small cement parking lots with islands of green where the weeds had broken through the pavement. It was an interesting mix of commercial and residential, as if the county's concern for zoning stopped at the border to the neighborhood.

These people were accustomed to living next to the establishments they patronized, a group of older women glaring with age weathered faces and cataract hazed eyes at a drug deal occurring on the corner. Not only had zoning forgotten this place, but also the police. Men stood out in the open exchanging a small baggy for a roll of bills, uncaring that they could be seen.

Thankful I'd rented a car rather than bring my own, I didn't have to be concerned about discovering my tires were stolen when I walked outside to go home following the first interview. I'd just rent another car if I had to.

Rainey's house was deeper in the neighborhood, a tiny clapboard number that had once been painted a bright white but now had streaks of brown where the

7

paint had been. I pulled into the dirt driveway to notice that the lot next door was nothing but weeds and a foundation where a house used to stand, burnt wood littering the ground that had been abandoned when the rest of the structure was carted away.

Anything could have brought it down: a meth lab, or space heater, a careless smoker falling asleep. Judging by the scorched circle surrounding the cement block foundation, the fire had been recent.

A dog barked in the distance as I walked the short distance to her porch, the door opening before I had time to knock. Rainey Day glanced up at me with blue eyes that were absolutely stunning in their clarity. The type of eyes that make a person do a double take, wide and shimmering with the sunlight that bathed them.

"You must be Justin- I'm sorry," she corrected, shaking her head, "I'm mean Mr. Redding. That's the polite way to speak to superiors, right?"

There was no way in hell this girl was a murderer. Not with a demeanor so subservient. The question was: how in the hell did she survive? "I'm not exactly your superior as I'm not employing you or grading your work."

Giving her my professional smile, I offered a hand in greeting. "And Justin is fine. Mr. Redding is my father."

She returned my smile and took my hand, her palm warmer than I'd expected, her fingers fragile. Squeeze too tight and you ran the risk of crushing her bones with minimal pressure. Delicate. There was no other word for her.

"You should come in," she waved her hand out in front of her. "The neighbors are already watching. They're nosy fucks who hate strangers."

Bending right (she was still favoring her left side in accordance with what I saw on the video), Rainey gave a pointed look at my car before straightening to peek up at me. "And around here, you are definitely strange. Don't feel bad when you're always being watched in this place. Morning, noon and night."

Twisting in place, I studied the new model four door sedan I'd rented, white with nothing flashy. It didn't have GPS or satellite radio. Standard features only type of rental. "It's nothing out of the ordinary." Our eyes met and she grinned.

"If it's not a motorcycle or a clunker billowing smoke out the back, then it's out of place around here. Come on in." She moved in front of me, swiping clutter from table surfaces only to toss it onto a side chair, not so much cleaning as rearranging. I made her nervous.

Taking a moment to study her, I noted her small stature. Not short, more average height, but while she was tiny in bone structure, she wasn't extremely skinny. She had curves. Her skin was without marks beyond her injuries from the party and whatever was beneath her left elbow. I still couldn't quite make it out.

Her hips swung when she moved, and she wore a pair of cut off jean shorts, the bottoms of her butt cheeks visible, with a shirt that - yes, my first assessment was accurate - was thin enough to showcase her lack of a bra.

Rainey Day, it appeared, was not shy of her body at all. Not that she should be. There was an appeal to her, something raw, primal, and carnal. She was the type of girl men would want without knowing why. A siren, her presence so natural and unapologetic that it brought one purpose to mind.

"So, are you another detective?" In person, her voice was even huskier, a hypnotic sound that made you want to listen to anything she had to say. Thankfully, I was in the business of listening.

"No, I'm a victim advocate."

She led me into a small sitting room, took a seat on the couch and directed me to sit in a chair opposite her.

Holding up a pack of cigarettes, "I hope you don't mind?" I shook my head and she lit one, the smoke blowing over her lips as she tilted her eyes up to study the ceiling. "Advocate, that's a fancy word."

"It just means I'm on your side. I'm a psychologist, and you've been through a harrowing experience from what I'm told."

Her laughter was as thick as her voice, full and unguarded. "You'll have to talk with smaller words to me, Doc. I'm not as smart as I look."

Rainey didn't exactly look like a rocket scientist. She looked like a helpless girl. "How long have you been living in Clayton Heights?"

"Five years," another billow of smoke. She ashed the cigarette in a cup on a side table next to her.

"And how old are you?"

Her brow lifted, head angling toward the folder in my lap. "Don't you have all my information in there?"

"I'd like to hear it from you." I needed to know everything from her. This girl held all the clues as to what happened in that house when her friends died.

A shrug of her shoulder. "I'm twenty-two."

Which meant she'd moved here at seventeen. Such a young age for such a rough area of town. "What happened the night your friends died?"

Rainey had given me one truth, had opened herself up that much. I changed the subject quickly with the hope she'd remain open. Instead, she shut down, her head bowing, her lips closing over the tip of the cigarette as she dragged the smoke into her lungs. It practically walked over her lips when she answered, "I'm not sure."

Sighing, I tapped my finger against the folder. "Not sure as in you don't remember, or-"

"Not sure as in it's all a mess in my head. I have bits and pieces of that night, a damn mess, you know?" She fluttered her hand. An unconscious habit. "It's scattered."

It was my job to keep her focused. "No, I don't know Ms. Day-"

"Rainey. Ms. Day was my mother."

Smiling at the reach for a connection, at her attempt to create a joke between 'friends', I nodded. "Rainey. I don't know. You know. And I need you to tell me."

"It's a long story. I don't even know where to start."

A bead of sweat slid down her neck from her hairline to pool in the hollow of her throat. It drew the eye lower, my gaze wandering to places that were unprofessional. Flicking my eyes up, I caught her stare, she knew. Her eyes softened, her lips pulling apart on a ghost of a smile. I cleared my throat, embarrassed for having been caught.

This woman would be a handful for any man. Perhaps I'd been wrong to immediately assume she was a victim. I wondered if the detectives had the same problem, if they'd called me in because they couldn't keep their attention from wandering to forbidden places. She blew out a puff of smoke, a small ring floating up to the ceiling above her.

"The beginning is a good place," I prodded, my voice gritty. "How did you end up at the party? How long did you know your friends?"

She was shutting down more, her body curling over itself. Abandoning the cigarette into the cup, Rainey refused to meet my eyes. "I'm not sure they were my friends."

Rather than filling in the empty space, I stayed quiet, allowing her to process her thoughts. A cryptic smile curled her lips when she glanced up at me again. "The beginning was the day I moved into the neighborhood with my mom. It all started then, I think."

"Where's your mom now?"

"Dead," she answered without a flicker of remorse.

"You have a lot of dead people around you, Rainey."

"We all die, just some of us sooner than others."

The statement was odd, and I wanted to explore it. It would have to wait. For now, I was willing to take whatever she would give me. Movement caught my eye; she was touching the mark beneath her elbow again.

Her fingers moved over it, and I had a clear view of five tally marks as if she was counting something.

Why five? What was so important she would carve the count into her skin? "Then let's start there."

Another smile. "I should warn you, Doc, I'm a bit of a slut. This story-" Her eyes closed, opened. "This story doesn't paint me in a pretty light. Not like all of the good girls I assume you're used to dating."

Despite the condemnation, she wasn't upset to make the confession. It was a simple statement as a prelude to her tale.

"I'm not here to judge you, Rainey. Just tell me what happened."

Lighting another cigarette, she drew in a deep drag then blew it out, her gaze distant as she began to talk.

CHAPTER TWO

A new start, a new Day.

That's what mom always said when it was time to pick up and leave. What she had told me since I was a little girl, crying to leave another home, another decorated bedroom, another school where I'd finally made friends. Mom had a problem with staying in one place, and it usually revolved around her inability to keep a job or a boyfriend.

This move was because of a man. They'd been together for several months, long for her, but like the others, he packed up and took off, his time with her done, his attention focused on something better.

It wasn't that my mom wasn't a pretty woman. She was. A little too pretty, which is why she went through so many men. She had her issues though, the type of issues that would draw a man in, at first mistaking those issues for fire, but then send him running when he understood it was a fire that was never snuffed out.

A frenzy of a woman, mom could go off the rails over nothing: an out of place towel, a pot hung on the wrong hook, a pair of shoes left in the center of the room instead of neatly lined by the door. Mom demanded the house be organized exactly as she wanted it. One mistake and that fire of hers could burn the skin. It sent the men running every time.

Not that I minded much. Although some of her boyfriends had been nice, there were others I hated.

We rolled into Clayton Heights in her antique station wagon, a clunker of a car she refused to call old, even if that's the truth of what it was. *Antique* like it was fancy,

14

like it wasn't a pathetic bygone of some other decade that was better left to a junkyard than driven on the road. The car sputtered and wheezed as we pulled into a dirt driveway in front of a small house, chain link fencing everywhere to divide the separate yards.

I glanced to my right as soon as we pulled up and noticed a man kneeling next to a motorcycle, sweat gleaming on his bare shoulders as he turned a wrench. The chrome of the bike shimmered beneath the bright sun, a fishing lure grabbing my attention.

Like mom, I had a way with men. Always had, but whether that was a good thing was anybody's guess. Certainly not when I was too young to understand what sex was all about.

"What do you think, Rainey? This looks like a good home, doesn't it? It's bigger than the apartment we just left."

It was a house. Not much more could be said about it, four walls and a roof that may or may not leak. Window AC units poked out from windows on either side of the building, old and rusted. There was no telling what you'd breathe in after turning them on. "Looks nice, mom."

"We'll clean it up, make the yard look nice and all. Make it our home, you know? One we'll stay in for a while." She said that with every new place. *We'll make it our home.* What she failed to add was *until we up and leave again following the next disaster.*

The door squeaked loudly as I climbed from the car, the man fixing his bike twisting to glance over his shoulder. Handsome, definitely older, probably my mom's age. Sure as hell didn't stop him though. His eyes ran up my bare legs like hands exploring the skin

15

and muscle, appreciation glimmering in his gaze as he dragged it up higher.

As hot as it was, I was only wearing a pair of cut off jean shorts and a halter-top that covered my tits but left my stomach bare. Our eyes met, and he nodded his head in a silent hello. Smiling, I turned to walk to the back of the car to help mom with the bags and boxes.

"The place came furnished, so that's a good thing. Should make it easy to settle in nice and quick."

She was oblivious to the neighbors standing around watching us. The man next door, a group of people on the opposite sidewalk. They were assessing us, getting a good look at who had moved into their grungy area of town. I didn't mind the attention. I was used to it. Lugging a garbage bag filled with clothes from the back of the station wagon, I followed mom up a short path to a cement porch with two cracked stairs. The yard was weeds more than grass, tall in some places closer to the fence.

Mom opened the door releasing a musty scent from inside, her hand waving in front of her nose. Dust motes hung heavy in the dappled sunlight bleeding in from curtains pulled in front of the windows. Mom paused, scanned her blue eyes over the interior and shrugged.

"It'll take a little elbow grease to clean it up, but I think this will do us some good." She turned, her eyes level with mine. "I'll need some of your help, Rainey. Work starts tonight, so while you're home alone you can sweep up, maybe scrub down the kitchen and bathroom before going to bed."

"Whatever you need," I answered, stepping deeper into the small living room. A couch and a few tables were covered with off-white sheets. "Do I have my own room, or are we sharing again?"

"Your own." She was proud to say it, as if separate bedrooms were a luxury she could finally afford. We'd had them before in some of the places we'd lived, but not all.

Our last apartment was an efficiency with kitchen, bedroom and bathroom all in one. We'd hung sheets to make it appear there were walls. I hated that place, especially when mom had her boyfriend over. He liked to turn his head and watch me when they thought I was sleeping and they were -

"This will definitely do. I'm so excited. Aren't you?"

Nodding, I glanced around, saw two doors down a short hallway. "Am I left or right?"

"Right. The bathroom is at the end of the hall between our two rooms. Only one, so we'll share that."

Opening the door, I moved into a small bedroom with nothing more than a thin mattress on a twin bed and a folding door closet, one hanger dangling on the bar.

The garbage bag of clothes thumped against the floor where I dropped it, a dusting of dirt floating up like low lying fog around my legs.

Crossing the room, I pulled the curtain aside to look out the window. There was another man in the neighbor's driveway now. He leaned against the side of the house smoking a cigarette watching the one still working on the bike. With messy brown hair, no shirt and a pair of jeans that hung low on his hips, he looked younger than the first.

The curtain fell back in place, and I ran out to help mom with more bags and boxes, the two men watching me walk between the house and car. Mom didn't notice them, she was too busy nesting in her head, dreaming of all the ways she would clean the house so it didn't look like the shithole it really was.

After clearing out the car, we locked ourselves inside, mom moving about pulling the sheets from the furniture. She wasn't the type to wait a few hours before settling in.

"I have to be at work at five tonight, Rainey. I'll get as much done as I can before leaving. Why don't you go put some sheets on your bed and get your room all nice? Hang up your clothes and such."

Five rolled around quickly, my mom waving goodbye as she pulled out of the driveway. I glanced at the neighbor's house again to see both men had gone inside.

Following their lead, I retreated into my new house, spent an hour unpacking boxes. After a while, I grabbed my pack of cigarettes and sat on the front porch to watch the sun roll down over the horizon.

Movement caught my eye, and I turned to see a new guy standing in front of the neighbor's house. *How many people did they have in there?*

He must have noticed me watching. Raising a hand, he called out, "You the new people living next door?"

I nodded, blew out a puff of smoke and watched him run around the end of the chain link fence to walk across my yard toward me. He was good looking with a fresh face and blue eyes, his brown hair a mess framing his head. Wearing baggy jeans and a white t-shirt, he strolled up to offer his hand. "The name's Rowan Connors."

Shaking his hand, I grinned. "Rainey Day."

He winced. "Ouch, no offense, but your name -"

18

My laughter cut off his comment. "I know. My mom is kind of an asshole. My full name is Rainey Summer Day."

Another wince, and he grinned. "That's even worse."

"Like I said, she's an asshole."

Sitting on the stoop next to me, he asked, "How old are you?"

"Seventeen, almost eighteen," I held the cigarette pack out to him. "Want one?"

He took it, tapped a smoke into his hand and used my lighter to start it. Smoke poured over his lips. "I'm fifteen."

Too young for me, but I'd already figured that out after he stepped closer. His shoulders weren't quite filled out, his chest scrawny, but his frame hinted to a bigger man waiting to develop. "How many people live in your house? I saw two other guys earlier."

Casting a quick glance at his house, he settled back on his arms, long legs stretching out in front of him. "Five. My dad, me and my three older brothers."

In the distance, the sun was ribboning the sky with a flash of color. Red, gold and pink kissing the day goodbye. "All of you in that small house?"

"We each have our own room. It looks small on the outside, but it's actually one of the bigger houses in this neighborhood. If we didn't each have our own space, we'd probably beat the crap out of each other."

Laughter rolled over my lips. "That's understandable." I canted my head, looking at him. "So, what do you all do to pass the time?"

A door slammed to our left, one of the guys I'd seen earlier stepping out to look around. Rowan's posture withered, his attempt to appear older snuffed out by

19

the presence of the other man. With a low voice he told me, "That's one of my brothers. The oldest."

As if he'd heard the comment, the man looked over, his brows shooting up his forehead to see Rowan sitting by my side. He made his way over, and I was able to get a better look at him.

Broad shoulders stretched a black t-shirt, full biceps challenging short sleeves. That was more like it, someone older who looked a lot like the kid beside me but had grown into his body. A jerk of his head in hello as he stepped up. He didn't offer his hand like Rowan had. "Who's this?"

I offered mine instead, "Rainey. And you are?"

Taking my hand, he pulled me up from the step, Rowan left forgotten behind me. Poor kid. I knew in that instant he was most likely an afterthought to his brothers, but then that's what happened when you're the youngest. He didn't say a word when his brother placed a hand at the small of my back and tugged me closer. "Jacob."

Rowan grew a pair just then. "We were hanging out, Jacob, so maybe you should go back -"

Leaning to look around me, Jacob shot his brother a look that shut him up. "Maybe you should go back and let the adults talk, kiddo."

I felt bad for Rowan, but knew he'd need to learn to throw his own punches. In truth, I didn't mind if he walked off. His brother was a hell of a lot more interesting.

"She's seventeen," Rowan argued.

"Almost eighteen," I added, "a month or two and I will be."

Jacob grinned, only one side of his pretty mouth pulling up. Damn if he wasn't gorgeous. He had brown eyes with flecks of gold, a rugged jaw with a dusting of shadow and straight white teeth beneath full lips. "I mean it, Rowan, get lost."

The kid pushed up from the stoop to storm off, his body retreating as Jacob's hand slid lower. "You party?"

My eyes slipped up to meet his. "Been known to. What do you have for me?"

Damn, that grin was everything my mom warned me to watch out for, so many promises lingering within it. "Whatever you need, but for starters, we have beer."

My voice dropped to a whisper. "Sounds good to me."

He squeezed my ass then dropped his hand to hold mine. I felt tiny in comparison to him, fragile. It was a good feeling.

Led over the yard and around the fence, I stepped up the porch stairs behind him and crossed it into the open front door of his house. Rowan hadn't been lying, it really was much bigger than where I lived.

To our left, a living room opened up, Rowan sitting on the couch and a guy I didn't recognize perched in a recliner, his feet kicked up and a joint hanging from his lips. He turned to look at us just as Jacob said, "You know Rowan, and that's my brother Frankie."

Frankie tipped his chin in my direction, his eyes quickly scanning me up and down. A cat's smile slowly stretched his lips, his shoulders rounding back against his chair.

He didn't say anything as we walked past, turned a corner and into a kitchen that was twice the size of mine. Glass clinked as Jacob grabbed me a beer from inside the fridge.

Popping the top, he handed it to me before caging me in with his arms against the counter. I took a sip of my beer, swallowing it while staring blatantly at his lips.

"Beer all you got?"

Another few times of seeing it and I knew I'd fall in love with that grin. Pure poison, an expression that whispered in your ear with a million dirty thoughts.

"I have other stuff to keep you occupied, but it will cost you."

Dragging my gaze up from his mouth, I met his eyes. "I don't have any money. Hate to admit it, but I'm always broke."

His fingers splayed over the back of my neck. "Then it's a good thing for you I take other forms of payment."

Jacob moved fast, but I didn't think he was serious. Teasing him, I asked, "Will you respect me in the morning?"

He laughed, his chest vibrating against mine. Pushing away from me just enough to look my body up and down, he answered, "I don't think you're the type to care."

Rowan walked into the kitchen, and Jacobs's head shot up.

"Get the fuck out of here, prick. You don't have anything this girl wants." He grabbed a bowl from the counter beside me and arrowed it at his brother, Rowan ducking out of the room just in time, the bowl smashing into pieces against the wall.

Muttering beneath his breath, "Fucking kid. The only way to get anything through his head is to beat the shit out of him."

I felt sorry for Rowan just then. Nobody wants to live in a house where you're the weakest. Guys like Jacob would eat him alive. Jacob grabbed my hand again, pulled me from the counter and out of the kitchen into hallway. He led me into a bedroom and closed the door. "I'll roll us a joint, but like I said, it'll cost you."

My bravery bled out in that moment. In truth, I played a good game, but normally never had to follow through. Not initially, at least.

Breaking up some weed on the top of a bureau, Jacob snatched a rolling paper from a pack. "I'm not joking, Rainey. If you want this, you'll have to work for it."

I clutched the beer to my chest, the cold bottle like ice against my skin. "What do you want me to do?"

"Strip or go home." He rolled the joint and licked the paper to close it. Turning, he leaned against the bureau and lit the tip. His eyes never left mine as he took a drag, one brow arching above his eye.

The scent hit me, and I craved the high. Living this life sober was like torture. At least with drugs, you had moments when you could pretend everything would be all right. I would give in to him even though I'd hoped he was kidding. I always gave in.

"Can we at least go to my house? There's nobody home."

He took another drag, blew it directly at me. "Why would we need to do that? There's nobody in this room besides you and me."

From beyond the door, I could hear the television, several deep voices rising up to compete against whatever movie they were watching. Jacob flicked his eyes to the door, back to me.

"If you're worried about them, they won't care." He stepped toward me, and I backed up. Damn, I wanted that joint so badly I could taste it.

"They won't know?" I glanced up at him, my voice unsure. He shrugged in response.

"Take off your shirt, if you can call it that. Looks to me like a scrap of cloth tied to you."

I felt cornered, out of control, but I'd gotten myself into this mess, and all I wanted was to get high. Refusing to meet his eyes, I set my beer down on a small table beside me, reached behind my back to untie the first string, reached up to my neck to untie the second. The halter-top fell silently to the floor at my feet.

"Oh, fuck yes, Rainey. You are stacked, aren't you?" Jacob's hand cupped one of my breasts as he handed me the joint. "You get one long drag for this."

I sucked in the first drag as his thumb brushed over my nipple.

Leaning down, he pressed his mouth to my ear. "You're making me hard. Touch me, and I'll let you take another drag."

Blowing out the first one that I'd held as long as I could in my lungs, my eyes closed to feel the instant relief of its effects. Jacob was kneading my breasts against his palms, pushing them together to rub his thumbs down the center crease. He didn't waste any time.

Plucking the joint from my hand, he laughed when I tried to reach for it, danced back a step to keep me just out of reach. His head tilted to the side. "You know what I want."

I did. It was the same thing every man wanted when they looked at me. Shame flooded my cheeks, but I

24

unfastened the button of my shorts and let them fall to my feet so I could kick them off.

In nothing but a thong, I glanced up at him. He stepped toward me and handed me the joint before grabbing my shoulders to turn me around. Slapping my butt cheek, he whistled.

"Damn baby, it jiggles just right. This body of yours is insane."

The joint crinkled as I breathed in another lungful, the cherry lighting up. Jacob pushed my hair away from my neck, his mouth running along my neck as both hands cupped my ass, his thumbs tucking beneath the sides of my panties, "Is this okay?" He tugged them down after I nodded, happy that he couldn't see my face. Not even twenty-four hours in the neighborhood and already I was the easy slut.

My panties hit the floor, his fingers exploring between my legs. "Keep smoking that while I take care of everything. Be good, and I'll send you home with your own when I finish. Sound good?"

I nodded, smoke pouring over my lips.

His body pressed against mine, his hands reaching around to play with my breasts some more.

"Say it out loud, Rainey. I need to hear you say it."

My eyes clenched shut. "Yes. It's fine."

He turned me around and dipped his head to lick one of my nipples. "Then take off my pants."

Before I could stop him, he plucked the joint from my fingers, freeing my hands. Jacob's brown eyes met mine when he took a long drag.

I'm already this far I kept telling myself while fumbling with his belt. Eventually I managed to unfasten everything, and his pants fell to the floor. He

25

kept his stare locked to mine. "You can touch me if you want."

Wrapping a shaky hand around him, I watched his head fall back, his lips parting to breathe out a billow of smoke. Jacob handed me the joint and took over.

Lifted off my feet so that my legs could wrap around his hips, he didn't bother with preparing me, but then, this was only about him, payment for what he had that I wanted and needed.

The wall was rough against my back, his hips dancing as I turned my head to smoke the joint down to my fingers. By the time I was finishing my joint, so was he, a steady thump thump thump as my butt hit the wall behind me. He never even kissed me, not once.

Growling deeply to climax, he pulled out in time to finish on my stomach, dropped me down to my feet, lifted his pants up enough to walk and crossed the room. Jacob snatched a towel from the floor, cleaning himself off before tossing it in my direction.

"Get dressed," he said without bothering to look at me. "I'll roll you up another one so you can go home."

I felt pure shame as I pulled my clothes on, waiting silently as he finished rolling another joint before handing it over. He opened the door to his room to see me out and slapped my ass as I passed him.

When we walked through the living room, Frankie laughed and howled while Rowan glared at me from his seat on the couch.

Their father must have come home while we were back in the room. He just shook his head, chuckled and murmured something under his breath before walking away.

I opened the front door and glanced back. Jacob smiled. "Any time you need something, Rainey, you let me know."

The door slammed shut behind me as I stumbled away into the night to head home. *What the hell just happened?*

After smoking the second joint, I finished cleaning the house and unpacking the kitchen. Tears soaked my pillow that night, cool against my cheek when I fell asleep.

CHAPTER THREE

Justin - Present

The memory was interesting, pathetic and sad. I felt sorry for her. Why she'd wanted to start her story there, I wasn't sure. It had nothing to do with how her friends were killed, how they all had ended up slaughtered inside a two-story house outside of Clayton Heights.

"Your neighbors," I asked, "were they in the house to the left?"

Rainey nodded, pulled a leg up to the couch, knee bent, her arm wrapping around the shin, completely oblivious to the shameless pose, her legs open, giving me the perfect view between them. From her story, I would believe she'd be more closed off, shy of her body after being so blatantly used.

"Yeah, their house burned down a couple months ago. It was awful. Scary, actually. I thought it would spread to my house too, but it didn't."

She was fidgeting to talk about it, her fingers trailing up her shin, body wiggling over her seat as if she couldn't get comfortable.

"Rainey, why did you tell me that story? What does it have to do with your friends dying a few nights ago?"

A heavy sigh blew from her lungs. "I thought you should know how everything started."

My brows knit together, a million questions I wanted to ask, it was difficult to pinpoint one. "Everything, like what? Do you know who killed your friends and tied you up that night?"

With a quick shake of her head she refused to meet my eyes, her hair falling forward to shield her face. She tapped at the mark on her arm again. "No. But-I don't know. I'm not sure where to begin."

"Let's talk about the party where your friends died. What is the last thing you remember about that night before you were attacked?"

Brushing the hair from her face, she peered at me from beneath her lashes. Her eyes truly were remarkable, beautiful even in the low light. They were innocent eyes, what you would imagine in the face of an angel, soft and unassuming. In my practice, a person's eyes tell as much about them as their body language and what they say, sometimes more because they can't control the manner in which they look out at the world. Truly a window to the soul.

"Um," snatching the pack of cigarettes, she tapped one out, lit it, "I was talking to Michael. I remember that. He'd come there with Megan, but she had fallen asleep on the couch, he wanted to-" Her voice trailed off, cheeks blushing pink.

I wouldn't make a suggestion as to where I guessed the story was going. To do so would be to lead her memory or run the risk of giving her a false one.

"Michael wanted to fuck." Blurting out the statement, she wrapped her lips over the cigarette, took a drag, blew it out. It was all very matter of fact, her body rigid, bracing to be judged. I was careful not to reveal my reaction through my facial expression. Seeing that, she added, "Michael was the reason I was tied to the bed. We were, you know, having fun. And then he left the room."

Whoever killed her friends hadn't been the one to leave her bound on the bed; at least they hadn't been the one to initiate it. We were getting somewhere. "What happened then?"

29

Why did the killer beat you up but leave you alive? It was possible they were interrupted. The killer got spooked and left. Anything was possible.

Flicking an ash, she raised her voice. "I don't know. I was messed up. I-"

"Okay," with a soft voice I changed the direction of conversation to calm her down. She wanted to talk about other things, so I went along with it.

"Why did you sleep with Jacob the first day you met him if you didn't want to do that? Did you want to sleep with Michael the night he died?"

Silence spread between us, heavily weighted. Rainey wouldn't meet my eyes again, but her leg moved, parting further open. She had no concept of the privacy of her body. Her voice was a bare whisper. "Because that's what girls like me do. That's what we're good for. It's just sex, right? Nothing special."

The words rolled off her lips like an early morning fog over water, lazy and thick. A man with a motive would agree with her.

I scratched a note on my yellow pad. "Do you enjoy it?" *Careful, Justin. Does it even matter?* I wanted to know.

"Not at first, but then you get used to it. Tell yourself you like it. I've had moments where it was fun." Her fingers traced up the inside of her thigh drawing my attention.

"Did you want to sleep with Jacob when you first met him?"

"I wanted to get high."

Lifting her head, she watched my reaction. I didn't give her one. Calm, collected, professional. That was all she'd receive from me. But that didn't mean I wasn't aware of the effect this girl would have on other men.

She was practically a sex doll, her body only complimented by her voice. Everything about her was free and on display. Rainey wanted to be seen.

"Are you a drug addict, Rainey?"

Another ghost of a smile. "I can quit anytime I want," she joked in a mock falsetto.

"Are you?"

Changing her position on the couch, she lowered her leg and bunched her shoulders forward, bracing her hands on either side of her body over the couch. It allowed the collar of her shirt to fall forward enough for me to see down it.

No shame. I was beginning to believe her actions were deliberate.

"What's the definition of an addict?"

"A person who can't say no. One who uses daily. Who destroys their life -"

"No," she cut me off. "Not me. I haven't done anything in a while. I really can walk away. But if it's there and I'm bored, why not?"

My pen tapped the pad on my lap. "Because people die from drug use or find themselves in situations much like you did with Jacob." Pausing, I watched her, noted the way she glanced to the side rather than look at me. She was hiding something. "Is that the only time you slept with Jacob?"

Her lips curled into a smile. "I thought you only wanted to know about the night my friends died." Head angling right, her eyes met mine. "Or would you like to know everything? Make up your mind, Doc."

"Justin," I corrected her.

A negligible shrug. "Whatever." Rainey's tongue licked across her lips. "Would you like to know the entire story, or just certain parts?"

31

With this girl, her odd behavior and complete lack of self-preservation, I understood that to know her as a person, to understand her capabilities and actions, I needed to hear everything she was willing to tell me. "We'll go through all of it, if you like."

"Then yes, I slept with Jacob again. Why not? It wasn't like he hadn't been there already." Her eyes were daring me to say something, to condemn her, to judge. When I didn't, she grinned to add another layer to the story, to peel back another curtain for me to see all the decisions she'd made in her life. "I slept with his father, too."

I had to breathe deeply not to widen my eyes on accident, had to take my time not to openly react. "Didn't you say his father was the same age as your mom?"

Nodding, she ashed her cigarette again, her cheeks caving in to take another drag and blow it out. Her lips curved seductively every time she exhaled the smoke. "Paul was forty-five, I think. Forty-three maybe. I don't know. But yeah, he was much older than me."

One breath in. One breath out. "Do you want to tell me about it? Did Jacob know you slept with his father as well?"

Dropping the cigarette in the same cup as before, she turned her body to lie back on the couch, her hands resting on her stomach as she stared up at the ceiling, one leg hanging over the side as her toe swung back and forth over the floor.

"Not at first he didn't. But I'm not sure he cared much. When he did find out, he didn't get upset or anything. The family wasn't the type to get jealous. The only person who ever got upset was Rowan, and I think it's because he knew they were using me."

32

Scribbling down names as soon as she mentioned them, I remembered the empty lot next door, the evidence of a house fire. "Rainey, what happened to your neighbors? Jacob and Paul and Rowan. Did they move away after the fire?"

For the first time since meeting her, I picked up remorse in her voice. "No. They're all dead. Frankie and Joel, too."

Frankie I recognized. "Joel?"

"Another brother. Jacob was the oldest. Frankie after him. Then Joel." She paused before admitting, "Rowan was the youngest."

So many deaths surrounding this girl...

I jotted down the new name. "Did they die in the fire?"

Her head rolled over the small end pillow beneath it. "No. Only Frankie. But we'll get to that."

Sadly, I had a feeling we would get to everything before the truth came out. I attempted to redirect her again. "Your friends at the party," checking the folder, I added, "Michael, Megan, Preston and Angel. How did you know them? What do they have to do with what you're telling me now about the family next door?"

Scratching at the mark on her arm, she answered, "I met them over there. Well, not Preston. I met him in school originally, I think. But the rest of them I met next door." She looked at me, hair hanging down the sides of her face. "Do you want me to tell the story? Or do you have other questions?"

Relaxing against my seat, I realized this interview wasn't going to be easy. "I don't have any more at the moment. Go ahead and tell me the next part of the story."

CHAPTER FOUR

Rainey - Past

Clayton High School left a lot to be desired. The building was wilting, every ceiling stained with leaks, and the hallways were as full of garbage as there were lazily wandering students. I assumed there were janitors that kept things tidy, but they didn't make rounds during the day to check on restrooms where every toilet was overflowing and the paper rolls were pulled out like long, wet streamers every damn morning, the floors mummified. Kids are assholes and also the reason I was practically stumbling home with a full bladder.

Clouds covered the sky above my head, concealing the sunlight, the warmth, the last days of summer ending as fall rolled forward. I'd left my jacket at home, adding another layer of crap to an already bad situation.

Being cold never goes well with having to use the bathroom and when I finally trudged up the dirt driveway to my house, I was so desperate to pee I almost burst. Mom's car was gone. She was working a double. I dug around in my bag looking for my house key.

"Fuck!" Dumping the contents out on the ground, I dug around in search for it, tears dripping from my eyes when I realized I'd forgotten to grab it that morning. Mom was usually home for a few hours after I got back from school. It wasn't habit to take it with me.

I tried the knob with the hope it would be unlocked, screaming and banging on the door to discover it wasn't. "Damn it!"

From behind me, "Is there a problem?"

Turning, I locked my knees together as if that would keep my bladder from bursting. Paul stood behind me, his expression bemused. Breathing out, "I have to pee and I forgot my house key."

He laughed, and glanced around. "There are plenty of bushes you could use."

I was bouncing at that point, hands between my legs like a toddler. "Can I use your bathroom real fast?"

"Be my guest."

Sprinting to his house, I tumbled through the living room and hallway, tripping over my own feet to get the bathroom. There are a ton of good feelings in the world, but nothing like sitting on a toilet in just the nick of time.

My bladder released and I moaned rather loudly, my torso folding forward over my lap with the relief that I felt. Finishing up, I washed my hands and walked into the living room to find Paul sitting on the recliner.

"Thank you," I called out, my hand on the front door to leave. I hadn't spent much time around Paul in the two months I'd lived next door to him. Plus, he knew I was trading sex for drugs with one of his sons. It was awkward being near him.

He cocked a brow. "Didn't you tell me you were locked out of your house?"

"Yeah, but I dumped my bag out on the front porch and I need to clean it up. Mom might have left a window unlocked or something."

"Let me help you. It shouldn't be too difficult to get you inside. These houses aren't the best." He stood up

35

from the recliner and I opened the front door, unsure how to tell him I didn't need the help.

Paul was a tall man and his legs were so long that he reached me before I had a chance to thank him but decline the offer. As soon as he stepped up next to me, the scent of his cologne hit my nose, masculine and musky. It wasn't a bad scent at all.

"Are you sure?" Peering up at him, I realized he was taller than Jacob, but only by a few inches. His body was larger, too. Not fat, the man was actually in damn good shape for his age, his arms strong from working on bikes and his stomach flat.

He wore a button down white shirt untucked from a pair of jeans, the hint of a black leather belt and heavy silver buckle showing every time he moved his arms and the shirt pulled up. When he nodded in response to my question, I ducked my head and followed him outside.

"How long have you been riding motorcycles?" My fingers ran over the chrome of his bike as we passed it, Paul glancing over his shoulder at me with a grin. His eyes were the same shade as Jacob's, his cheeks and jawline dusted in stubble. There wasn't one grey strand in his brown hair, but in the shadow of his beard, there was.

"Longer than you've been alive probably. My dad rode and my grandfather. I couldn't imagine being trapped inside a metal box while driving down the road. I like the wind."

Tall weeds tickled my legs as we crossed through my yard. Mom still hadn't gotten around to doing anything with it. Then again, the weeds and islands of dirt weren't exactly out of place in this neighborhood. Just about every house had the same problem, the decay of urban neglect and underpaid people with too many hours at their jobs.

While Paul went around the perimeter of the house checking windows, I crouched down on the porch to repack my bag, tucking the last book inside as he stepped up beside me.

"Apparently your house was built better than mine. I can't find a way in without breaking something."

Slumping down onto the cement, I glanced up at him. "It's no problem. I can wait out here until mom gets home."

He squinted his eyes at me and rocked back on his heels.

"Doesn't your mom work until late at night? It's not safe for you to be out here all alone when the sun goes down. You can hang out at my house. The boys are all off doing their own thing until later, but you can watch television to pass the time."

I wasn't exactly comfortable with the idea.

"Plus, I know you think it's Jacob that does the dealing at my place, but he gets it from me, baby girl. I'll roll you up something while you wait."

After the day I had, a joint sounded like the best medicine to make it all go away.

Mrs. Cleft had called me out in the middle of class to answer a question I didn't know. She made me look like an idiot in front of everybody when I didn't have the answer. I wasn't smart, could barely read, much less remember anything. Mom never paid any attention to my grades, so neither did I. Instead, I muddled through, showed up every day so I would have something to do, and so child services wouldn't be called on her for failing to make me go to school.

"I don't have any money to pay for it."

"It's on the house." His brown eyes locked to mine. "But just this once."

What else was there to do? It was supposed to be a good day, but it all had turned to shit. "Well, it is my birthday. Can we just call it a birthday present?"

"Today's your birthday?"

I nodded, a smile stretching my cheeks.

"How old?"

"Eighteen."

Paul's eyes brightened, his face lighting up with a white-toothed grin that reminded me of Rowan's. His youngest son didn't talk much or smile that often, but in the moments we had alone, he did. I saw Rowan in Paul's face now and knew his youngest would look just like him when he was older.

"Well, welcome to adulthood, baby girl. I've got something special since it's your birthday."

Taking my bag from my shoulder, he walked me to his house and tossed it on the couch as we passed through the living room. His sons' rooms were all on the right side of the house while his was through a doorway off the living room on the left. Following him in, I glanced around. It was twice the size of Jacob's.

"Take a seat while I set this up." Paul pointed to a bench against a wall, one just tall enough to sit on while lacing up your shoes.

The room was silent between us, except for the drawer he pulled open and the crinkle of a plastic baggie. I saw the flash of something metal in his hand followed by a high-pitched scraping sound like nails against a chalkboard.

Waving me over, he pointed down at a mirror with white powdered lines streaked across it. "You ever done coke before?"

"No." The most I'd ever done was drink alcohol and smoke weed.

"Well, these two lines are for the birthday girl and these two over here are for me." Paul handed me a dollar bill that was rolled into a tight straw. "Just put one end to your nose and follow the line while breathing in deeply. It'll help if you cover the other nostril while doing so."

Shifting my weight between my feet, I looked at the lines and back at him. "What will it do to me?"

"Just make you feel good. Speed you up a bit. I didn't give you much."

The truth was I liked to pretend I was hard, that living a life constantly moving around had made me street smart like a lot of people I knew. But when it came to stuff like this, I didn't know much. Not until somebody taught me.

My mom did drugs and so did every man she dated. All my friends did. Just about everyone I knew did, so it never occurred to me there was something wrong with it.

"Okay." Taking the dollar bill from his hand, I pinched my fingers around the paper to keep it from unwinding. I plugged a nostril with one finger and stuck the bill up to the other before bending over the mirror.

The powder burned when I breathed in, a bitter taste dripping down the back of my throat immediately after. Paul laughed when I scrunched my nose and shook my head.

"You'll get used to it. Go ahead and finish the other so I can do mine."

The second line wasn't as bad as the first. Handing him the bill, I stepped back, waiting to fall over or

39

something. I didn't feel any different and retook my seat on the bench while Paul finished his lines and turned to lean against a wall, his arms thick across his chest. His brown eyes glimmered in the sunlight pouring in through a window.

"How's it feel?"

A shake of my head, the movement causing the collar of my shirt to fall to one side and slide over my shoulder. His eyes followed it. "I don't feel anything."

Paul's grin was just as poisonous as Jacob's, every one of the Connor men had it, a smile that drew you in and made you want to return it.

"Give it a minute." He shifted against the wall, planting his feet at shoulder width. "Tell me about yourself, Rainey. The only thing I know about you is that you live next door."

There wasn't much to tell, but within a few minutes I was talking fast, a jumble of words pouring over my lips in a fast rushing stream. I didn't even know what I was saying.

A smile stretched my lips that matched Paul's, and while I continued blubbering on about God knows what, Paul turned to put more lines on the mirror, calling me over with a crook of his finger when done.

With bouncing steps, I crossed the room never having felt so damn happy. This stuff was so much better than weed. Instead of being lazy, I felt like dancing. Laughter rolled over my lips after I finished the next two lines. I pressed a shoulder against a wall and watched Paul finish his.

"Thanks for this," I said, "you have no idea how much better my day is after doing these lines. This is so much better than smoking a joint."

Taking a step closer to me, he backed me against the wall and ran his finger over my bare shoulder, his eyes following the motion of his hand. "What's going on between you and Jacob?"

My stomach flip flopped, my neck craning to look up at him. "Nothing."

The corner of his lips tugged up. "Are you two dating or anything?"

I shook my head, swallowed, felt dizzy on my feet all of a sudden. "No. It's just-"

"Sex for drugs?" His eyes met mine, pupils tiny, the lids hooded.

Biting the inside of my cheek, I admitted what he already knew. "Yeah."

His nostrils flared as he inhaled sharply. "Have you ever been with a real man? One that knows what to do with a woman's body?"

It was just a fingertip against my skin, but I was hyperaware of his touch. My heart was a trapped bird beating its wings beneath my ribs. "No."

Leaning forward, he trailed three light kisses over my shoulder. "I mean Jacob is a good guy, but he's also a little punk. You're never in his bedroom very long, which tells me he's not worried about you."

Paul's left hand traced down the center of my body, stopping just above my shorts. "Why don't I tap out another few lines and show you what I know you're missing?"

Blinking my eyes, I glanced down at the floor. This is what all men wanted from me, even ones old enough to be my father. The only problem was I liked what the coke was doing for me. I wanted to be touched and wasn't so out of my mind that I wouldn't know what was happening. It was an impulsive answer. "Okay."

41

The glimmer in his eyes told me he liked that answer. "You don't have to if you don't want to. I mean, the door's right there, if you want to leave."

What I wanted was two more lines. Shaking my head, I told him, and he obliged me, letting me finish mine before telling me to go sit on the bed.

From what I knew of being with Jacob, from what I remembered from my past, this would be done and over with pretty quick. Then we could go watch television or whatever. Maybe he'd give me a few more lines before we left his room. It was worth it. It had to be worth it.

He sniffed loudly as I took a seat on the side of the bed, my legs practically glued together, my shoulders hunched forward, my body vibrating from the rush of the drug.

It was almost impossible to stay still.

Paul walked over to me, his steps heavy against the ground. Crouching down, he grabbed my knees and pulled them apart, his eyes on mine the entire time. "I'm not going to hurt you, baby girl. Just the opposite. But I can't make you feel good if you block me from certain parts of your body."

I let him spread my legs, my eyes watching his palms rub up the inside of my thighs. His thumbs rubbed between my legs and I moaned.

Everything was so sensitive. I'd never felt this good before. He lifted my shirt over my head, a masculine sound coming from deep in his chest. "I have to say, Rainey, the good lord built you right. Do me a favor and take off your bra."

My hands shook as I reached behind me, my chest pushing out while Paul watched. As soon as I freed the hook, the straps slipped from my shoulders, my breasts exposed as I let it fall.

His mouth closed over the nipple of one while his hand molded the other. Closing my eyes, I tried to forget how old he was, tried to imagine it was a boy like Jacob making me feel so good. I moaned, shy about the sound because I'd never made it before. Not like this.

Pulling his mouth away. "You're trembling, Rainey. Just try to relax. I'll take care of everything."

I knew what we were doing was wrong, but I couldn't say no. I didn't know how. Maybe, just maybe, if I did this right, he would give me more of his coke, or he would send me home with a joint. I thought it might be my fault men always wanted this from me. They always told me my body was just right.

"Lie down," his voice was pure gravel.

This part was the same. *Lie down, take off your pants, let me move between your legs for a few minutes then I'll be done.* I could do this. I thought I wanted to do this. Just as long as I could close my eyes and pretend it was somebody else. This moment, it reminded me-

No. I wouldn't let my mind go there. Not now. Not while I was feeling good.

He pulled off my pants next and my underwear. Dropped them to the ground, forgotten in a small pile over brown carpet. He was still crouching down and tried to spread my legs again, but I held them together.

"What are you doing?" My head popped up to look at him.

"It's fine, Rainey, just lie back and let me do this for you."

"Do what? Shouldn't you be on top of me?"

Paul gave me the funniest look. "Haven't you ever had a man go down on you before?"

I shook my head. "No. Is that the same as when I do it?"

Murmuring under his breath, "Jacob really is a fucking prick." His eyes locked to mine. "Lie back. Let me show you."

Legs shaking, I did as he said, my eyes wide open and staring at the ceiling when I felt his breath on my thighs. In the next second, his tongue flicked out and my knees squeezed on either side of his head. He pushed them back open, stuck his tongue inside while his finger rubbed at a spot above his mouth that made my hips buck up.

"What? Oh." I think I lost my mind, a tingling rushing over my body as the room began to spin.

It felt different, like my insides were tightening up. When he switched places between his mouth and his hand, sucking on one part while his fingers slipped inside me, I cried out, my body shaking as my fingers fisted the blanket. Every muscle in my body tensed, his pumping fingers felt so good. He stopped as my body relaxed, pushed up to his feet and looked down at me.

"By the look on your face, I would say that's the first time you've ever come."

I thought it was. Sex had never been like that before. Paul rubbed a thumb over his bottom lip. "Turn over on your belly. I'm going to take you from behind."

I did as he said, listened as he stripped off his pants. Grabbing my legs, he pulled me down so my knees fell down to the carpet and only my chest was on the bed. Rubbing a finger between my legs, he pulled it up to play with my asshole. I jumped, but he held me in place with a hand splayed over my back.

His voice sounded so big above me. "I don't want what my son's already taken, Rainey. I plan on taking something else. Just relax, baby girl, I promise I'll make this feel just as good."

CHAPTER FIVE

Justin - Present

This interview was dangerous. Sitting there, listening her go into so much detail, it affected me in a way that was wholly unprofessional, completely debased, frightening for how I was feeling. I should have felt sorry for her, but my mind was going other places simply because of the sound of her voice, the way her fingers slid slowly up and down the tops of her thighs as she spoke.

Shaking myself of the feeling, I cleared my throat. "What he did to you; were you okay with it?"

"I didn't say no," she answered, her hair splayed over the side of the couch where she was still lying down. "And it was the first time I ever orgasmed. He was right about that. The first thing he did at least. The other, when he-" Rainey visibly shivered. "That hurt," she admitted on a soft voice.

"I'm sorry that happened to you." And I was. Rainey had been used over and over from what she was telling me. But how did it all fit in to what happened to her friends? Why did any of this matter?

Rainey touched the marks on her arm again. I opened my mouth to ask about it, but she spoke before I had the chance. "I lied to him, you know? To Paul."

Scribbling a note down on my legal pad, I stared at her hand rubbing back and forward over the mark. "What about?"

"About being with an older man."

It occurred to me that when she spoke about her neighbors, Rainey's voice was soft, reminiscent. It changed when she admitted she'd lied, the smooth cadence becoming clipped and brittle, harsh and cold.

"I've been with older men before."

Sitting up, she lit another cigarette. The girl was a damn chimney and I had no doubt I'd leave her house with stage three lung cancer.

"I've been with five, to be precise. Five that may have been older than Paul." Her hands were shaking, her eyes unfocused. Rainey appeared to be on the verge of tears. The collar of her shirt slid over one shoulder much like she'd described it doing with Paul.

When she didn't enlighten me further, I prodded her along, gently like a mother would a temperamental toddler. "Who were the five older men Rainey?"

My eyes flicked to the mark on her arm, back to her face. Maybe this is the answer I was looking for, the reason for the scars.

Blowing out a breath, her eyes followed the cloud of smoke, watched it bloom through the room as it swirled, spread and morphed. "My mom's boyfriends."

Was there anybody who hadn't used this girl? I shook my head, made a note, then glanced up at her, attentive and willing to listen. "Do you want to talk about it?"

We were so far off from the details of the party the night her friends died, but maybe this was something I needed to know.

Grenshaw wanted to clear her, but the deeper we got into her life, the more her personality developed. There was more to her than a simple, dim-witted girl who lived in a bad part of town.

Rainey's hand shook so bad I worried she would drop the cigarette. "There's not much to talk about. It happened so long ago. Not all of her boyfriends were bad. Just five of them. They took advantage, you know? I was a little girl."

"How old were you?"

"The first time happened when I was ten. He didn't do anything to me beyond touch. But he made me do things to him. The others - Well, they were all different in what happened, but I never liked it. Never. Even if they claimed I did."

Jotting this new information down, I kept my voice casual, inoffensive. Interested, but not too much. I didn't want to scare her so that she retreated into her shell. "They told your mother that?"

A shake of her head. "No. My mom never knew. I never told her, but that's what they would say to me when I complained."

I had to ask given her recent history. "And are these men dead, too?"

Her head snapped up, her eyes furious. "No. They left. Just like all of my mom's boyfriends do. They found something better. I wasn't upset to see them go even though she cried like it was the end of the world, uprooted me to *start again*. A new start and new Day and all that."

Rant finished, she slumped over exhausted, her energy tapped.

I wanted to check in on them, see if she was telling the truth that they left and weren't skeletons lying in a ditch somewhere. "Do you happen to remember their names?"

A shake of her head and she tossed her cigarette into the cup. It fizzled to meet the water, the only sound in the silent room.

"All the names blend together after a while. It's my fault, though. For whatever reason men see me and

48

think of sex. Even when I was little. I developed early, so I always looked older than I am."

"It's not your fault, Rainey. You were abused by those men. They had no right to do what they did and were wrong for doing it. What they did was criminal. Never blame yourself."

She didn't respond, her eyes wandering the room, mind processing our conversation. I hoped what I told her sunk in, that she would stop this cycle of letting men use her.

Softly, "Are they the reason for the mark on your arm? The five tally marks?"

Immediately, she touched the scars. "I don't want to talk about that."

Dropping the subject, I attempted a new direction, her past was upsetting and convoluted. "Let's go back to the night of the party."

Sadly, the topic of her friends being bludgeoned to death was far less emotional for her. "You told me Megan was asleep on the couch, and Michael tied you to a bed to presumably have sex with you. Where were the other two people? Preston and Angel?"

"Upstairs," she breathed out. "Having sex."

It matched what the crime scene photos showed. They were found naked in the same room, Preston on the bed and Angel slumped against a wall. "Were they dating?"

Rainey laughed, a one burst chortle that stretched her lips into a grin. "No. Not really. Preston was-"

Her voice trailed off. "He was a jerk. Angel was using him to get off, but she wasn't the type to date someone like him. Not after Joel."

The name was familiar. "As in Joel, one of your neighbors?"

49

Crossing one leg over the other, Rainey leaned back in her seat to stretch her arms above her head. It caused her chest to arch forward, the shape of her breasts obvious beneath her thin shirt. "Yeah, Joel Connor. The one closest in age to Rowan."

Lowering her arms, "He was really pretty. Dirty blond hair with blue eyes. Rowan said he looked a lot like their mother. His face was sharper than Jacob and Paul. Not as round. Although Rowan got the best mix of them all. He was pretty, too." Pausing, she drifted off, her thoughts in the past.

"Anyway, that's how I knew Angel. She dated Joel. Up until he died, at least."

"Were you good friends with her?"

Laughing, Rainey shook her head, her hair slipping over her shoulder to tumble down to her waist. "Not at all. She hated me, actually. We tolerated each other."

Yet, they were at a party together? Interesting. "Why did she hate you?"

Blue eyes peered over at me, soft and wide, the rims red and a bruise deepening on the side of her face. "Do you really want to know?"

"It would help me understand things better."

Grinning, she settled back in her seat and crossed her arms over her chest. "Okay, Doc, I'll tell you, but just remember you were the one who asked."

CHAPTER SIX

Rainey - Past

Things had been going pretty good for mom and me in the new place. Mom was working two jobs while I finished high school. I offered to get a job as well, but she didn't like the idea. The area was bad and I didn't have a car, so she preferred I stayed close to home.

Rowan had come over to hang out several times and mom thought he was adorable. She'd joke around and pinch his cheeks, pretend like he was the son she never had.

In a way he was. I'd adopted him as my little brother, sheltered him under my wing when his brothers treated him like crap. He played along, kept my secrets about what went on at his house. He was the only person who knew I was having sex with both Paul and Jacob.

Well, Paul technically knew, but he didn't say anything to Jacob. The only reason Rowan knew was because he'd caught me coming out of Paul's room one night.

Poor Rowan. He wasn't happy about what I was doing, and I knew he felt left out. All of his brothers were of age, but he was the baby of the family, an accidental pregnancy that wasn't intended, but happened a few years before his mom died.

He wasn't like his brothers, though. He was kind, a gentle soul, the type of person who deserved a good girl that would treat him right. I think Rowan was the only friend I ever had in life, someone I could talk to who wouldn't judge me or use me for anything. He genuinely cared how I felt. If I was happy or sad. He worked to keep me happy.

He was still a kid, though, and for that, I didn't listen to him much. His opinions were sweet, but they didn't carry weight in my mind. There was no possible way he could understand what I'd gone through in my life, why I preferred getting wasted and playing the role of a girl who was only there to be used.

Several months had gone by and my neighbors were having a small get together at the house, nothing big, a few friends and that was it. As usual, I was on the couch (I was at their house more than I was home, but loneliness will do that to you) when Joel walked in with his arm around a girl. It was surprising to see Joel with her.

The woman was my age or possibly a little older, she had mouse brown hair clipped close, a pixie cut, longer in the front than back. Her eyes were a little too far apart, her nose a touch too small, the slope of it noticeable. With a round face that didn't have much definition, she had thin lips that smiled when she looked at Joel but pulled into a tight line when she turned to look at me.

Leaning over to Rowan, I plucked a headphone from his ear. He was always listening to music, probably would have been a great musician if anybody ever paid enough attention to buy him an instrument. Tipping my chin, I nudged his shoulder with mine and asked "Who's that?"

His blue stare narrowed on her. "Angel Maxin. She was in a grade ahead of you. She's a bitch."

"What's Joel doing with a girl like her?"

Rowan rolled his eyes, smiled, the expression not quite real. "Don't tell me you plan on fucking Joel as well."

I gaped at him, stunned and little hurt. It wasn't like Rowan to take shots at me. Realizing his mistake, he threw an arm around my shoulders and tugged me into a hug. "I'm screwing with you, Rainey. Don't take it personally."

It still hurt to hear him talk about me like that. Even if I deserved it.

"Hey," he grabbed my chin and turned my face to him. "I'm sorry. I didn't mean it."

"Oh, isn't that cute? It looks like the slut next door is going to fuck the baby brother, too. You certainly do get around. But maybe Paul and Jacob just see you as a matter of convenience considering you're always within reach."

My head snapped up to see Angel standing at the entrance to the living room, Joel walking in behind her. Slipping his arm around her waist, he passed her a joint and blew out a cloud of smoke.

"Nah, Rainey isn't into Rowan, is she? Rowan cries himself to sleep about it every night. Probably jerks his dick so much thinking about her that the damn thing will fall off before he ever gets the chance to use it with an actual woman."

Joel laughed, his eyes locking on me in a way I recognized. It was cold that night, early January, the snow flutters outside warning of a bigger storm to come. I had on a pair of tight jeans and a long sleeved shirt, but as usual, I'd neglected to wear a bra. I hated the damn things; they were too constrictive. So, unless I was at school where dress code demanded them, I usually went without.

53

The heaters in the house attempted like hell to keep up with the chill, but breezes would blow past and my nipples would become hard points because of it. That's what Joel was looking at, my breasts, even though he had a girl right next to him.

Angel had a nice body despite her face, and I thought if she were to grow out her hair, it might help balance her features more. But at that moment, she was as ugly as could be, her features twisted in mockery and hate, her eyes squinted from the joint they were smoking. She couldn't stand to see me in the house.

Jacob walked into the room while I sat mortified that my secret wasn't just known in the house, but also by people outside of it.

"Did I hear my name?" He was high, they all were. All, but me. Not that I didn't want to be; I just hadn't made payment for it yet.

Joel laughed again, slapped Jacob on the shoulder and said, "Yeah, Angel called out Rainey for fucking you and dad, and now Rowan looks like he might come across the room at us."

I had been so worried about what Angel knew and said that I hadn't looked at Rowan. Turning, I saw so much anger in his eyes that it scared me. Touching his hand, I attempted to pull his attention my way, but he glared across the room at his brothers, his body tense, hand shaking over the couch.

"Hey, it's fine."

He didn't answer me.

"Wait a second. What?" Jacob's eyes widened, his weed-addled mind finally comprehending what Joel had said. His eyes snapped to me, a slow smile stretching his lips. "Is he lying? Are you fucking my dad too?"

I thought he'd be mad, but he laughed instead, shaking his head like he couldn't believe it. "Damn girl. You have no shame do you? How does old dick taste? Do you like the added wrinkles? Ribbed for her pleasure or some shit, right?"

Tears stung my eyes, a chorus of laughter filling the room from Jacob, Joel and Angel. Rowan turned to me and at the sight of just one of those tears, he pushed up from the couch, would have charged across at his brothers if I hadn't reached out and grabbed his wrist.

He was still too small to fight them, and they taught him that lesson every chance they could get. I didn't want him getting hurt because of me, not when he got hurt so often for other reasons.

Rowan was too damn good for this family and if I could have willed him into another life - a better life - I would have.

Joel must have been too messed up to understand what he was doing, he wasn't the type to make things worse.

Closer in age to Rowan, he tended to try to calm things down. But not that night. He was having too much fun, probably trying to show off in front of Angel.

"Man, she doesn't suck dad's cock. She takes it up the ass from him. I saw her walking funny one day after leaving his room, like she crawled off a horse or something."

His laughter boomed through the living room, like a damn gust of oxygen stoking the flame of Rowan's rage. Rowan tried to break free of the hold I had on his wrist, so I knew I had to get him out of there. Jacob and Joel would hurt him.

Forcing out more tears wasn't hard. What they were saying was embarrassing, especially with Angel standing there. I cried, not caring that they all could see me. I only cared about getting Rowan's attention. He turned when he heard me, his palm cupping my cheek with such tenderness that it made me want to cry for an entirely different reason.

"Come on," he said, his voice soft despite how angry he was. "Let's get out of here. You don't deserve this."

Joel, Jacob and Angel were laughing even harder as we left. But I got Rowan away from them and that's all that mattered.

We ran over to my house because it was so cold outside and I'd forgotten to grab my jacket. By the time we walked into my living room, my body was tight, my boobs swollen from the cold, nipples erect. Rowan's eyes kept wandering there and I couldn't deny what Joel had said was true.

Rowan wanted me. Wanted to be with me like his dad and Jacob. But he wasn't the type to force it. We were friends, and he respected that. Respected me.

After grabbing some sodas from the fridge, we went back to my bedroom to hang out. My mom wouldn't be home until late that night, so we had a few hours to hang out and chill. He calmed down once we were away from his brothers.

"I'm sorry what they said to you."

Looking at him, I smiled.

He reached forward to wipe what was left of the tears from my eyes. "I hate to see you cry, Rainey. It does something to me. It makes me mad because you're better than that."

I wasn't, but I didn't argue with him. He would just keep insisting. It was weird to hear someone who actually believed I should value myself. My mom always told me I should, but she was my mom. They're supposed to say those things. Plus I thought she was afraid I'd turn out like her, lots of boyfriends with nothing to show for it.

The joke was on her, I guess. I never had an actual boyfriend, just people I fucked. She thought I was a good little girl, a virgin. I let her think that. The truth was too sad for her to hear.

"Rainey, I'm serious. You should have a guy that cares about you. That sees you as more than a girl to use and toss aside. But you don't make people see you that way. You let them hurt you. It has to stop."

I shook my head, grinned, even though the expression was sadder than anything. What he was saying: it sounded true, but I knew differently. The whole time we sat talking, all I wanted to do was go back to his house and get high. I didn't think Jacob cared to hear about Paul and me, which meant I could still pay him for the drugs by letting him fuck me or going down on him.

I preferred it when he just wanted oral sex. It didn't hurt as much. He was never the type to prepare me for the other and it burned at first. It was too dry.

Rowan touched my cheek again, his eyes glimmering with how much he cared. It made me uncomfortable because I didn't deserve his concern. It only hurt him. I should have been paying more attention, should have kept some distance between us. If I had, he wouldn't have been close enough to lean forward and kiss me.

As soon as his lips met mine, I jumped in place, his hand sliding to my hip to steady me. Jacob never kissed me and neither did Paul. It was just sex to them. But

57

Rowan, he kissed me softly, his lips moving over mine slowly until his tongue swept along the crease. I wasn't thinking. I was too surprised at the way it felt to be kissed. I thought it might be the first time anyone had ever done it.

My mouth opened and his tongue danced against mine, his body pushing forward even more until he was lying on top of me. I liked the feeling, the slowness.

Eventually, his hand swept up my shirt, cupped my breast, his thumb rubbing circles over my nipple. I could feel him grow hard against my thigh, and it freaked me out for some reason. His palm was cold against my breast, which made it tighten more. He moaned, must have thought I was into it.

Rowan was too young for me, still fifteen at the time, although his birthday was coming up.

He spoke against my mouth as his hand continued playing with my breast. "I'll treat you right, Rainey. I won't hurt you." His hips started moving, dry humping my leg. Even that was slow and soft. Tender and caring.

It was too much. He was just a friend. I didn't look at him that way. What we were doing was wrong and I shoved him away, sat up. I hated the rejection I saw in his eyes. "You're too good for me, Rowan. I'm not the kind of girl you should be with. I'm too fucked up."

Looking away from me, I could see his jaw tick, his teeth clenched in anger. And although he was in the middle of feeling hurt and pushed away, all I could think about was getting next door again, paying Jacob for another high.

"Come on," I said. "It's been an hour. We should go back. I left my jacket and my mom will be mad if I don't go get it."

Rowan nodded his head and brushed his hand over his face. I realized then that he'd cried because I pushed him away. He cared about me that much. Nodding his head again, he didn't say anything, just stood up and grabbed my hand to help me to my feet. The walk over to his house was slow despite how cold it was. I was giving him time to calm down.

Paul had arrived home during the time we were at my house. As soon as we stepped inside, he tossed money at Rowan. "Go get me a pack of smokes."

The stores in our neighborhood never carded. They didn't give much of a damn about the laws and how old someone had to be to buy cigarettes. I wondered why Paul would make Rowan go, but then I looked at the doorway leading to his bedroom and saw a woman peeking out.

Knowing what they were doing, I was jealous. Paul had the coke. All Jacob ever had was weed. I'd developed something of a craving for the white powder, which was why I continued sleeping with Paul.

Rowan snatched the money from the air and looked at me. He wanted me to go with him, that much was obvious. I shook my head, told him to go without me. Joel was sitting in the living room by himself and I was happy to see Angel was gone. It meant I could give Jacob what he wanted so he would roll me a joint. Rowan would get in the way of that. He tended to try to keep me away from his brother.

Rowan stormed off and Paul didn't say a word to me as he returned to his room and shut the door. I heard

59

female laughter rolling out into the living room. They were partying. He was most likely doing the same thing to her that he did to me.

Walking through the living room, my eyes met Joel's and I could see how fucked up he was. He tended to drink a lot and when he smoked, he was so out of it he would stare off into space. It was fine by me because I just wanted to do what Jacob wanted, grab a joint, and go home. I walked back to his bedroom to find him sitting on his bed. Music was playing, something hard and fast.

He looked up at me and shook his head, a smile tugging at his lips. "I didn't know you were the type to keep it in the family."

"I'm sorry. I should have told you, but-"

"Don't worry about it, Rainey. I don't care. It's not like I have feelings for you or anything. You're just pussy."

It stung, his words. Not like I didn't know already, but it still hurt to hear them.

Jacob was rolling a joint, not really looking at me when he shrugged a shoulder.

"Actually", he said, his fingers working the paper to twist it up, "I'm happy to know you don't mind spreading it around. I want you to do something different tonight for your fix. Because of you, Angel and Joel got into a fight. She stormed off. Not sure why. You're just a slut, but now Joel's in a pissy mood." His brown eyes lifted to mine. "You're going to fix that while I watch."

I stilled in place, not really happy with what I thought he was saying. "I don't think that's a good idea. I can just -"

"You can just do what I tell you to do or you can leave. Dad's busy with another bitch so you can't go to him for anything." He held up the joint. "Do you want this or not?"

He knew I wanted it. His room smelled like weed and it made me want it more. "I do."

Lips pulling into a grin, he stood up from the bed. "Then take a seat. I'll be right back."

This wasn't fair to me. I knew it, didn't like it, but went along with it. Nothing made sense in my head anymore. I looked up when two sets of shuffling steps entered the bedroom. Jacob kicked the door closed, but it didn't latch, popped open a crack when he and Joel stepped forward.

Joel was leering at me, his eyelids heavy, his eyes bloodshot, but his grin told me he was all too happy to oblige his brother. Jacob moved to his radio and turned the volume up some, just enough to drown out the sound of the television in the living room.

"Well," he said, lighting a joint while Joel stood staring at me, "Are you going to party with us or what?"

My voice was soft. "What do you want me to do?"

"Taking off your clothes would be a good start."

When I hesitated, Jacob said, "I tell you what: Since there's two of us, I'll roll you two joints. It's only fair." He nudged Joel's side. "Right, Joel?"

Joel nodded, his eyes locked on my chest.

I closed my eyes and peeled off my shirt, Joel's lips parting slightly when my chest was bare to his eyes. Jacob gave a low whistle.

"Didn't I tell you, man? Her tits are fucking perfect. Rainey doesn't even need a bra. They're high and tight

61

all on their own. Jump up and down for us, Rainey. Make them bounce."

My feet didn't leave the floor, but I shook my body enough to make my chest move around. Joel's eyes were glued to them. He was so fucked up it was like he was mesmerized by the way they wiggled. Jacob's voice was low as he took a drag from the joint and blew it out. "Go touch them, brother. You know you want to."

Joel crossed the room, his hands reaching to grab my tits, push them together, pull them apart. He ducked his head and sucked a nipple into his mouth, bit down on it with his teeth. My stare remained locked to Jacob from over Joel's shoulder. He grinned, leaned back against a wall as he continued smoking. "You want it, man. So just take it. Rainey won't say no."

I was beginning to wonder if Joel was even aware of what Jacob was doing. If he was, he didn't seem to care. He just kept playing with my breasts like it was the first time he'd seen a pair.

Jacob angled his neck, still staring straight at my face.

"Tonight's going to be a little different. You're normally so quiet when we fuck and I hate that about you. It means you're not enjoying it. So, tonight, if you want what I have to give you, you're going to be loud, Rainey. And while my brother here fucks you, it's going to be my name you call out. Since you like to keep it in the family and all. Now tell me you want this because I'm not forcing you. It's your decision. Fuck Joel or walk out the door."

Nodding my head, I silently agreed.

"I need to hear it, Rainey."

"I want this," I whispered.

Jacob smiled, a full watt smile this time, dimples and all. "Go ahead, Joel. Take off her pants and fuck her. Get that pussy Angel wouldn't give you."

Joel pulled the button of my jeans, unzipped them and shoved them down my legs. He didn't even bother pulling them off my ankles before shoving me on Jacob's bed.

"No, Joel, not that direction. Turn her around and on her stomach. I don't want to watch your ass bounce while this happens; I'd rather see her tits and face."

Joel did as his brother said, his moves uncoordinated and rough. Jacob kept his eyes locked to my face as Joel got on his knees behind me and tugged down my underwear. He was pulling his own pants off next, notching the tip of his dick up against me.

"Now, Rainey, push up with your arms and hold yourself there so I can see those gorgeous tits on you move. Keep your eyes on me, beautiful, and use my name. I want to hear it loud and clear."

It was hard to keep the position he wanted, but I did it, my arms shaking as Joel thrust forward a few times with just the tip. Jacob laughed, "Stop playing around and give it to her. She wants it."

He pushed in fully, his hands grabbing my hips as he began to move. Skin slapped against skin, my body moving back and forth with every thrust. Jacob's eyes watched my breasts and his tongue peeked out at the corner of his mouth. "Make noise, Rainey."

While Joel was thrusting inside me as hard as he could, I called out Jacob's name. "Yes. Oh, yes. Jacob that feels so good."

"Make me believe it. Ask for it harder. Joel can do better than that."

63

The mattress was squeaking beneath us as his cock filled me over and over again. "Harder, Jacob. Please, harder!"

"That's more like it," Jacob crooned. He took another drag of the joint when a noise to our side caught our attention. Our heads turned in unison, my heart sinking into my stomach to see Rowan standing at the crack of the open door, his eyes locked on what Joel and I were doing. I thought Jacob would slam it shut, block Rowan from his room, but instead he reached over to pull the door open wider. Joel continued fucking me, oblivious to Rowan's presence, grunting with every thrust.

Jacob laughed. "What do you think, little brother? Like what you see? It's too bad your dick is still too small to make her scream like that." He turned, cupped his ear, "Keep up the noise, Rainey. I can't hear you."

I couldn't look at Rowan while doing what Jacob wanted. It hurt my heart too much. Remembering the way he kissed me, the tenderness, forced a tear from my eye. "Yes, Jacob! Harder!"

Joel sped up and Jacob taunted Rowan more. "Hear that? That's what a girl sounds like when you're giving it to her good. Maybe one day you'll make a girl scream like that. Take a good look, Rowan, I'm sure you'll have lots to think about tonight while jerking off."

He laughed and slammed the door shut, dropped the joint into an ashtray and walked over to the bed. Crouching down, he reached forward to grab my tits in his hands, squeezing them while Joel kept going.

"Hurry up and finish. I want to get Rainey out of here so we can go do something else more interesting, like watch television or some shit."

Joel grunted one last time, pulled out and came on my back. Jacob winked at me, stood up and crossed the room to roll up the joints he'd promised me. After climbing from the bed, Joel tossed me a towel to clean up and left the room.

Ten minutes later and Jacob handed me two joints, but held up a third. "Want this too?"

I clenched my eyes shut, hating myself, but nodded. He unzipped his pants, shoved his cock against my mouth and said, "Then open up."

Taking him into my mouth, I used my hand to work his dick while sucking him off. He finished quickly, laughing as he pulled out. "Damn, Rainey, you're getting better at that." The third joint fell into my lap. "Now get the fuck out of my room."

I didn't see Rowan when I left, and I was glad for it. Facing him after what he just saw would have broken me apart.

He really was too good for that family. Just like he was way too good for me.

CHAPTER SEVEN

Justin - Present

I left Rainey's house around four that afternoon. As she promised, there were neighbors milling about, their eyes scanning from my car to me, back to my car.

It wasn't unusual for them to be curious, not with the story Rainey was telling me. There was no doubt in my mind that the neighborhood knew what was going on in that house. Opening the door to my car, I paused and glanced at the empty lot where the Connors' house used to be. Only one of them died in the fire from what she said, so what happened to the others?

Needing more information, I drove out of Clayton Heights, happy to discover I still had all four tires and nobody had stripped my car. There was still time for that to happen.

My interview with Rainey had just begun and I would be at her house every morning to continue it until I had enough information to give my report.

Traffic was tedious due to the time of day, my mind wandering over what Rainey had already told me. Listening to her was difficult, she had a habit of rambling over moments she found uninteresting, but then diving into clear and particularly painful detail regarding the sexual activities she carried on with her neighbors. Some victims had a tendency to remember everything while others were unable to recall, their minds blocking out the moments that hurt them, that left them helpless to the whims of whatever monster caused harm.

Rainey was a mixture of both. Her recollection of the night her friends died was all but absent, while she carried on with excruciating detail regarding the way she was used by the Connor men. I was still confused as to how it all fit together.

Perhaps it was something as simple as having met her friends at that house. Perhaps these memories had nothing to do with the night her friends died and Rainey was so lonely she needed someone to listen to her talk.

She had no one. Her mother was dead. Her friends. It was clear to me that she was a person who needed human contact, who would undergo abuse so she didn't have to feel alone. I wondered if she was using my position as a psychologist to work out whatever problems were in her head, if this entire interview was simply a platform for her to talk without ever having the first intention to tell me what happened the night her friends died.

Anything was possible with her.

Pulling into the police station parking lot, I gathered the file and my notes of the first several hours I'd spent with Rainey. The station was quiet for the most part, very few people wandering between cars and the building.

It was a good night to speak with Detective Grenshaw and attempt to pin down the information I needed before continuing the interview. Walking quickly through the lot, I let myself in the glass double doors and made my way to the front counter.

A receptionist stared up at me, the collar of her prim white shirt buttoned all the way to her neck, her dark brown hair pulled into a strict bun. The pearl chain of her glasses swung slowly as she moved her head. Thankfully she recognized me from that morning.

"Good afternoon- or I guess good evening, Mr. Redding. It's a little late in the day to say afternoon, isn't it?"

Unlike Rainey, this woman had some strength to her, but even then, she still straightened her posture to see me coming, her hand reaching up to make sure her hair was in place. Behind her glasses, green eyes met mine, open and expectant.

I didn't consider myself a great looking man, but I'd never had an issue finding a date or picking up a woman for a one night stand.

Tall and broad, I took good care of my body. I ate a healthy diet, worked out to keep myself fit, preferring to jog every morning for several miles to clear my head. It was my preference to keep my black hair tamed by a professional cut, but in the moments I let it grow long, it tended to curl like my mother's had.

Women approved of me, although I couldn't understand why. When I looked in a mirror, I saw a stern face with sharp cheekbones, my lips rarely pulling into smile. Yet, like now with the receptionist staring up at me as she continued to squirm over her seat, women were drawn to me like moths to a flame. They were available, often simple and easy.

What interested me was the complete lack of the same reaction in Rainey. I didn't believe her mannerisms were played up due to my presence.

No, Rainey was a natural flirt, either by genetic design or because she'd learned to use her body to get what she wanted. Having spent time with her, I had no delusions that she saw me as something special. She had motives, I just needed to figure out what they were.

"It is rather late in the day," I answered. "Is Detective Grenshaw available? I'd like to talk to him about a case."

The receptionist flashed me a toothy grin.

"About the Day girl, right? I'm telling you, I knew that girl was a handful when she and her mom moved into the neighborhood. What those Connor boys did to her. It was disgusting. They tried to keep it quiet, but everybody knew. I'm not one to wish harm on anyone, but they all got what was coming to them."

Surprise lifted my brows. "You live in Clayton Heights?"

She nodded, her cheeks coloring pink.

"I hate to admit I do. I live a street down from Rainey's house. She is such a pretty girl, but to know how she was being used? It's disgusting. I hope now that they're all gone, she'll do something with her life."

The receptionist shook her head. "I read about what happened at that party a week ago. Absolutely horrible. Those poor kids. Rainey is fortunate she survived."

Keeping my opinions on that to myself, I reminded her, "Could you let the Detective know I'm here?"

"Sure thing."

Without glancing away from me, she picked up the phone and pushed a button. She announced my presence and slammed the phone down, grimacing from the noise she hadn't intended to make.

There was no need to be so nervous around me. I was just an ordinary man who had no intention of knowing her as more than what she already was. My fingers drummed over the counter, a sigh of relief blowing over my lips when Grenshaw opened the door and waved me back.

"Have a good night," she called as I walked away. I waved, keeping my attention on Grenshaw's back as he led me to the room staged for the case. Dropping his weight heavily into a chair, he leaned back, the springs squealing beneath him.

"Before you tell me anything, I have to ask this: Were you walking funny when you left her house?"

I paused mid-step, arched a brow in question. "Excuse me?"

Grenshaw scrubbed a hand down his face in an attempt to hide his grin. Broad shoulders shaking, he wasn't as capable of hiding the laughter bubbling up his chest.

"I'm sorry," he said, his expression twisting with humor, "It's just that listening to Rainey is like watching porn. We called you in because of it. I know you didn't watch the full interview because you weren't in the room long enough, but you have to admit the girl all but shows you how she fucks. My partner and I both walked out of there with our pants a little bit tight, if you know what I mean."

Knowing exactly what he meant, I didn't appreciate it. Not for Rainey. "She's the victim of sexual abuse. Are you telling me you were turned on by what she had to say?"

His eyes widened, expression melting to be met with my lack of amusement.

"Listen, I don't know if she told you something different than what she told me, but Rainey let those guys do what they did to her. And the way she describes it? Fuck. It sounds like she's reliving it all in her head with her fingers between her legs. I don't think she considers it abuse."

"But I do," I responded bluntly.

70

"You're right that something is off with her, so for those men to take advantage the way they did, it was a form of abuse. They were hurting her. Humiliating her. And I'm not sure if she delved deeply enough into it during the interview she had with you, but in mine, she admitted the sexual abuse she'd experienced in her life started with her mother's boyfriends at the age of ten."

Grenshaw could have been doused with a bucket full of cold water and it wouldn't have sobered him up quicker. "Shit..."

"Yes, shit, for lack of a better word. So rather than getting hot and bothered over the information she's given us, perhaps it would be better to take a closer look at the girl we're dealing with. Rainey knows something. She just hasn't told us yet."

Stretching his neck, he ran thick fingers over the scruff along his jaw. "Do you think she had something to do with the murders?"

I took a seat, slapped the file folder down on the table and breathed deeply.

"No. Not yet. She didn't give me much about the night of the party, but what she did tell me was that Michael was the person who tied her to the bed. Apparently Megan had fallen asleep and since she was unavailable to have sex, he turned to Rainey."

Grenshaw's brows lifted up his head. "He went for the sure thing."

"He did," I agreed. "But that's not the point. Whoever killed those kids wasn't attempting to abuse Rainey by keeping her bound. When first reading over the details of the party, I thought perhaps the killer was also a sexual deviant. That he, or she, decided to keep the last victim for a little more than just beating her to death."

Pausing, I traced my finger over a tear in the file folder. "It doesn't make sense. Why beat her up but then leave her alive?"

Eyes pinned to an evidence bag on the table, Grenshaw said, "My opinion?" He looked to me and I nodded. "Maybe she gave it up willingly. She's not the type of girl to keep fighting if that is what the killer was after. He might have roughed her up, and when she complied without complaint, he chose not to kill her."

"It's possible," I answered, my thoughts already moving past the party. "Tell me what you know about Rainey's previous neighbors. The Connors."

A groan slipped from his mouth, deep and weighted with what I assumed was hatred for the entire family. "Every single one of those bastards was a major pain in my ass. If she's mentioned them, I'm sure you know they were drug dealers."

"I do. Rainey told me they sold and used marijuana and cocaine."

"To start with, maybe. Try adding in pills, heroine, meth. Whatever they could get their hands on to hustle, you know? It didn't stop there either. The dad, Paul, was running guns. Jacob was on track to become a serial killer. Frankie had a tendency to punch first and ask questions later. Joel was accused of taking advantage of drunk high school girls a few too many times and Rowan-"

He stopped. Shook his head. "Well, Rowan didn't live long enough to become a problem. The kid died two days before he turned eighteen."

Rowan's death must have destroyed Rainey. She was always careful when talking about him, her voice softer. There was remorse and pain when Rainey

72

remembered the only boy she considered a friend. "How did he die?"

"Car accident. From what the family told us, and what we determined at the scene, Rowan had driven someone to Chicago. It was a cold night. There were ice patches all over the roads. He was probably driving way too fast and lost control of the car on his way back. We thought the impact would have killed him, but the medical examiner found he was still alive when the car caught on fire. Rowan burned to death a few blocks from his house."

The manner of death was unsettling. "Was Rainey ever informed how he died?"

He shrugged. "The family may have told her."

It was enough to mess with any person's head, enough for a person to snap knowing someone they cared about died so horribly. "What about the others?"

"About eight months after Rowan died, Joel was found naked and stabbed to death in an alley near the front of the neighborhood. We never solved the murder. Another few months passed and Paul and Jacob were shot to death in a drug deal gone bad. They were gunned down in their house. Lastly, a few months ago, Frankie died when the house burned down. It was determined to be arson."

Nodding, "I knew about that. Rainey told me she was worried that her house would catch fire as well."

"Yeah. She reported seeing someone run from the house. But that didn't give us much. The Connors had a lot of enemies. It could have been anybody, even competition for their drug turf."

It was a short list of many different ways to die. Without a pattern, I discounted Rainey as having anything to do with it. Grenshaw looked like he was half asleep, his eyelids heavy.

"Go ahead and do what you need to do for the rest of the night, Detective. I'm going to do some work in here. I'm continuing Rainey's interview in the morning.

Standing, he hitched up his pants and tapped a hand on the table. "Good luck with that."

Pausing before he left the room, he said, "Do me a favor and forget about the comment I made about Rainey. I had no idea about what happened to her as a child."

"Already forgotten," I assured him, my focus on the notes I'd made on my notepad.

Left alone in the room, I underlined and highlighted patterns I could clearly see, the one sticking out the most being the marks on Rainey's arm.

The number five was important for some reason, but there were already so many possibilities as to what it could mean.

She'd lived in Clayton Heights for five years.

She lived next door to five men.

There were five adults who'd abused her as a child.

I would include the five victims on the night of the party, but the scars were healed. She wouldn't have had time for that to happen if she'd carved them into her skin within the past week.

What did the five marks mean?

By the time I left the station I was exhausted. The only sleep I accomplished that night was fitful, my thoughts returning to Rainey and the stories she told me.

Regardless of the lack of rest, I arrived at her house the next morning at eight sharp. Rainey was waiting at her door for me, a steaming cup in her hand.

Hair messy as if she'd just crawled out of bed, she had no issue standing at her open door wearing only a pair of loose running shorts and a cut off shirt, her flat stomach visible, the shirt practically see through. As I suspected would be the case, she'd neglected to wear a bra. Briefly I wondered if she would walk around completely naked if it were socially acceptable.

"Morning," she yawned as I climbed up the two steps to the porch.

"You look tired," I observed. "Did you sleep at all last night?"

Round eyes peered up at me, the blue shimmering in the early morning light. "I slept fine. I'm just not a morning person." Full lips pulled into a generous grin. "Would you like some coffee before we start talking again?"

I wasn't a coffee drinker and I never accepted anything from subjects. Especially ones with significant drug problems. "No, I'm fine. Thank you."

Nodding her head, she led me back into the same room as before, her hips swaying again, bottom bouncing in a way that drew the eye. It was difficult not to look when Rainey was in front of you. Everything about her screamed sex. She wasn't shy about it either.

Taking the chair from before, I prepared my notepad and waited for her to sit on the couch in front of me. She held her mug between both hands as if using it to keep warm.

"You look cold. Are you sure you don't want to go put on a sweater and pants before we begin?"

Please, I thought. It would be a lot less distracting.

"No," she answered, her voice hazy from sleep. The sound was even more appealing. "I'm fine. I don't wear a lot of clothing."

That much was apparent.

"We left off with your story of the first night you slept with Joel. But I'd like to go back to the party again now that you've had another night to think about it. Have you remembered anything more?"

Rainey shook her head, ran her fingertip down her neckline, her arm pushing her breasts together. Lips slightly parted, she stared at me for a few seconds. "Not much else."

"Okay. Well, we can try again later."

Pulling my eyes from her, I fought to keep my focus on my notepad rather than on her body. "I looked into some of the information you gave me last time we talked and I learned how your neighbors died. Is there anything you want to tell me about that? Or maybe how their deaths affected you?"

From her spot on the couch, Rainey cleared her throat. "I'm not sure how I feel about them. It didn't bother me when most of them died. People die, you know? Rowan's death bothered me."

She became quiet. Thoughtful. "It bothered me a lot."

I glanced up. "Would you like to talk about it?"

"No. Not right now. I think we should just continue where I left off. There's a lot more to this that you don't know."

Rolling my neck over my shoulders, I clicked my pen and readied myself for what I assumed would be another day of horrifying memories of her sexual experiences. It was the last thing I wanted to hear about, but also what made Rainey who she was.

76

"Fine, Rainey. Go ahead and tell me what happened next."

CHAPTER EIGHT

Rainey - Past

After what happened with Joel, I got into the habit of sleeping with him as well as Jacob and Paul. They all were dealers and it became a matter of who was home and who wanted payment. Everybody in the family knew what was going on and I stopped caring about it, except for how it bothered Rowan.

As the months went on, he was getting moodier, his temper constantly on edge with his family while he was growing closer to me. Rowan and I talked a lot. He often followed me home when I left their house at night and would sit with me on the porch while I smoked whatever I got from his brothers.

He never tried kissing me again, and I was happy for that. I felt horrible about what he saw happening in Jacob's room and had avoided him for a full week after, but when we hung out again, Rowan didn't mention it.

I think he knew I would avoid him more if he kept bringing it up.

Our friendship was close. He would open up to me about the fights he had with his brothers or even problems at school, and I would tell him about my problems at school or things that happened to me before my mom moved me to Clayton Heights.

Mom liked him so much that she would let him sleep on the couch on her nights off, especially if we were up late watching movies. All of us fell into a good place, all except Rowan and his brothers.

It wasn't unusual for him to show up at my window late at night with a black eye or a busted nose. Jacob had even broken one of Rowan's ribs during a fight.

78

While Rowan would admit to the arguments that led to their violence, he would never tell me what the arguments were about. But I knew.

It wasn't too difficult to believe that Jacob or Joel were making fun of me, comparing notes or even poking fun at Rowan because it was obvious he had a crush on me. I kept reminding him to let it go, that nothing was worth getting beat up over, but he never listened.

It was spring and we were on break from school. I was hanging at their house more often than not, all of us getting on each other's nerves because the house was so full most of the time. During the day, there wasn't much to do but get high, and I couldn't be at my mom's house since she was home sleeping.

I'd fallen into a schedule of sorts, switching back and forth between Paul, Jacob and Joel on different days. It wasn't the best situation, and it killed me to see the look on Rowan's face when one of them would call my name to go back to their bedroom.

Rowan could tolerate Jacob and Joel for some reason, but his face would get red, his hands fisting when it was Paul that called me back. Something about my being with his dad really got under his skin. He was always waiting on the couch outside Paul's door for me to come out. The worst part was I knew the walls were paper thin.

You could hear everything that was happening in the living room when I was in Paul's room, so I knew Rowan could hear everything that was happening between us.

Sometimes it hurt when Paul first pushed inside my ass and I would cry out. I didn't have to see Rowan to know he was angry to hear my pain.

One time a loud thump shook Paul's wall and we came out to find that Rowan had punched a hole in it. Paul himself beat Rowan down for that. He told Rowan that if it happened again, he would make him watch us the next time.

I cried that day. God, how I cried.

What I was doing was ruining Rowan. He was a happy kid when I first met him, but within a year, he was always angry. His grades were dropping in school and he started smoking weed all the time. Taking it from his brother when he could, he would give it to me on the days he didn't want me going to his house to get some of my own. But Jacob caught on and stopped giving it to him.

It was a Thursday afternoon. Paul had just left with a few of his biker friends to go on a run or whatever, they were usually gone for a few days at a time and Joel was off with his girlfriend, Angel. She still hated me for being around the house all the time, and I had a feeling she knew about Joel and me even though he swore she didn't know anything.

He'd sworn everybody to secrecy and oddly, the brothers were careful to stay silent about us when Angel was around. Even then, she had to know.

Joel wasn't exactly careful not to touch me when Angel was around, and his eyes were usually on my breasts or butt. If it bounced when I moved, he watched it, Angel scowling at his side.

I'd just left Jacob's room after giving him oral sex for a joint and sat down next to Rowan on the couch. He offered me a breath mint, which had become an inside joke between us. Taking it, I smiled and he just shook his head. "You're better than that," he reminded me on a whisper.

"I know." I whispered back.

Comments made, we settled in and were watching a stupid movie about aliens (Rowan loved sci-fi) when Frankie came storming into the house. The door slammed behind him, the walls shaking. He shoved a hand through his hair and dropped down into the recliner next to us.

Out of all the brothers, Frankie scared me the most. He was a grenade with the pin pulled, a bomb with a fuse sizzling as fire rushed down the length of it. Anything could set him off. Drugs didn't mellow him out either, not even weed.

If anything, they made him worse.

As soon as he sat next to us, a gust of air hit me like a ton of bricks, the smell of alcohol making my stomach roll. I didn't have much to do with Frankie, avoiding him as much as possible, but tonight he glanced over at me and made a point to look me up and down.

"What the fuck are you watching, Rowan?"

Jacob walked into the room just as Frankie was asking the question.

Leaning a shoulder against the wall near the couch, he laughed and said, "I think Rowan likes to watch this shit to see alien tits. Seeing as how he never gets to play with them in real life, he has to add more to his spank bank than just fantasies of Rainey. She lets me play with them though, don't you? She likes it when I play with them."

Already, I didn't like where the conversation was headed. Touching Rowan's leg, I gave him a silent reminder to stay calm. He hated it when Jacob made comments like that. His skin was mottling red and I watched as his jaw ticked a few times. The grind of his teeth was so loud it hurt to listen to it.

81

"Seriously though, Frankie, you should see Rainey's tits. They are so round and heavy that I had to fuck them the other night. I came all over her chin afterward. Didn't I, Rainey?"

Rowan's thigh muscle flinched beneath my hand, his body so damn still that I was worried he'd jump up and do something. He was always beat the worst after an argument with Frankie because his older brother loved to fight. At least once a month, Frankie was arrested for hurting someone. Why he wasn't in prison yet was anybody's guess. Violence thrummed just beneath his skin, morning, noon and night.

"What do you say, man? Would you like to see them? Rainey will do just about anything for a joint."

"Cut it out, Jacob." Rowan's voice was so soft, I wasn't sure anybody besides me had heard him. Unfortunately, I was wrong.

"What was that, kiddo? I couldn't quite hear you."

I wished that Paul or Joel were home. At least with them here, I had some help protecting Rowan from the worst of it.

"Rowan, please," I begged under my breath, my hand squeezing his leg, a reminder for him to let it go.

Jacob laughed. "That's what I thought. Back to what I was saying, Frankie -"

"I said cut it the fuck out!"

Rowan's voice boomed through the living room, pure rage undercoated with hatred. I think of all the brothers, Jacob was the one Rowan hated most. The oldest versus the youngest, and the rest of us were caught in between. While he yelled his demand, Rowan picked up the remote control and flung it in Jacob's direction. His aim was off, the hard plastic cracking against Frankie's cheek instead.

The fire finally reached the end of the crackling fuse. Frankie launched forward, knocking me to the side as he grabbed Rowan's shirt, blood exploding from Rowan's nose from the first sickening crunch of Frankie's fist.

I screamed, tried to pull Frankie back while he continued wailing on Rowan. The coffee table was knocked over, a glass shattering against the floor. Jacob laughed as he slowly rounded the recliner into the living room to get involved.

Tears streamed down my face to hear the continuous thud of Frankie's fist against Rowan's face, and when Jacob pulled his brother away, Rowan was covered in blood. Still, Frankie was chomping at the bit to keep going, a growl emanating from his chest as he thrashed to break Jacob's hold.

"So, here's the thing, Rainey..."

Speaking over the noise, Jacob stared at me, his lips pulled into a smirk that made it clear he'd intended for this to happen. He was always causing problems, always picking at everyone until they were at each other's throats.

"Frankie will probably end up putting poor little Rowan in the hospital if somebody doesn't do something about it. And the best way that I know how to calm Frankie down is to give him another focus he can use to drain all his pent up energy. Considering you're the reason this fight happened, I think you should take Frankie back to his room and spread your legs. You should be that new focus because I won't be able to hold him for long."

His eyes flicked to his youngest brother. I followed the path of his gaze to see Rowan barely conscious, one of his eyes already swelling shut while blood continued to pour from his nose.

Frankie lunged again, Jacob barely holding him by the back of his shirt collar.

"So what do you say? Are you going to follow me back to Frankie's room? Or am I going to let him go? It's your call."

My pulse was hammering in my throat, anger and fear mixing inside my veins that had me stuck in place with no idea what to do. I knew Frankie; he wouldn't stop. I also knew Jacob and if I said no, he would let Frankie go, would sit back and laugh while he continued beating on Rowan.

I had to protect my friend, had to do something to make this all stop. "I'll go back there."

"You sure?" Jacob canted his head, his bicep flexing to continue holding his brother. "You can always say no."

"I said I'll go!" It was the first time I'd raised my voice to any of them, but I was panicking. If this was the only way to get between Frankie and Rowan, then it's what I would do.

Jacob grinned. "Then let's go."

Frankie was stumbling over his feet, blood dripping from his hand as Jacob led him down the hall to his room. Shoving him inside, Jacob turned to glance at me, a glimmer in his eyes that made it clear he was enjoying every bit of what he'd done. He held his arm out for me to walk into the room. "Ladies, first."

Rolling my shoulders back, I walked into Frankie's room and heard the door slam shut behind me. Jacob banged on it twice and yelled through the wood, "You two can thank me later." He was laughing as he walked

84

away, the sound fading the farther he got down the hall.

I turned toward Frankie, legs shaking, my hands fisting and releasing. He was breathing heavily, his eyes narrowed with anger. It occurred to me that if I didn't do something, he would shove me aside and go back into the living room. Closing my eyes, I shed another tear, my hands wrapping over the bottom of my shirt so I could pull it up and over my head. Frankie stilled, his eyes locked to my chest as a smile stretched his lips.

"Jacob wasn't lying." Blue eyes lifted to meet mine. His eyebrows climbed up his forehead. "Were you planning on standing there all night or are you going to take the rest of it off and get the hell over here?"

My fingers flicked the button of my shorts open, pulled the zipper. Slipping my thumbs beneath the sides of my panties and shorts, I shoved them off my hips, let them slide down my legs to the floor and kicked them away. Frankie ran a slow trail down my body with his eyes.

"Fuck yeah," he growled, crooking a finger to beckon me forward.

Forcing one foot in front of the other, I was within arm's reach when he wrapped an arm around my waist, spun me and slammed me up against a wall. His fingers shoved between my legs at the same time his mouth closed over my left nipple. A small yelp volleyed across my lips when he bit down, not caring if it caused me pain.

"That hurts," I complained.

Pulling his lips free, he looked up at me, released my waist from his arm and gripped my other breast so hard that my head fell back against the wall, my teeth

85

clenched. "You'll get used to the pain, baby. I like it rough." Another hard squeeze and he spoke against my ear, "Seriously though, your fucking tits are amazing. Take off my pants and spread your legs."

When I didn't move fast enough, he released my breast to wrap his hand over my throat, his other hand still moving between my legs, his fingers rough. "I said take off my fucking pants, Rainey. You're into this, right? Into me?"

I nodded, struggled to breathe. "Yeah, Frankie. I want this." What else was I going to say?

My hands went to his pants and I fumbled the button a few times before unfastening it and ripping down the zipper. I shoved the material off his hips and he kicked it away into the same pile as mine. Frankie was already hard; the violence turned him on.

Lifting me by my ass, he slammed me back to the wall again and shoved inside me with one thrust, his hips rocking against me as he moved his hand back to my breast. The wet sound of our bodies coming together was a beat beneath his grunts.

"Fuck yeah. You are such a fucking slut. Now I know what everyone else sees in you."

My butt and back kept thumping against the wall. Frankie put enough distance between our bodies that he could look down and watch where he was sinking into me, his brows pulled together, teeth clenched as he slammed harder and harder.

"That's a good little slut," he growled, not caring that I was fighting not to cry. "You like that, bitch? Tell me you fucking like it!"

"I like it," I lied, my arms wrapping over his shoulders.

"Yeah, you do."

86

He dropped me to the floor suddenly, pain shooting up my tailbone from the impact. "Now crawl over to my bed and bend over the side. I want to ride that shit from behind."

I did as he said, ignoring the pain in my back and between my legs. He walked behind me as I crawled, grabbing my hips when I bent over the side of his mattress and buried my face into the blanket.

Wanting to cover my ears to keep from hearing the horrible names he called me, I just lay there and took it. Unlike Jacob, he didn't come quickly. It kept going and going until he got so frustrated that he wasn't satisfied with just one hole any longer.

Frankie's hand gripped my hair and he pulled out, slid his dick up, notched it at my ass and laughed to shove inside. It wasn't like Paul. He didn't work his way in there slowly and I silently screamed, my mouth opening in response to the pain.

Another ten minutes and he finished. It took me longer to crawl to my clothes and pull them on, every part of my body on fire. He didn't try to help. Didn't clean me up. Just fell onto his bed and went to sleep while I struggled to get my clothes back on.

When I stumbled out of his room, Jacob stood in his doorway with a joint in his hand and a smirk on his face.

"Thought you might need this."

I took it and kept walking, Jacob talking at my back.

"You did good, Rainey. Probably stopped Frankie from fucking up Rowan permanently."

When I turned the corner into the living room, Rowan was sitting on the couch holding an ice pack to his face. He glared at me as I walked past, pain and

barely restrained anger flooding his normally friendly
eyes.

CHAPTER NINE

Justin - Present

I blinked, angled my head right to crack my neck, blinked again and cleared my throat.

Keeping a professional demeanor in the face of a story such as that was near impossible. It wasn't the same reaction Grenshaw had joked about before he understood Rainey's truth. This was more a saturation of shock, an utter and intolerable, disbelief that Rainey could speak about such an experience without so much as an ounce of doubt that what she had allowed Frankie to do to her was wrong.

Carefully, I chose my next words. "Did you, by any chance, feel that what happened that night was abusive?"

Flicking the ash from her cigarette into a new cup, Rainey peered over at me, her face a mask of confused innocence. "Well, of course."

Relief washed my over body. At least she had that much sense.

"I mean, Frankie could have killed his brother by hitting him so hard. They were always abusing Rowan, all three of them."

Pain returned, a pulsing electric spear drilling into my left temple. Reaching to rub at it, I stared across the room at a woman who sat with one leg crossed over the other, her toe pointed, foot bouncing.

Tapping my pen against my lips, I attempted another angle.

"I meant towards you, Rainey. Frankie's behavior. Did you continue having sex with him after he treated you so poorly?"

89

Shaking her head, she pulled her lips into a tight line. "No."

Oh, thank God...

"Paul basically gave Frankie the riot act for messing me up so bad. He told both of us that we weren't allowed near each other again. He didn't like having to wait for me to heal. Apparently his other women weren't as - I don't know. Willing?"

I was beginning to agree with the police receptionist and Detective Grenshaw. It was a good thing that all the Connors were dead.

Appealing to her emotions was the best approach. It was clear Rainey wasn't concerned for herself, but for Rowan she felt something. Whether it was a protective instinct or simply that he'd been a friend, he was the key to her heart.

"Let's pause here and talk about what was occurring between you and the Connors. Per my notes, we're what? A year into your life in Clayton Heights?"

She nodded. "Sounds about right."

"You move into this new neighborhood with your mom. You meet the new neighbors and immediately begin a sexual relationship with the oldest brother, Jacob. Sex for drugs, right?"

Another nod, her eyes meeting mine, open and honest.

"Within a few months, you're sleeping with the father. Also a sex for drugs relationship. Another few months after that and you're sleeping with Joel."

"That's right."

"And then this incident occurs with Frankie. You've slept with an entire family at this point."

"All of them except for Rowan." A slight grin, sheepish. "I warned you I was a slut."

Holding up a hand, I sucked in a breath to temper my reaction.

"First, you need to stop referring to yourself that way. In my opinion, you made some poor decisions (*incredibly stupid decisions*, I didn't say) and by calling yourself a slut, you are basing your view of yourself, valuing your worth, on those decisions. But those decisions don't make up for who you are. They are events. Memories. Mistakes. But they are only *parts* of Rainey, not *all* of her. Do you understand what I'm saying?"

Pulling her lower lip between her teeth, Rainey stared at me dumbfounded. "I think so."

"Good," clicking my pen, I broke our stare. "Okay, good. We're getting somewhere. So, if we're a year into your life in Clayton Heights, I'm assuming Rowan was sixteen around the time of the event you just described."

Her expression softened, eyes drifting so much that I knew she was seeing the past rather than the present.

Shifting her body over her seat in a sinuous move that stretched her legs and arched her back, she smiled with just the corners of her lips.

"Yeah, he was. Mom and I had baked him a cake on his birthday. He was so surprised. Nobody had ever done that for him before. You should have seen his face. We even had a present, wrapped and everything. But," she laughed softly, still trapped in a memory, her hands fluttering over her thighs with butterfly touches. "Neither my mother or I could bake. The cake was a disaster. I'm not sure if we messed up on the ingredients or what, but it was awful."

Rainey's faraway gaze lifted to mine.

"Rowan ate the entire thing and swore it was the best cake he'd ever tasted. He was like that. Kind. Not like his dad and brothers. They would have probably tossed that cake in my face or against a wall. But not Rowan."

A click of my pen. "Did Angel and Rowan get along? You've mentioned she was Joel's girlfriend and Joel took it easy on his younger brother, would intervene in fights and such. What was the relationship there?"

"Why do you ask?"

Because I'm not here for the story of your life, I'm here to find out who would have killed her and your friends. "Just because."

A dismissive shrug of her shoulder.

"They didn't have much to do with one another. Normally when Angel was over with Joel they stayed in his bedroom, fucking most of the time, I'm sure, but also because he was afraid she'd find out he was also having sex with me. He didn't bring her around a lot, and when he did, he kept her in other rooms. Any time she was near me, she would call me all sorts of horrible names. It pissed Rowan off, but so did everybody else."

"If she hated you so much, how did you end up at a party with her?"

"Megan invited me. I'm not sure that Angel knew I was going to be there."

My head shot up, surprise and relief that she was finally giving me something about that night. "So, you and Megan were friends?"

"No," shadows raced behind her eyes, "Megan hated me, too. Probably more than Angel."

"Why?"

"Because she was Rowan's girlfriend and I'm the reason Rowan died. It was my fault -" A choked sob cut through her voice.

Fighting to regain her composure, her pale skin turning red around her nose, Rainey straightened her spine, the sleeve of her shirt falling from her shoulder, the material dipping so low that one breast was almost entirely exposed. She didn't appear to notice.

I did...and I hated myself for it. She was the type of girl that made you want to look.

Forcing my gaze to my notepad, I asked, "What was your fault?"

"Rowan got into that car the night he died because of me. He was upset because of me. He died because of -"

Knowing she wouldn't finish the thought, I redirected her once again. "So if Megan hated you, why would she invite you to a party?"

"We worked together. I got a job at the diner down the street a few months ago. She was trying to let go of the past. And she was dating Michael, so, I don't know, I guess it had been so long since Rowan- I don't know. She just did."

Dragging my gaze back to her, I found that the shirt had fallen farther down, the entire left breast exposed. It was -

"Rainey, would you mind lifting your shirt up, please? I'm not sure if you noticed but -"

She glanced down, laughed, lifted the strap of her shirt to her shoulder. "Sheesh, Doc. It's just a breast. Most men like looking at them."

"I'm not most men, and we're not in the type of relationship where I should be looking at them, understand? Your body is your body and it's not meant for display unless you want to show it to somebody."

"Who says I mind now?"

Tilting my head to the left, "Rainey."

She gave me a full smile. "I'm just messing with you. I really don't mind though. There were days when I would walk around topless at the house next door. After Rowan died, I did. Why not? They'd all seen them. Touched them. Sucked on them. It didn't much matter anymore. Not after Rowan was gone."

"We should stay on track. Let's talk about how you ended up at a party with two girls who didn't like you and you don't seem to have liked much."

"I liked Megan. She was good for Rowan. Kept him busy and out of trouble. Maybe that's why I went to the party with her? I liked her."

Or you were just lonely...

"Did Megan have any enemies you know of?"

Leaning against the couch, Rainey slid her palms down her thighs, her legs parting as she did so. "No. She was a sweet girl. Well, I mean, she had her moments. Mostly around me. She didn't like that I was at the house so much, but I preferred it over there. Especially after my mom found a new boyfriend."

Jotting that information down, I looked over at her. "Was the new boyfriend mean to you? Did he-" I wasn't sure I wanted this answer, not with everything else I knew about her. "Did he-"

"Mom and him had sex a lot. I mean, that was great for her, she seemed to really like him, but the walls in this house are as paper thin as the neighbor's house. You could hear everything. It made me uncomfortable. So I preferred being next door."

My brows shot up. "Oh? Well, that's good, I guess. So, the boyfriend, he was-"

"He's dead now. Died in this house actually."

94

Why was I not surprised? "And how did he die?"

"We haven't gotten there yet."

"In the story, I assume?"

Rolling her eyes, "Yes, Doc, in the story. Don't you know that stories are supposed to be told from beginning to end? Jumping around will only confuse things."

Except we were taking a long and winding road to the night I wanted to discuss. How any of this had anything to do with the party, I couldn't wrap my head around. Rainey needed someone to listen to her, and she'd chosen me to be that someone. As such, I would do her the favor.

"Okay. Then back to the story. At this point, you've slept with everybody but Rowan. You mentioned Megan was his girlfriend. Was that the reason you never slept with him?"

A curious expression flashed across her face. Lips demure, eyes soft, her chest expanding with a deep breath. "I never said I didn't have sex with Rowan. I just hadn't done so by the time I'd already been with everybody else. Megan didn't like me because she knew I'd been with Rowan. I was his first."

"Did you fight with Megan about Rowan?"

She glanced up at me, laughed softly. "We haven't -"

"Gotten there yet, I know. Just tell me the next part of the story then. Tell me about Megan."

CHAPTER TEN

Rainey - Past

Have you ever looked at a person, really looked at them, and knew they were the best thing in your life?

That was how I felt when I looked at Rowan. I don't know why God felt I was anywhere near good enough to know a boy like him, but for some reason Rowan had been tossed in front of me, a gift from the universe, I suppose, an angel without wings. I often wondered if I'd been younger or if Rowan had been older when we met if things would have been different.

Maybe I would have hooked up with him that first night and been his girlfriend instead of just a friend. He was the type of boy I would have been faithful to, the kind that smiled at you and made you feel like the prettiest girl in the room.

That's why I wasn't surprised when he started having a lot of girls chasing after him as he grew older. By the time he was a month away from turning seventeen, he'd filled out in the chest and shoulders, was catching up to the size of his brothers and was even taller than Frankie and Joel. He worked out, ran in the afternoons after school and considered joining the track team.

His face was always scruffy, a dusting of dark hair along his strong jaw. When he smiled, his dimples would sink down creating little dark pinpoints next to his mouth. I really did love him, but I knew I would destroy his life. He needed a good girl, one who would worship him and keep her legs closed for everybody but him.

That girl wasn't me. He knew it and I knew it.

After the fight with Frankie, Rowan and I hung out over at my house mostly. But I still wanted drugs, so we agreed that when I was over at his house, he would stay in his room to keep from getting so upset about the way his brothers treated me. He'd learned to walk away when Jacob attempted to start fights, and he was happy his dad had demanded I stay away from Frankie. There were some good moments within all the gloom of our lives.

One day in the fall, it was getting cold outside. I was just walking home from the corner store when Rowan came running up behind me, wrapped his arm around my waist and lifted me from the ground. I squealed from surprise, laughing as he kissed my cheek and mussed my hair before putting me down. He'd just left school, but by that time, I'd dropped out. I wasn't smart enough to graduate and since I was of age, my mom wouldn't get in trouble if I didn't go.

"What's got you in such a good mood?"

He winked at me, nudged my shoulder with his. "A girl."

Instantly, I felt jealous, but I kept that to myself. He deserved to be happy about someone else. "Oh yeah? Who is she?"

Walking down the sidewalk on our way home, Rowan launched into detail about the girl who'd put such a big smile on his face. "Her name is Megan McCormick, and she's beautiful. She has blond hair and blue eyes." He lifted his hands to his chest, "She's stacked." I rolled my eyes and smacked his shoulder.

"Please, like you don't know men look at that."

"You know I do."

His eyes darkened for a second, and I knew we were walking a fine line to even talk about it. "So she's got great tits? What else?"

"She's smart," he answered, beaming with pride, "Why she wants me, I have no clue, but she smiles a lot, is constantly touching my arm or shoulder. I think she wants me to ask her out."

"You should." In a way, this girl already bothered me and I hadn't even met her. Rowan wasn't hurting for female attention, but the girls who chased him had never caused him to turn his head. Not away from me, at least. I had a feeling this one would.

"I might. If I do, I'll never bring her around the house. Not with the way my brothers are. They'll screw with her and I'll get angry."

Nodding my head, I mentioned, "That's smart. Keeping her away from them. When are you going to ask her out?"

He hitched the strap of his backpack up his shoulder. "You think I should?"

Laughter bubbled over my lips. "I already said you should. Don't you ever listen to me?"

Serious suddenly, "You're the only person I listen to, Rainey. If I could lie back and listen to you talk all day, I would. I love your voice. It's soft, like a lullaby. Sometimes when I get angry or worked up and you're not around, I think of your voice to calm myself down."

Glancing at him, I grinned, but felt sad at the same time. "What's Megan's voice like?"

His eyes grew distant. "Higher pitched than yours. But she's short, I mean *tiny*, the kind of girl you can pick up and toss over your shoulder."

"There you go. Some women like the caveman approach."

"Do you?"

The question knocked me off balance. "I don't know what I like. Nobody has ever asked. They just do what they want and I go along with it."

His jaw tightened, hand clenching over the strap of his backpack. "Maybe you should figure it out and then only mess around with guys who are willing to give you what you like."

Rowan's house and mine came into view. Rather than going to his, we walked up the dirt path to mine, across the porch and inside. As soon as we made it through the living room, we heard the mattress squeaking in my mom's room, the grunts and moans that meant she and her boyfriend, David, were going at it again.

"Let's grab a few sodas and go over to your place. I hate listening to them."

Rowan's expression fell. He'd been hoping we could stay at my house for a while, just the two of us. "Yeah, okay."

Walking into his house, we found that Joel and Frankie were home. Frankie for the most part ignored us. He was on the recliner watching television, most likely high as a kite or drunk. Joel was in the kitchen making something to eat. As soon as he saw me, he grinned and tapped his leg like someone would do when calling a dog. Rowan grumbled beside me and said, "I'll be in my room."

Our eyes met and I nodded before walking up to Joel. "Where's Angel?"

"Not here," he answered, his eyes looking me up and down. "Jump up on the counter."

"Why?"

"Because I said so. You want something, don't you?"

99

"What do you have?"

"A few joints."

"Okay." Planting my hands on the counter at my sides, I lifted myself up, butt clearing the edge so I could sit on the surface.

"Take off your shirt."

I blinked my eyes. "Out here in the open? Why don't we just go back to your room?"

He laughed. "Everybody in this house has seen you naked already. I don't know why you'd give a damn about whether you are out in the open or not. Now take off your shirt. I want to play with your tits."

Breathing out on a huff, I slipped my shirt off, dropped it on the counter beside me. He cupped my breasts, buried his face in them, his thumbs brushing the nipples.

"I wish Angel had your rack." Joel's eyes peered up at me. "I always think of your tits while fucking her. Stay right there. I want to do something."

Turning, he opened the freezer, pulled out a jug of ice cream.

"What are you doing?"

"Having fun, just sit still."

Rolling the side of the cold container over one of my nipples, he used his fingers to toy with the other. "Arch your back so they stick out more."

I glanced around to see if Frankie was watching. His eyes were glued to the television. Rowan was in his room. Paul was gone as well as Jacob. We were pretty much alone so I did what he said. Joel pulled the container away, staring at my tight nipple, then dropped the container on the counter beside me and opened the top. "Unbutton your shorts and play with yourself while I do this."

100

"Joel-"

"Just do it, Rainey. You want the joints, don't you?"

"I do."

"Then finger yourself while I play with your tits." He glanced up at me. "Haven't you ever masturbated before?"

A shake of my head and he grinned. "Well, there's a first time for everything. Get moving."

Unbuttoning my shorts, I unzipped them, unsure what to do next. Joel pulled the sides wide open. "I want to be able to see what you're doing. Now shove your fingers down there and play with yourself. Stick them up inside and pump your hand. Like a guy would do."

Doing as he instructed, I felt heat rise in my cheeks, a blush turning my entire body pink.

"Lean back on an elbow so you can get good and deep. Yeah, like that. Fuck, just like that."

While I was touching myself, Joel took two fingers and scooped out ice cream. He rubbed it over one of my tits and watched me for a second before bending over to lick it off. "Moan, Rainey. Why do you always have to be so quiet?"

Probably because I was scared someone would walk in. Parting my lips, I let my head fall back and moaned. "Harder. Fuck yourself harder," he demanded.

Dipping his fingers in the ice cream, he scooped out more, rubbed it over my nipple and then sucked it off.

The front door opened and closed, heavy steps shaking the floor as someone walked into the kitchen. I turned my head to see it was Jacob, tried to pull my hand from my pants, but Joel grabbed my wrist to stop me. "Don't worry about him. Just keep going."

Jacob laughed, walked up to the counter behind my head and molded my right breast with his hand while Joel sucked on the other. "Well, isn't this interesting. Didn't expect to come home and find a slut fingering herself on the counter."

I clenched my eyes shut, not liking the way they were both messing with me. My hand kept moving and they were cheering me on, telling me to go harder and faster. "Work for it," Joel would say. "What's she getting for this?" Jacob asked. "A few joints," Joel answered.

"What the fuck is going on?"

Rowan's voice caught all our attention, three heads snapping his direction, Jacob and Joel laughing while my eyes widened with surprise and shame.

"Nothing much, little brother. We're just having some fun. Want to join in. Clip your virgin wings?" Jacob's voice was a low hum. He was always teasing Rowan.

"I'm not a virgin."

I pulled my hands from my pants and sat up, covering my chest with my arms.

"Oh yeah?" Jacob asked. "You dicked somebody? I don't believe it."

Rowan's cheeks flared red, his eyes meeting mine. "It's none of your fucking business."

He was lying. Everybody knew he was lying. If Rowan had ever been with a girl, he would have told me. I was sick and tired of people always making fun of him, always holding how good he was over his head.

"You know what?" I said, shoving Joel away from me and jumping down from the counter. "I'm tired of this shit."

Still without a shirt, I marched across the kitchen and took Rowan's hand. One tug and I was leading him to his bedroom. Jacob and Joel howled behind us.

"Go get it, little brother. About damn time."

Shoving Rowan into his room, I slammed the door behind us. His eyes were locked to my chest when I turned around and I remembered I had no shirt. What did it even matter? Joel was right. It's not like everybody in the damn house hadn't seen them already.

"Well," I looked up at him. "Go ahead and touch them, Rowan."

"Rainey-"

"Just do it. You know you want to. I know you want to, and I'm sick of your brothers calling you out for not being with somebody. If anything, we can stop that at least."

He stepped back, ran his hand through his hair and blew out a breath. "You're better -"

"Than this. Yeah, I know. You keep telling me that. But I'm not, Rowan. You are. But I'm not. So, if this is what I'm good for, you might as well just get it over with. You'll need the practice for when you're with someone else. And it will stop your asshole brothers from constantly making fun of you, so there's no reason why we shouldn't."

Crossing the room, I stepped up to him, my eyes locked to his as I grabbed his hand and placed it over my breast. "Like that, Rowan. You've done it before. At my house, remember?"

His fingers squeezed, heat blazing behind his blue eyes. Reaching forward I touched him over his jeans and discovered he was already hard. It didn't take much with him. Not when it came to me.

103

Softly, I whispered, "Now touch the other one while I take off your pants."

Other hand lifting, he touched me so tenderly that I shivered. This wasn't a man using my body like everyone else, Rowan worshipped me with the way he placed his hand on my body. I didn't deserve it, but I would let him if it meant I could stop Jacob and Joel from always making fun of him.

"Yeah, baby, like that," I prodded him, my fingers unfastening his jeans and shoving them down his hips. Our eyes remained locked while I wrapped my hand over his cock, his body flinching immediately. "Do you like when I touch you?"

Rowan nodded, his tongue licking over his lips. "Rainey, when I said I'm not a virgin, I was -"

With my free hand, I placed a finger over his lips. "I know. And we're going to fix that. Okay? You just let me take care of it."

Nodding, he looked down between us, at his hands molding my breasts, at mine working slowly over his dick.

"Can I kiss you?"

Not understanding why, I wanted to say no. His kisses were too precious, his love too good for a girl like me. But I knew he needed it. "Yeah, Rowan. You can kiss me."

Leaning down, his mouth brushed over mine, his hands squeezing harder as I kept a steady stroke with mine. Long and slow. He wouldn't last. I knew that. Not if this was his first time and I knew his brothers would laugh if we left this room too soon. Silently, I promised I would give him everything he needed, would make sure he walked out of this room with his head held high.

Tongues dancing, Rowan moaned into my mouth, his hips moving, the rhythm not quite there. He needed help. I would be the one to teach him.

I broke the kiss. "You just stand right there. Let me take care of this first part and then we'll go again, okay?"

Rowan's brows knitted together, but he didn't stop me, just watched me like I was some beautiful goddess as I dropped down to my knees in front of him. "Rainey."

"Shhhh, let me do this."

His fingers weaved through my hair as I licked the tip, my lips parting as I took him inside my mouth, my hand still working the shaft.

"Oh, fuck," he whispered above me. I tipped my eyes up to see his head had fallen back. Bobbing my head, I watched Rowan with fascination as he learned what it was like for a girl to go down on him.

Blue eyes peered down on me, our stares locking, my lips pulling into an odd smile as I sucked and licked, my hand still pumping.

"I'm going to-"

He tried to pull away, but I reached behind him and grabbed his butt, taking him deeper into my mouth. His first orgasm was quick, just like I knew it would be. The second would take a little longer.

Eyes wide, he watched me as I pushed up to my feet. "Well?" I smiled shyly, not quite sure what he was thinking. Rowan just stared at me like he'd never seen me before, his body tight, his hands fisted at his sides.

"I think I love you, Rainey Summer Day. I think I've loved you since the moment we first met."

My heart hammered, jumped into my throat and slammed down again. "Rowan, don't say that-"

105

He lunged forward, his fingers wrapping over the back of my neck, his mouth closing over mine as he led me back against a wall.

Our mouths sliding together, he gripped the back of my thigh and lifted my leg up to wrap over his hip. Our breath collided, his hands moving everywhere as he kissed me like he would die without it. I placed my palms against his chest wanting to push him away, but at the same time wanting to pull him closer.

I think I love you too, Rowan...

I didn't say it. Just thought it. It would be wrong to lead him into thinking we could ever be together. He needed someone better, like Megan.

It was a good thing we were getting this over with now before he was officially with her. I promised him and myself that once he had a girlfriend, I would never let this happen again. And maybe once he realized I wasn't anything more than a girl who men liked to fuck, he would focus his attention on a new girl, one who deserved his love, his kisses, his touch.

I pulled away, my chest beating against his, both of our breath labored. "Lie down on your bed, baby. Let me show you what sex is like. And when we get done in here, your brothers won't have another fucked up thing to say about you."

Reaching over his head, he tugged his shirt off, my eyes tracing over the definition of muscle in his shoulders, arms, chest and stomach. Damn, this boy was fine. Absolutely, stunning. He'd grown up, all right. Had put on weight and toned his body into something women would drool over. Placing a palm against his chest, I looked up at his face.

"I like it when you look at me. Your eyes get all big and I know you like what you see. We can be together, Rainey. Just you and me."

Shaking my head, I smiled. "It's you and me right now. Okay? Just right now. But when we leave this room, we're friends again. That's the way it has to be."

"Why?"

My heart broke. "It just does. Now go lie down. Let me take care of you."

Stepping backwards, he kept his eyes on me. Eventually sitting on the edge of his bed, he waited for me to step forward and take off my shorts and panties. They fell to the floor, I kicked them from my feet, and Rowan couldn't stop staring at me like I was a shooting star flaming across his sky. "You're beautiful."

"So are you. Now lie down." I tilted my head, smiled. "Don't make me tell you again."

Grinning, he shoved back on his bed, stretching over it with his head landing on a pillow. I stepped up, watched him watching me, and then crawled up on hands and knees to straddle the tops of his thighs. He was almost erect again. I wrapped my fingers over him and stroked to help him get ready. Keeping our stares locked, I leaned over and kissed the tip, smiling when his cock jumped in my hand, growing even more. When he was full and long, I pushed up on my knees, notched myself above him and asked, "Are you ready?"

Rowan was star struck, his mouth parted slightly as he nodded his head.

"Touch my breasts while I sink down on you. Squeeze them in your hands."

He did as I asked, my body lowering so slowly that both of us moaned to feel how perfectly he fit inside me. Seating him all the way, I kept from moving at first, allowed him to feel what it was like to be inside a woman, my hands flat against his stomach as he stared up at me. "How do you like it?" I squeezed my inner muscles and he flinched, his eyes clenching shut and his lips pulling into an odd grin.

"Rainey, you're killing me."

"Well, then put your hands on my hips and work me above you. Kind of like jerking off, but with a girl instead. You set the rhythm you want, Rowan. Or just hold on while I do it."

His hands slid from my tits to my hips, his blue eyes opening to watch me move above him. I went slow at first, pushed my body up until just the tip was inside and then slid down again to let him fill me.

Rowan wasn't a virgin any longer, and I thought maybe it was meant for me to be his first time. I took away his shyness, showed him what it was to be a man when a woman looked at him with lust in her eyes. His head rolled over the pillow as I continued to move with a slow roll of my hips, forcing him deeper. "You can't come in me, Rowan."

"I know."

"Okay, just let me know if you think that's going to happen. I'll pull off."

It was pure luck that I wasn't pregnant yet. Jacob and Joel were decent about pulling out, and Paul and Frankie weren't exactly in the right spot to make a baby. But Rowan, he didn't have enough experience yet to know when to stop. I would be the one to let him know. I could tell. It was impossible to count how many times I'd noticed a guy about to finish and thought *oh, thank you, they're almost done.*

Except I didn't want it to be done with this guy. I wanted this moment to last forever.

"Fuck, Rainey, you feel so good. I didn't know - I mean, I knew - but I didn't. Fuck."

He was cute when he rambled. I bounced faster, pushing down harder, one of his hands released my hip and his thumb worked my clit. My head fell back and I moaned. "Rowan?"

Laughter shook his chest and stomach. "It's my turn to take of you now." When our eyes met again, he grinned and blushed. "I've watched porn, Rainey. Do you like this?"

That familiar tightening inside me happened again, my body moving against him, rubbing against his thumb and I came, the climax so hard and violent that I fell forward and moaned into his chest. With one hand, he brushed my hair from my face, our bodies still working together. Then he surprised me by flipping me over and taking control of our dance.

With one arm he held himself above me as he stared down at my face, his hips still working, sweat beading down his chest. "I'm making love to you, Rainey. That's what this is. I can never just fuck you, not like them. Do you feel the difference?"

My eyes started to water as another orgasm snuck up on me. Rowan wiped a tear from my cheek. "It can always be like this. You and me." His hips worked harder as he watched me, his arm wrapping beneath one of my legs to push it up and out. He sank deeper, never once breaking our stare. "Please, Rainey. Tell me you'll be with only me."

The climax took me, a tidal wave of pleasure rushing through my body so furiously that I shook beneath it. Carnal moans crawled up my throat, Rowan's name a prayer on my lips as he continued to move even faster. He was almost there. Almost done.

This could never happen again.

Another minute and he pulled out, his release hot on my stomach. He sank down against me despite the mess, his mouth slanting against mine as he kissed me deeply.

Speaking against my lips, he begged, "Please, Rainey. Just you and me. I promise you I'll take care of you. I promise I'll always protect you."

My eyes blinked the tears away, hot drops falling down my cheeks. "I can't, Rowan. I'm sorry. You deserve better than me."

"You are better. Why do you refuse to see it? I will love you more than anybody, Rainey, I promise you that. Just...please."

Shaking my head, I cupped his cheeks and pressed my forehead against his. "No, baby. We can't. You need to ask that Megan girl out and if you like her, you should be good to her and make a life with her, okay? Just forget about me. I'll always be your friend. I'll always be your first. But that's all I'll ever be."

Staying in his room for another two hours, I had sex with him one more time. When I left, he followed me to the door, leaning a shoulder against the doorframe while watching me turn the corner into Jacob's room to earn another joint in nothing but my panties and shorts.

CHAPTER ELEVEN

Justin - Present

There was something very wrong about Rainey, so infuriatingly wrong that I wanted to shake her and slap some sense into her. I almost wished Rowan was alive so I could pat the poor kid on the back and sympathize with him for his desperate love of a girl that would never admit she loved him back.

Staring at her, I noted the pain in her eyes, the longing, the heartache of a memory that she'd shared with me with adoration in her voice. Of all her experiences, that was a good one, that memory was something I had no doubt she held onto with both hands clenched, refusing to let go.

So why hadn't she accepted that a man could truly love her, and chose to be with him?

"He treated you well," I observed aloud.

Nodding, she knocked a tear from her cheek. "He did. Rowan was my best friend. He was everything."

Placing my pen down, I shifted the notepad from my legs to the arm of the chair and leaned forward. "You know, I have to ask this, Rainey. Why didn't you stay with Rowan? I know you think you weren't good enough for him, you made that clear, but why? What have you done that's so bad, you don't deserve to be with a good guy who cares about you?"

Her fingers swept over the mark on her arm, the five tally marks, a count she was keeping of something.

"I just wasn't good for him, Justin. Not for him. Not then. I went from a boy's room who loved me, who made love to me, and walked into his brother's room to let him fuck me against the wall between their rooms.

That's how screwed up I was. Rowan had just finished pouring his heart out to me, had just been with me for his first time, and I screamed out Jacob's name while my ass thumped against the wall, Jacob laughing the entire time reminding me that's what it was like to be with a real man. Should I remind you about those walls? Rowan would have heard the entire thing. He sat on the bed we'd just had sex in and listened to his brother *'fuck me good'*. Rowan deserved better."

Mirroring my posture, Rainey leaned forward, her arms tight to her body so that when her shirt draped forward, I could see straight down it. It was automatic, my eyes drifting lower. I stared without thinking.

"You want to fuck me good, too, Doc?"

Head snapping up, my eyes locked to hers. She grinned, blue gaze sparkling. "I'll let you. I let everybody. The only difference is I've learned to like it now. Rowan taught me how to like it. That's how good he was. If I was going to abuse my body, then I might as well get something out of it. Some form of pleasure, you know? I slept with Rowan four more times after that first experience. Four more before he died. And those four times taught me everything I needed to know about my body and what could be done with it."

Sitting back, I scrubbed a hand down my face. "Rainey, I'm sorry, I shouldn't have-"

"Don't worry about it," she said through her soft laughter. "It's like I told you. I won't say no. Not to you. Have you looked in a mirror recently?" She whistled. "You're a pretty man, Doc. Pretty like Joel and Rowan. There's a bedroom in back."

I shook my head. "I'm not here for that, Rainey. I'm here to help you."

"There are a lot of different ways to help a person. I know I had sex a lot back then, but lately, I've been good. I've kept my legs closed. I'll make something of myself."

"You were about to have sex with Michael on the night he died. A night we should be talking about instead of what happened with your neighbors."

She lit a cigarette, the first she'd had in a few hours. "What do you want to know?"

This was good. We'd redirected back where we needed to be. But when I looked up to speak to her about that night, she smiled and blew out a cloud of smoke, carnal knowledge in a pair of eyes that had been innocent just a few minutes ago. Rainey stretched back against the couch cushion watching me, daring me to take another inappropriate peek at her body.

"Did you see the murderer that night? You must have. He attacked you as well as the others."

Silence stretched between us, our stares locked. I wouldn't glance down, wouldn't take the bait she'd cast and was now reeling in like the master fisher she was. A knowing grin stretched her lips, slow and feline. "No, I didn't. I must have been asleep. We were drinking and smoking pot, which tends to knock me out, especially after work."

Frustration flooded me. "Do you have any idea who it might have been?"

Another puff of her cigarette. "It's coming back to me. Slowly."

Outside the windows, the sun was hugging the horizon, the bright day transitioning into late afternoon. I was surprised to see how much time had passed. "Can you tell me anything unusual that happened that night?"

"Preston was a dealer, not when I met him at first, but after the Connors died, he took over. He left that night for about an hour. It was uncomfortable as hell because that left Michael, Megan, Angel and me in the living room together. And since Michael and Megan were all over each other, she was straddling his lap and rubbing all over him, that left Angel and me staring awkwardly at each other, not sure what to say or do."

Grabbing my pen and notebook, I made notes. "What happened after that?"

Rainey stretched her legs out in front of her, the movement catching my eye. I turned my head toward her just enough to get caught. She grinned. "Preston came back pissed off for some reason. He was yelling and hitting walls. Angel took him upstairs to calm him down. I think something went wrong with a deal."

My pen scribbled furiously over the paper. "So someone could have followed him back?"

"Could have," she said, the strap of her shirt falling from her shoulder again revealing the swell of her left breast. Canting her head, she followed my gaze. "You sure you don't want me to take you back to my room? You look, I don't know, hungry."

What I was feeling at that moment was beyond the professionalism I'd learned in school. Never had I experienced this. Never had I crossed a line, even in thought, when it came to a patient or subject I was interviewing. But there was something about Rainey. She was a woman created solely for the purpose of temptation. Everything about her, *everything*, brought out primal instincts that were more animal than human.

What made her dangerous was that she knew it.

Clearing my throat, I lifted my eyes to her face. "I should go. It's getting late and I still have to report to the detective what we talked about today before heading home. We can continue this tomorrow. Same time."

She nodded, standing up from the couch to walk me to the door. As I stepped outside, Rainey leaned a shoulder against the doorway, her eyes darting past me to a neighbor standing across the street. The man stared back at us, curious, his gaze slipping to Rainey, a smile stretching his lips as if he knew what we had been doing.

Behind me, Rainey said, "Damn neighborhood. Everyone knew what was going on with me and the guys next door. Now they watch me like a hawk. I don't have many visitors, but when I do, they assume I'm having sex with them."

The man stared for another few seconds, the bill of his baseball cap shadowing his face. He waved and Rainey waved back before tugging the strap of her shirt into place. I cocked a brow at the sudden sense of modesty. Turning, I watched the man walk away.

"Do you know him?"

She tipped her eyes up to mine. "People move in and out of this neighborhood all the time. When they're down on their luck, they move in. When something goes right and they can go to a better place, they move out. All different people, but all the same."

Exhaustion overtook me. "Have a good night, Rainey. I'll see you tomorrow."

She watched me walk to my car and drive away.

On my way home, I stopped by the station, updated Grenshaw on how Rainey knew Megan, and also about Preston and the deal that went wrong. I walked into

115

my apartment a few hours later and dropped my file folder and notepad down on a small breakfast table in the kitchen.

I was exhausted, bleary eyed, my shoulders aching from sitting in a chair all day. Stripping off my shirt, I walked into my bathroom to turn on the shower. Dropping my pants, I stepped beneath the hot spray, a moan escaping my lips at the instant relief. Dipping my head beneath it, I looked down the length of my body as water poured over me, thoughts of Rainey filtering through my thoughts.

A siren, there was no other way to describe the girl. Her long brown hair was thick and always tangled like a woman who didn't quite care. It curtained her pale face, causing her blue eyes to pop, the color stunning. Her body, dear God, her body was as amazing as her neighbors always claimed. When she talked about Paul, or any of the older brothers, her husky voice was always matter of fact about the acts that occurred between them, but when she talked about sex with Rowan...

My hand was gripping my cock, self-hatred pouring through me as I pumped the shaft. In my mind, I saw Rainey's lips, her breasts, heard her voice inside my head so clearly it was like she was standing in front of me talking about how it felt to have a man touching her. It made me want to touch her so I could experience it for myself.

Cursing under my breath, I climaxed into the spray of water, my forehead pressing against the cool tile, my eyes clenching shut with every bit of shame I felt for thinking of her in that moment.

Sleep didn't come easy, dreams forced me awake several times, my body lunging up into a seated

116

position. This case was getting to me, and despite two full days of interviewing Rainey, I wasn't even close to discovering the truth.

I contemplated walking away from it on my drive to her house the next morning. Stepping aside so they could bring a female psychologist in to finish what I started.

Rainey was waiting for me again, mug in hand, her clothes just as skimpy as before. "Good morning. I'm making some breakfast in the kitchen, if you'd like to join me?"

"I won't eat, thanks, but I can stand in there with you while you finish. We can talk about the party and the deaths of your friends."

She flashed me a funny look. "That's a bit awful to be talking about over breakfast, don't you think?"

Chuckling, I nodded my head. "Fine. It can wait until after you eat."

Rainey led me into the kitchen, set her mug on the counter and slapped some bacon into a hot pan. Instantly it sizzled and popped. While doing that, she attempted to mix some pancake batter, but the bowl spilled over when she reached for it.

"Shit." Grabbing paper towels, she attempted to clean the spill, smoke rising from the cooking bacon.

I rushed over to help. "Here, I'll flip the bacon while you clean up that mess."

"Thanks," she said, crouched over the floor, wiping up a small pile that had spilled over the counter. The bacon finished while she was cleaning up the last of it. I went to pull the pan away, but bacon grease splashed up onto my finger.

"Ouch. Shit."

She raced over to me, grabbed my hand. "Oh, I'm so sorry."

Pulling my finger to her mouth, she sucked the tip of it, her tongue swirling the end, blue eyes tipping up to meet mine. We stared at each other, her lips wrapped over the tip of my finger, every male instinct in me rising to the surface.

I yanked my hand away, "Rainey."

"I shouldn't have done that. I'm sorry. Let me get you some water for that burn. Or butter. Mom always used butter."

"It's not that bad," I insisted. "You should finish your breakfast so we can get back to the interview."

Her head hung down. "I'm sorry. It's just that I'm nervous about today. What I have to tell you."

"Did you remember more about the night of the party?"

She shook her head. "No. But where we are in the story. It's a bad part, Doc. I've never told anybody. Well, Rowan knew. But, nobody else."

A bad part. As if all the rest of it hadn't been bad. "You should eat and I'll go wait in the living room."

Shaking her head, she walked to the stove and turned off the burners. "No. I've lost my appetite. Plus, I spilled most of the pancake batter."

Guilt flooded me. It was a constant back and forth with this woman. One second I would swear she was completely void of common sense. But in the next, I would stake my professional reputation on the fact that she was playing a game, one she knew how to play to get exactly what she wanted out of men. There was never an in between. She was innocent or conniving, expertly so.

118

"At least eat some of the bacon. There's no reason for it to go to waste."

Plucking a slice from the pan, she lifted it to her lips, wrapped her lips around it like she had my finger and bit down. The crunch filled the silence in the room, the corner of her mouth curling. "Yum, that tastes so good. I can't get enough sometimes."

The slice slid further into her mouth and I turned around to walk into the living room, my thoughts going to a shower I would regret for the rest of my life.

Focusing on my notes until she joined me to take her place on the couch, I dove directly into the interview. "You told me last night that Preston was dealing and you thought a deal had gone bad. That, perhaps, someone had followed him back to the house. Correct?"

"Yes."

"What did he say when he first returned to the party? Did he mention any names that you may or may not have recognized?"

Silence caused me to glance up, her eyes studying me. Thoughts of the shower again, my hand wrapped over my -

Damn it. I had more control over myself than this.

"Did you hear my question, Rainey?"

"Yeah, I'm sorry. It's just that you're so smart. I wish I were as smart as you. I bet you read a lot."

Her finger traced down her neck, the motion catching my attention. "You probably do crossword puzzles with a pen because you know you'll never mess up. That's attractive in a man. Intelligence. Rowan was intelligent, although not many people knew it. He was really smart, always teaching me things."

Like how to enjoy sex... I inhaled to keep my mind from going there.

Pausing, I knew she'd continue deflecting if I asked questions about the party. This interest she had in me at the moment needed to stop. The conversation was going in the wrong direction. "What are you nervous about telling me, Rainey? The bad part you claimed we're at in the story?"

Her expression shuttered, shoulders hunched forward and her gaze danced away. Staring out the front window, she dropped the vixen act, truth coming out of her in the defeated posture of her body.

"Tell me about it, what you consider bad." In truth, I was more than interested to know what was so horrible this particular girl would consider it as out of the ordinary. At the same time, I wasn't sure I wanted to know. There was no telling with her.

Tears welled in her eyes, taking me by surprise. "Rainey?"

Lips pulling into a thin line, she slapped them away, her hand going to the mark. "I'm bad, Doc. I'm a horrible person. And there's not a damn thing I can ever do to make it stop."

Interest piqued, I wondered if she was about to confess something that might implicate her in a crime. If so, then it would be our answer as to whether Rainey was capable of murder, if there was even the slightest chance she had more to do with her friends' deaths than she was letting on.

"Tell me about it, Rainey. Why do you think you're bad?"

If ever there was a loaded question, it was the one I'd just asked.

CHAPTER TWELVE

Rainey - Past

Rowan turned seventeen a few months after we'd been together. Life had really turned around for him. After what happened between us, he'd asked Megan out.

The two of them hit it off immediately. It was strange how it happened, one day Rowan was there all the time and the next he was gone, always off with her. He was happy. Thrilled, really, always smiling, his eyes bright, his head held high. For his seventeenth birthday, my mom and I baked a cake again, making sure to get it just right, but he never came by to eat it.

Megan's family was better off, she lived in a decent neighborhood and they invited him over for dinner. It was all a little over the top if you asked me, but they bought him a used car, told him that they preferred him picking Megan up for dates in a vehicle that was safe rather than walking everywhere. I think she really loved him, wanted to marry him, which was ridiculous at that age, but sweet.

I'd see him every once in a while when he was home. Rowan stopped hanging out at my house as often, so we didn't get to talk much, and while I was at his house, I was busy earning my next fix.

It became a stupid habit, my sleeping with Paul and Rowan's brothers so they would get me high. I think I was close to addicted, but not to the drugs as much as the escape, because when I was there, I wasn't home being stared at by David.

My mom had been so happy when he moved in, and I was happy for her, but I couldn't trust it...trust him.

David had never done anything wrong. He hadn't touched me or hit on me, nothing like that. It was his eyes that bothered me the most, they followed me. I always felt like I was being watched, like that feeling you get when you *know* somebody is looking at you. Your body tingles and their stare becomes hands examining all the places they wanted to see but couldn't.

When I was at home, I stayed in my bedroom as often as I could. Mostly, I was next door. The first month David lived with us, it wasn't a big deal, but eventually he started asking questions.

"It looks like it's going to rain today." Mom was standing in our kitchen staring out a window, playing the short ends of her dark hair through her fingers. She had the same blue eyes as me, but hers were always bruised beneath, exhaustion from working so often wearing on her as she got older.

David stood at the sink washing dishes while I opened the fridge to grab a soda. They were the only thing I ever went in the fridge for. Mom used to keep them on the top shelf, but since David moved in, they were kept on the bottom all the way in back. I had to practically crawl inside to get to one.

Dressed in a pair of cutoff shorts and a halter top, I bent over to grab one and bumped my head on one of the wire racks.

"Careful, Rainey. You'll knock yourself out if you move so fast."

Twisting in place, I peered up to see David looking down at me, his hand busy cleaning a plate as his eyes scanned where my shorts had ridden up the cheeks of my ass. A chill ran up my spine and I abandoned the soda to straighten up and close the fridge.

"What time do you get home from work tonight, Mom?"

"Late, sweetheart, but don't worry. David will be here if you need anything." She turned to look at her boyfriend, her skin practically glowing. "Won't you?"

Smiling, David placed the bowl he finished washing in the drying rack. "Of course." He was silent for a second, his brown eyes flicking my direction for just a second before looking back at mom. "Although, I'm not sure that's a problem for Rainey. She spends a lot of time next door. Doesn't come home until early morning."

"So?" Leaning against the counter, I crossed my arms and stared up at him. David was tall, at least six foot four inches, but he was skinnier than me. I knew mom and him partied every once in a while because I could smell the smoke coming out of their bedroom. Weed mostly, but given how thin he was, I assumed he did other stuff as well.

"So," he answered, picking up a plate and dipping it in the soapy water, "People will wonder why a nice girl is constantly hanging out at a house full of men."

"Oh, she's just over there to see Rowan. He's close to her age. You've met him before," my mom insisted.

Completely snowed, my mom, often so far off in her made up reality that she didn't see the truth right there in front of her. I'd taken advantage of it more times than I liked to admit.

"Then why can't Rowan come over here? And when he does, why don't they watch television in the living room instead of hanging out in her room? Plus, didn't Rowan get a car?"

Mom's head popped up from the plant she was watering. "That's right, he did. His girlfriend's family bought it for him."

David grinned and I wanted to slap the look off his face. "That's strange because Rainey hangs out over there even when Rowan's car isn't in the driveway. Why would she be over there when Rowan isn't home?"

"Why are you talking about me like I'm not in the room? I'm friends with Rowan and his brothers, so what? It's better than being here all the time."

Spritzing the leaves of a Ficus tree that was half dead, mom turned to me. "Rainey, that's no way to talk to an adult."

"I am an adult!"

"Maybe in age, young lady, but not in any other way that counts. You haven't kept a job for longer than two days and you're still living under my house and my rules."

That was the first time mom had ever mentioned rules. "What rules?"

She set the sprayer down on the counter and stared at me.

"Rowan is a good boy, Rainey, but his brothers and father aren't. I can tell just by looking at them. They're constantly throwing parties over there."

Sharing a look with her smirking boyfriend, she said, "I think David's right. You should spend less time at their house. If Rowan's home, he can come visit you at our house. It's not like it would be any different."

I was pissed, my face flaming red and my hands shaking. "This isn't fair. I'm old enough to make my own decisions."

Her eyes met mine. "When you are paying your own bills, then you are old enough to do what you want, Rainey. Until then, you will respect the rules that David and I give you."

"This is bullshit!" I yelled, spinning on my heel and storming toward the back door.

"Where do you think you're going?"

"Over to see Rowan." I shoved the door open. "Oh look. His car is there. I guess I'll go let him know about these bullshit new rules."

"Be back in an hour," my mom called after me. I didn't answer, just stormed across the tall weeds, followed the line of the chain link fence and rounded the corner into the neighbor's yard. I was over there so often, I didn't bother knocking on the front door anymore, just let myself in whenever I felt like it.

It was still early in the morning, nobody awake yet, so I wound the halls and walked into Rowan's bedroom. He sat up as soon as the door closed behind me.

"Rainey?" Rubbing the sleep from his eyes, his hair was a mess and his chest was bare. His body was filling out even more and I couldn't help but look. "What are you doing here? Is everything all right?"

Tears streamed from my eyes, my entire body shaking because of how angry I was. Rowan snapped to attention, all the sleep haze gone the instant he saw I was crying.

"Hey," he opened his arms. "Come here."

Wrapped in his strong hold was the only place I wanted to be. I practically jumped into the bed, my back against his chest and his arms locked around me.

"Tell me what's wrong."

"It's David. He's a fucking asshole and he pissed me off."

Rowan's body tensed. "David, your mom's boyfriend?"

I nodded.

His voice dropped to a dangerous pitch, a warning of the violence I knew was inside him. "Did he do something to you, Rainey? He didn't touch you, did he?"

Rowan was the only person who knew about my past, about the other boyfriends that had done things to me when my mom wasn't home. Just like me, he didn't trust David because of it.

"No, nothing like that."

Muscles relaxing, Rowan hugged me tighter to his chest. "Good. Because I'd hate to have to kill him, which you know I would. What did he do to piss you off?"

"Told me I can't come over here anymore. Not even to see you. He said if we wanted to hang out, it had to be over there instead of here."

Quiet for a minute, he finally said, "I don't necessarily see that as a bad thing."

I twisted around to face him and slapped his chest. "Damn it, Rowan. You're not supposed to agree with him."

"Sorry, but you don't need to be around my family as much as you are. It's not good for you."

His blue eyes peered over at me, our mouths so close I could feel his breath on my face. "I've been telling you that since I met you. And call me selfish, but I don't mind having you all to myself. At least, I'll still get to see you."

"You're always with Megan."

126

"I don't have to be."

"Rowan," I warned.

"Rainey," he grinned at me, adorable for how sleepy he was.

"Her family bought you a car. I think that counts as proof that she's better for you than I'll ever be."

His thumb swept the back of my neck, my body shivering because of it. "She could buy me an entire fleet of cars, a new house and a yacht, and it still wouldn't make her better. Megan's not you. She never will be."

The silence between us felt heavy. Lying there, we stared at each other, a dappling of light filtering in past his curtains.

"I've missed you," he whispered.

I was crying again, but for a new reason. "I've missed you, too."

"Hey, hey, hey," he wiped a tear from my face. "What are these for? I've never seen a man make you cry."

It wasn't a man that had done it. Not these tears, at least. It was Rowan. The way he looked at me. The way he talked to me. The way he loved me when he should have loved someone else. "It's nothing."

"It's something, Rainey Summer Day."

I grinned. "Stop calling me that."

"It's your name. A shitty one. But still your name."

My smile stretched wider and he returned it. "That's better. I've missed that smile."

Silence again, his lips hovering inches from mine. I knew what he wanted before he asked. Rowan's eyes had a way of glimmering when he watched me, they had a way of expressing every desire in his head.

"Can I kiss you, Rainey?"

Every thought in me screamed no, but still my head nodded yes. My body never agreed with my mind, and my heart was the biggest traitor of all.

Leaning forward, Rowan brushed his mouth against mine, the kiss tender, just a touch of skin against skin.

Yet, it wasn't enough. Nowhere near enough.

We were magnets to each other, constantly drifting together before shoving apart. Two birds dancing in the sky. Cold air and hot, blending until we became the perfect storm.

His mouth opened and his tongue slid against mine, our bodies melding together as his hands explored my body.

"Rowan-"

"You can't tell me you don't want this." Fingers slipping up my shirt, he cupped my breast, his thumb rolling the nipple. "You respond to me, Rainey. Every damn time."

"I respond to everyone."

Anger narrowed his stare. "Not the way you do with me. I don't care how many times you fuck Jacob against my wall; I know the truth. I know what it sounds like when you actually want someone inside you."

My eyes closed and his mouth was on mine again, his body rolling over to cover mine as his hips worked between my legs. Breaking our kiss, he ran his lips down my neck, ducked his head lower to run soft kisses over my chest. "Rowan, you have a girlfriend."

Untying the straps of my halter, he answered, "A minor inconvenience that I can correct as soon as you tell me you're mine."

He made quick work of pulling the scrap of cloth from my body to drop it on the floor beside the bed, his hand moving down my stomach to unbutton my shorts.

"I've already told you a thousand times that if you want me, I'm yours. I'll take care of you, Rainey. Protect you. Love you."

It was a mistake coming to his room, but I always ran to Rowan when I needed support. He was the only person who could comfort me. The only one who made me feel wanted and safe.

I wrapped my hands over his shoulders as he pulled my shorts and panties off my legs, my clothes getting lost in the sheets as he palmed a breast and kissed me again, positioning himself between my legs.

Blue eyes met mine, nothing false or cruel about them.

"If we do this, Rainey, it's just me. You're not getting anything out of this, not working for drugs or whatever else. This is just about being with me."

Nodding my head, I wrapped my legs around his hips as he pushed inside me, his lips parting slightly, his eyes becoming soft. "Oh, Rainey. God, yes."

And then he began to move, our eyes locked together, our bodies moving in perfect rhythm. I tried to look away, but he gripped my chin and directed my face back to his. "No, I want you to stay with me while we do this."

It was too much, looking at him, feeling him love me with long, slow strokes that sped up in pace, pushing me closer and closer to a release I didn't deserve.

Still, it rolled over me when it hit, my legs tightening around his hips, my back arching as he stared down at me with pure adoration in his eyes.

This man loved me. With every bit of his body, his heart and his soul. He would do anything for me, be

129

anything for me. He would keep every promise he made to me because that's who Rowan was.

He pulled out when it became too much, his own release quick, a grunt bursting from his lips. I cupped his cheeks, planted a soft kiss on his mouth. "You're too good for me."

The boyish grin he flashed reminded me of the day I first met him on my front porch. "That's funny, I was thinking nobody could ever be good enough for you. Not in my opinion, at least."

"I have to go. My mom said an hour, and with David acting as her cheerleader, she'll come marching over here just to prove a point."

Lying on his side, Rowan pushed a stray hair from my face. "Will you be home alone with him tonight?"

I nodded.

"No. You won't. I'll come over later. Sneak in your window and keep you safe."

Almost telling him no, I changed my mind at the last second. "Okay. Are you sure you can come over?"

"I'll always come find you, Rainey."

"Promise?"

"Promise."

Getting dressed, I left his room without looking back at him. Guilt was nagging at me, the knowledge that he would ditch out on his girlfriend any time I asked him to. And asking that of him was taking advantage. I did it regardless.

The day passed slowly. We ate dinner around six, David giving me a soda in a glass instead of the can claiming it was more grown up. I rolled my eyes at his insistence, but mom went along with everything he was saying.

Mom left for work as soon as dinner was over, leaving me and David standing at the sink together washing the dishes.

While scrubbing a pan, my arms felt weak and my head was becoming woozy, the room spinning just a touch. I dropped the pan, and David looked at me. "You feeling okay?"

Blinking my eyes rapidly, I attempted to bring the room into focus. "Yeah, I'm -"

Everything was spinning, but I tried to grab the pan again, my hand dipping in the water as I rocked slightly forward.

"Rainey, you don't look okay."

David's voice sounded like it was coming from deep in a cave, echoing around me while my body slowed down, my eyes rolling closed before I forced them open again. I fell backwards I think, David catching me before I could hit the ground.

Hovering above, he stared down at me, but it wasn't concern I saw in his face.

"You won't remember any of this. I promise. And if you do, you should know you did this to yourself."

Lifting me from the ground, David cradled me against his chest, his steps slow as he walked me back to my room. Every sound was hollow, my head so heavy that it was a fight to keep it against his chest rather than falling back over his arm.

"...always over there...skimpy clothes...everyone knows...slut..."

He was talking to me, but his voice was going in and out. It didn't matter whether I heard every word he said, I knew what he was doing. Outside, I was struggling to move, but on the inside, I was screaming. *Not again. Please, not again.*

He laid me down on my bed, crouching beside me, and brushed my hair from my face.

"...won't remember...like it...wanted this..."

My head rolled over the pillow, stomach sour. It took effort to breath and all I could hear was the steady thud of my heart like a drum in my skull to the beat of my inner voice begging him to stop.

A breeze blew across my chest and I knew my top was off. Hot hands touching, his voice saying something. I just closed my eyes and felt water drip down my cheek into my hair. One tug at my waist. Another. I was cold all over as my legs were lifted up.

"David, no, stop..."

I think I said it, but my tongue was thick in my mouth. Legs parting, I forced my eyes open to see a blur hovering next to me, touching me, staring at me like I was a free for all. A burst of laughter. Maybe I was. I thought I was going to puke and my head rolled sideways, a face at my window. Familiar. Angry as all hell.

In truth, I couldn't be sure what I saw. All I knew was that someone was touching me, and then they weren't. Shouting, like thunder though the house, a flash of silver. Two blurs facing each other. The silver scared me.

Not Rowan. Please not Rowan.

I couldn't keep my eyes open any longer and as those blurs stood facing each other in my room, I closed my eyes and drifted off somewhere else.

CHAPTER THIRTEEN

Justin - Present

There was keen sense of self-loathing I felt while listening to Rainey reveal the details of what David had done to her. Prior to this, every story she told had been consensual, effortless, a mutual agreement that her body could buy her what she thought she wanted and needed.

Speaking of her experiences with Paul, Jacob, Joel and Frankie, Rainey wasn't emotional, the opposite in fact, as if she were discussing a business arrangement made in a boardroom. She saw nothing wrong with what she had done with them.

While remembering her experiences with Rowan, her voice changed, softened, the corners of her lips tilting up in a ghost of a smile because those memories she cherished. I had no doubt Rainey, in all her confusion and denial, truly loved Rowan Connor.

Her voice changed again when speaking of David. It was clipped and harsh, angry and devoid of the usual seductive lilt she commonly spoke with during her other memories. Disgust poured out of her with every tear, and her hatred of him created in me a hatred of myself.

It was just a shower. A moment alone. But what I had done while thinking of her went against every moral fiber inside of me. She was a victim, had been abused her entire life, and I had allowed my thoughts - my body - to go to a place that victimized her further.

There were professional regulations in place to protect patients from doctors for a reason, this being the most important. Taking advantage, even if just in thought, was wholly and entirely wrong.

"You're crying," I observed.

She slapped away a tear, lit a cigarette, refused to look anywhere but out the front window.

"Rainey, I hate to ask this seeing as how upset you are, but did David rape you that night?"

Silent for a few seconds except for the inhalation of smoke followed by the exhalation of a heavy cloud, Rainey grinned, the expression bitter.

"Rape is a heavy word, Doc. To be honest, I don't know what he did that night, whether he actually went through with it. I woke up in a sleep shirt and underwear the next morning. I remember that. But after Rowan came in my room, I passed out. Whatever David had slipped in my drink-"

She looked at me then, her eyes glistening with tears, "We assume that's what he did. Slipped something in my soda at dinner."

I nodded.

"Anyway, whatever he gave me knocked me out cold. I have no further memories of that night."

The tip of my pen scratched over the notepad. I wanted to look further into David's death as well as her mother's. "Did Rowan ever tell you what happened that night?"

Another heavy drag from her cigarette, the cherry at the end glaring red, and she nodded.

"I, uh, David wouldn't let me go over there for a day or two after. He had my mom convinced Rowan was giving me drugs, that I'd come home fucked up and he caught Rowan trying to have sex with me. I had no clue what happened. I could see Rowan's car in the driveway, saw him standing outside looking at my

134

window, but he never came over. Not at first. My mom had those two days off and I thought maybe it had something to do with her being there."

"What happened when she went back to work?"

More tears, a soft keening from her chest as she curled over herself. "I asked to go see Rowan. And-and-" Rainey shook her head as if she were attempting to shake the words free. I was surprised to see her so upset.

"It's okay, Rainey. Take your time. Tell me when you're ready."

Breathing heavily, she took a few minutes to calm herself down, her expression shifting from mortification and pain into something far colder. Eyes distant, lips a thin line, she went so still that it surprised me. Her voice was practically robotic.

"David said he'd let me go over there, that he wouldn't tell my mom, but the only way he would keep my secret is if I fucked him and pretended to like it. He said he thought about me when he was with my mom. Wanted it to be me. And as long as I gave it up to him first, he didn't care if I went next door to give it up to the neighbors."

Keeping my tone of voice calm, I asked, "Why didn't you go to your mom and tell her what he was doing?"

"She wouldn't have believed me. Mom was the type to believe life was one big fairy tale. She believed her boyfriend over me. Always had."

"Then why didn't you call the police?"

A burst of harsh laughter shook her shoulders. "You don't call the cops where I live, Doc. That's just one of those unwritten rules. Too many people could get in a lot of trouble. I risked Rowan and his family if I called the cops on David."

135

"So, What did you do, Rainey?"

She flicked an ash, curled her arm over her stomach. "What do you think I did? Same thing I always do. I gave him what he wanted. Right here on this couch. Bounced up and down on top of his lap shouting his name like I had never had it so good before. Thankfully, Jacob had taught me how to fake it. Always demanding I scream his name to mess with Rowan's head. So I bounced, you know? Right here where I'm sitting now. He was sitting and pulled me backwards on top of him, reached around me to grab my tits like they were handles or some shit. I made sure he liked it because I was that desperate to go see Rowan. I was that desperate to go get high and forget the entire thing had even happened. Bounce, bounce, bounce. *Oh yeah, Daddy, give it to me harder.* He demanded I call him Daddy. But whatever. Same shit, different day." She cringed. "At least I didn't have to look at him. He didn't care much about my face."

Jesus...

"I'm sorry, Rainey. That should have never happened to you."

She grinned. "You say that a lot, Justin. *I'm sorry.* You didn't do anything wrong. You have no reason to apologize."

In my mind, I did. The only difference was she didn't know it with me. "Did he let you go next door after that?"

Nodding, she relaxed against her seat.

"Yeah. I burst through their door, my eyes all crazy, I'm sure, and Rowan jumped up from the couch immediately. He knew just by looking at me. Grabbing my wrist, he dragged me back to his room. Held me while I cried. Promised to never let it happen again."

Rainey paused, smiled, took a drag and blew it out.

"Rowan told me that the night David drugged me, he saw through the window and came inside to stop it. But David had a gun, held it right at him and told him that if he didn't leave, he'd shoot and claim that Rowan was the one who drugged me. He would lie and claim that he walked in on Rowan raping me. That he had no choice but to kill him. And since everyone in the neighborhood was well aware about what went on in their house while I was there, the police would believe him. He had an entire street full of witnesses.

"Then he told Rowan that he would be dead and wouldn't be able to stop David from doing it to me night after night for as long as he wanted. Rowan left. He was smart. He knew to wait it out. He planned on coming back over to my house the next night, but my mom was home. He was waiting, you know? Just waiting to do something about it. That night was the first my mom wasn't there, but I did what I did before he had the chance to come over. Hell, I was probably bouncing on David's lap before she even had the chance to pull down the street. It was all a matter of timing."

"So, the boyfriend, he was-"

"He's dead now. Died in this house actually."

Recalling what Rainey had told me previously, I had a feeling I knew where this story was going. "What happened after you talked with Rowan?"

The shutdown was immediate, her energy spent, her hands shaking. "I can't talk about this anymore. Not today."

My eyes drifted to the window following the direction of her gaze. Neighbors stood on the sidewalk across the street watching her house. It angered me

137

how they always watched her. The same man from yesterday stood among them, his hands shoved in the pockets of his jeans, the bill of his cap shadowing his face. A few feet from him was an older woman walking her dog. Next to her, an older man pacing.

I sighed. "I tell you what, Rainey. Why don't we conclude this interview for today? You need some time to calm down, to gather your thoughts. Is there anything I can do for you before I leave? Will you be okay by yourself?"

Not wanting to leave her, I struggled with calling someone in to counsel her. She shook her head. "These are all just memories. I've lived with them this long already. I'm fine. Just don't want to talk anymore. Not today."

Moving slowly to gather my things, I waited until I knew she'd calmed down. The neighborhood audience dispersed as I walked out the door and to my car, my head turning just enough to watch them in my peripheral vision. Rainey hadn't walked me to the door like she normally did, so I wasn't worried about them catching sight of her so upset.

The drive to the police station was a slow crawl, my legs heavy as I walked at a snail's pace inside the building. I couldn't fake being pleasant with the receptionist, rejection heavy in her eyes when Grenshaw came to the front to lead me through the halls to the room.

A dry erase board was set up, all my ideas as to what the five marks on her arm could mean written in black. I stared at it as Grenshaw took his seat and folded his hands behind his head.

"You look like you've seen a ghost. Did she finally tell you what happened?"

Inhaling sharply, I set my folder and notepad on the table, sat on the corner of the wood surface and stared at a man who was as exhausted as me.

"No. We didn't talk about the party. Not today. After the story she told me, I thought it best to leave and begin again tomorrow morning."

"What did she tell you?"

I was quiet for a brief moment, feeling uncomfortable sharing Rainey's secrets, but if it somehow led to what happened at the party, I had no choice but to divulge the information.

"Her mother's boyfriend may have raped her. She's not sure, but he certainly coerced her into agreeing to sleep with him at one point."

"Son of a bitch," Grenshaw growled, a sheen of angry red coloring his face.

"She told me he died in the house. Do we have information as to how that happened?"

Pulling a laptop across the table, Grenshaw flipped the top, typed in several lines of information before scrubbing a hand down his face.

"Yeah, we do. It says here that David Gibbons died by drowning. The toxicology report showed opiates in his system, pharmaceutical, not street. He was found the following morning by Eleanor Day, Rainey's mother, when she returned home from work. Looks like he passed out and drowned in the bathtub."

Looks like... Good choice of words, but I had my doubts. "What about her mother? How did she die?"

He typed in a few more lines of information. "Heroine overdose. A few weeks after David. She was found by Rainey with a needle in her arm, vomit puddled on the floor by her face."

I wondered about the circumstances of that as well.

"What do you think, Justin? Is it possible Rainey does have it in her to kill? I recognize the look on your face. You think she had something to do with David's death, don't you? Possibly her mother's?"

Shaking my head, I continued staring at the dry erase board. I needed to add another five:

Five years in the neighborhood.
Five older men that abused her as a kid.
Five neighbors.
Five victims at the party.
Five times she slept with Rowan.

She was counting something, there were simply too many choices as to what it could be.

"We haven't reached that point in the story yet. Once we do, I'll let you know."

Grenshaw and I spoke for an hour before I left and returned home. Unlike the night before, I didn't touch myself with thoughts of Rainey in my head. Instead, I stood in the shower hating everything about this case.

Toying with thoughts of turning it over to someone else, I understood I was too deep at that point. Rainey could view a new psychologist as a rejection and shut down entirely. We needed her to keep talking.

After very little sleep, I drove to her house the next morning, parked in my usual spot and walked up the dirt path to her porch. She opened the door as I was crossing it, her body covered in nothing but a long shirt.

"Good morning, Justin. I finished breakfast early so we don't have another disaster on our hands." Her blue eyes were bright again, all the pain I saw in her yesterday completely absent.

"Thanks for that, Rainey. Let's take our seats and get back to it. We still have a lot of information to cover."

Leading me back with a swing of her hips, she glanced over her shoulder to see if I was watching her. I had been careful to keep my eyes directed to the top of her head, refusing to look down at where the shirt ended just above the backs of her knees.

She took her seat and I took mine, our eyes meeting from across the room while she lit a cigarette and I arranged my notepad. "Are you feeling better today?"

A feline smile. "Much, actually. Sorry about breaking down yesterday. That was a hard memory to discuss. The worst is over now."

Inclining my head, I wrote the date on the top of a clean page and settled back in my seat. It was pointless to bring the party up, I knew she wanted to continue with the story. I was interested to do so as well, if for no other reason than to discover if she was involved in David's death.

"Would you like to tell me what happened after you spoke with Rowan? We left off quite abruptly yesterday. Is there more to what occurred that night?"

Nodding, Rainey scratched an itch on her upper thigh, the movement dragging the hem of her shirt up her lap. Beneath her shirt, she wore blue panties. I forced my eyes away.

"I'm ready to talk about it now."

With pen poised, I smiled.

"The floor is all yours, Rainey. Tell me what you would like me to know."

CHAPTER FOURTEEN

Rainey - Past

"I'm going to fucking kill him."

Rowan paced the floor in front of me. I was sitting on his bed, my hands shaking, fear crawling over every inch of my body to see the tiger's prowl as he moved, the sharp turns as he reached the end of the room to walk the opposite direction.

Calming him down was important. I thought a joint might do it, but I couldn't go sleep with anybody to pay for it. Not with the way Rowan was behaving. Not after what he knew had just happened.

"It's no big deal," I lied. "Just sex, Rowan. I'm kind of used to it if you haven't noticed. It was no different than what Jacob or Joel have done. As long as I keep David happy, he'll let me come over here and see you. That's good, right?"

Inside I felt like dying, but I had to play it off. Had to keep him calm. Rowan was yanking at his hair, every muscle in his body tense. I had no doubt that if I said the word, he'd march over there and beat David to death without thinking. Now that I knew David had a gun, I couldn't let Rowan do it. If something happened to him, it would destroy me. I'd fucking snap to lose the only person I'd ever loved.

Rowan stopped suddenly, turned to me, his pupils so large that his eyes looked pure black. It scared me.

"You need to take a shower."

"What? Why?"

"I need him off of you, Rainey. I need to scrub you clean and figure out what to do about this."

Opening my mouth to argue, my words were cut off when Rowan picked me up from the bed and tossed me over his shoulder. Carrying me out of his room and down the hall, he didn't even react to Jacob hollering about fucking me good as we passed his room. All Rowan did was walk me into the bathroom, set me on my feet, slam the door and turn on the water.

"Take off your clothes."

"Rowan-"

"God damn it, Rainey! Take off your clothes and get in the shower!"

I flinched at how loud he'd yelled, my hands moving quickly to strip off my shirt and pants while he did the same. Both naked, we stepped over the rim of the tub and Rowan took a washcloth and soap, immediately soaping me up to clean every inch of my body. He took his time, not missing an inch. He couldn't stand to think that anything of David remained on me.

Kneeling down, he was careful when washing between my legs, his focus intent, his shoulders shaking because of how angry he was. I balanced myself by holding on to his shoulders, eventually letting go with one hand to run my fingers through his hair.

"Hey, it's fine. He didn't hurt me, Rowan. You need to calm down."

Scrubbing my legs, he didn't bother to look up at me. "What I need to do is make sure that son of a bitch never touches you again. He's dead, Rainey. Tonight. I don't give a fuck what you think about it. I'm taking care of you just like I promised you I would."

Rowan stood up and I had to crane my neck to see his face. Gone was the sweet boy I'd always known and in his place was a dangerous man that had every

143

intention to kill someone else. Reaching, I cupped his cheek. "Please calm down. For me?"

His jaw clenched, his eyes locked to mine. "Turn around."

"Rowan-"

"Turn around and let me clean the back of you. Stop arguing with me about this."

Spinning on my heel, I pressed my palms against the tile while he took his time cleaning me. Knowing I needed to do something before this all went horribly wrong, I waited until the washcloth was between my legs to buck my hips and moan. Honestly, I wasn't turned on, just scared, but I knew how to make a man think I wanted him.

"Rowan," I breathed out, my voice a plea for him to drop the washcloth and use his fingers. He slapped my ass - hard.

"Not even funny, Rainey. I know when you want something. Remember? I'm not fucking stupid. Stop trying to distract me."

"Well, somebody needs to distract you. The way you're talking, I'm scared you actually plan to go over to my house and kill David."

"I do," he answered calmly, the washcloth rubbing down the back of my leg. "By the end of tonight, he won't be breathing any longer. I don't give a fuck about going to jail for it either. Not after what he did to you."

Rowan stood and turned me around to face him, crushing my body against the shower wall with his own. He glared down at me, his chest hard against mine.

Watching me silently, he traced the line of my jaw with his thumb. "Nobody, and I mean nobody will hurt

144

you like that anymore. I won't let it happen again. I'll kill every last fucking one of them."

"You're talking crazy."

His eyes closed and opened again, the lashes water spiked and dark. "I don't care."

Lowering my voice to a whisper, I told him, "I'm not worth it, Rowan. Really, I'm not." Tears stung my eyes, his gaze tracking one as it rolled down my cheek. Leaning down he kissed it softly, his body still pinning me to the wall.

"Yeah, Rainey, you are. You've always been worth it. One day you'll see yourself the same way I do, and you'll be so mad at yourself for letting people treat you the way you have. It ends. Tonight."

Shaking my head, my lips quivered. "I won't stop using my body for drugs, Rowan. I don't mind it."

"Rainey-"

"You have Megan. She's good for you. She can help you become something so you can get the hell out of this life. I'm nothing. I'll only drag you down and it looks like I'm already doing it. You're talking about killing someone."

He grinned, the expression hard instead of adorable. The boy I knew wasn't here. This person was a stranger. "I'm telling you I'm killing someone, because it's happening."

Terror rolled through me on a deep shiver. Not that Rowan was capable of killing someone, but because I was worried something would happen to him. "He has a gun."

"Then I'll take that risk."

My eyes closed, my pulse hammering in my throat. There was no way to stop him. I couldn't overpower him, and his brothers would just egg him on. I had no other choice than to keep him from getting himself killed. "Let me help you."

"What?"

My eyes flicked open to lock with his. "Let me help you. If you go in there to beat him to death, he'll shoot you. Either that or you'll go to jail. I can't let that happen. You're too special to me. It would kill me if I lost you."

A finger traced my lips, his eyes searching mine. "What are you suggesting?"

I shrugged a shoulder. "He likes pills, Rowan. I can go over there and get him fucked up-"

"No-"

"Shut up and let me finish."

He stilled against me, his arms caging me against the shower wall.

"I can get him to take a pill or two, and when he is weak, you can come over and we'll shove the entire bottle down his throat. It will look like an overdose."

Rowan's forehead fell against mine. "And how do you plan on convincing him to take the first few?"

"How do you think? Same way I convince everybody to do what I want."

"No." Stepping back, he shook his head. "I won't let you fuck him again."

My eyes peered up at him. "I won't. I'll let him think it's going there, but I won't have sex with him."

Rowan looked pained, his shoulders hunching forward, but then his body straightened again and he punched a wall. Turning away from me, he rested his forehead against the tile, was quiet for a minute. He turned back. "Fine. I'll trust you to do this. But I'll be outside looking in the window. If I even think you're about to fuck him, I'm coming in."

146

Not liking the plan at all, I went along with it. I had to protect Rowan. "Okay."

We climbed out of the shower, dried off and got dressed. I put on what I already had while Rowan dressed in black from head to toe. The dark color looked good on him. Made me see him differently than I normally had. The boy I'd known was grown now.

I left his house without him, but knew he was sneaking through the yards while I walked in my front door and found David sitting on the couch watching a movie. He was surprised to see me.

"Back already?"

Casually, I took a seat beside him. I wanted to vomit when his hand slid up my leg. Thankfully the pants prevented him from touching my skin. "Yeah. They didn't have anything over there and I remembered that you might have something. I was hoping you could give me a pill or something."

David laughed, his head turning so he could look at me. "It'll cost you."

"I know," with a smile, I added, "Daddy."

He grinned, his eyes dropping to my chest before crawling up again. "Stay here. I'll go get them."

As he walked away, I called out, "Are you going to take one with me? It's never fun doing it alone."

David didn't answer and I worried that my plan wouldn't work. Rowan was outside and he would lose his patience eventually. Thankfully, David came back with the bottle in hand. He took two in front of me and tipped the bottle my way. I reached for it, but he snatched it back before I could grab it. "Nuh uh, little girl, payment first."

Bile crept up my throat, but I forced a smile. "Sit down. Let your little girl take care of you."

Pure slime was in his grin. I'd never hated anyone as much as him. Shoving down his pants, he spread his legs.

"Take off your shirt and kneel in front of me. I want to watch your tits shake while you give me a hand job. You'll get one pill for that. But don't finish me off. I want those lips wrapped around my cock when I come."

It took everything I had not to vomit, but somehow I managed to keep it down while stripping off my shirt. Glancing at the window, I imagined Rowan was about two seconds from coming in that door, gun or not. With a smile on my face, I lowered my body to my knees between his legs, my hand wrapping over his shaft. Pumping quickly, I kept my eyes locked on his face.

He reached to cup my cheek. "What are you supposed to call me?"

"Daddy," I whispered, my fingers gripping tighter because I wanted to rip the nasty thing right off.

His head fell back against the couch, hips bucking as disgusting grunts volleyed from his lips. Fingers in my hair, he said, "Yeah, baby girl, just like that."

My hand started to cramp at the same time his head lifted, his eyes dazed. "Suck my cock, you little bitch. Show Daddy how much you like him."

A dry heave shot up my throat. Swallowing to keep from actually throwing up, I licked my lips and bent forward to take him into my mouth. The front door slammed open before I had the chance. Rowan's patience had run out.

Unfortunately, David wasn't as out of it as I'd hoped he would be. But he didn't have his gun, and with his pants around his ankles, he couldn't move fast enough to get away from Rowan.

"You sick son of a bitch!"

I practically rolled right as soon as Rowan lunged forward. Grabbing David by the collar of his shirt, he shoved him down onto the couch and held him with one hand, using his other to grip his cheeks and force his mouth open. "Empty the bottle in his mouth, Rainey!"

Grabbing the orange plastic container, I fumbled the lid a few times, struggling with the child lock, but eventually opened it and dumped it in David's mouth. He fought to spit them out, but Rowan held his mouth shut. "Hold his nose closed so the son of a bitch swallows."

I did as I was told, my heart beating so hard I thought it might come through my chest.

Rowan's voice was hollow. "Go fill the bathtub."

"What?"

"Go do it!"

Pushing up to my feet, I ran down the hall and started the bath. I heard a struggle behind me, watched Rowan dragging David down the hall, his hands reaching for doorjambs and his legs kicking out. Moving out the way, I stood and watched as Rowan stripped David's clothes off him while holding him still somehow. Once he had David naked, he dropped him in the water and held his head beneath the surface.

I didn't move, couldn't, not with the amount of shock I was feeling. David kicked and screamed beneath the water. It was splashing over the rim as bubbles came to the surface.

After a few minutes, he finally went still and Rowan let go of him. David's body floated limp, his eyes wide open.

"Go get some towels, Rainey. We need to make it look like he fell asleep in the bath."

Running from the room, I grabbed towels out the closet, brought them back and handed them to Rowan. He began mopping up the floors and walls, his eyes still crazy black and his body moving quickly. Once it was all done, he told me to put the towels in the dryer.

It took me a few minutes to make it through the house into the small laundry room near the kitchen. I started the dryer and wound my way back to find Rowan standing over David's body, still as a statue staring down at him. Steam rose up from the bath water.

Speaking softly, I asked, "What do we do now?"

He twisted around to look at me, his gaze dark, mouth a tight line, and his shoulders somehow larger in the tiny room. "We wait here for the towels to dry so we can fold them and put them back in the closet. Then you can come stay with me at my house, let your mom find him when she gets home."

The house was so silent, I could hear the dryer running in the distance. "I can't stay at your house, Rowan. If I sleep there, mom will know I had something to do with this. I'm not supposed to be over there."

His expression twisted, anger flooding his eyes. "I'm not leaving you to sleep in the house with a dead body."

"I have to. We'll close the door and I'll just go to sleep. Plus, mom is going to lose it when she gets home. Someone needs to be here for her."

Despite everything, I loved my mom. Yeah, she was clueless, and because of her, I had a lot of bad things happen to me, but she didn't know. I never told her. I liked to think she would have done something to stop it if she knew.

"Fine, but I'm staying here with you until she gets home. I'll sneak out the window when she pulls up. I'm not leaving you alone with him."

It wasn't like David could hurt me again. He was dead and he wasn't coming back.

For the first time since I'd met Rowan, he scared me. Something in him had changed and I wasn't sure if it was because he couldn't protect me from David the first night when I was drugged, or because he'd killed someone to protect me now. "Okay. Let's hang out in my room, like we normally do."

Rowan followed me to my room, his booted steps heavy, the floor vibrating beneath my feet. He shut my door and leaned against it, his eyes studying me. Once again, and sadly as usual with me, I was naked up top, my breasts exposed to him.

"You're so beautiful," he whispered. "You have no fucking idea how beautiful you are."

The sound of his voice was off, so dark and deep that I shivered in place. Standing there in front of him, I'd never felt so naked in my life. Raising my arms to cover my chest, I stopped when he shook his head.

"No, Rainey. Let me look at you. I love looking at you. Even when I close my eyes, all I see is you."

I dropped my arms, my legs trembling. This was Rowan, the sweet, kindhearted boy I loved. Yet, in that moment I feared him. The adrenaline was wearing off and I was suddenly so cold.

His lips parted as he stared at me, those blue eyes I knew so well slowly taking in my body as heat blazed behind them. He'd grown so large, twice my size at least, and it had never occurred to me how strong he was until now. Nobody would pick on him anymore. Not without getting their asses handed to them in a fight.

"Can I touch you, Rainey?" His eyes lifted to mine. "Is that all right? For me to touch you?"

"Always," I whispered, unable to put any strength in my voice. "You can always touch me."

He stepped forward and I stepped back out of instinct. He would never hurt me. Not Rowan. But what I saw in him now was the predator that had always lingered just beneath the surface. He wasn't a monster like his family or David. Not him. He was something else entirely.

Pain shot through his eyes when I moved, his hands fisting at his sides. "Do I scare you now?"

Shaking my head, I forced my mouth to move. "No. It's just -"

"Just what?"

"You're different, Rowan. A man, I guess. You've grown."

Blue eyes held mine, the darkness in them seeping away, but not entirely. His lips pulled into a tight smile. "You need a man. I've become exactly what you need. You, Rainey. Not for anybody else. Just for you."

I drew in a rattling breath. "Touch me."

Rowan moved forward and I held my ground, craning my neck to look up at him as his hands cupped my breasts. He was shaking, his skin so cold that I knew I had to fix him somehow. "Rowan?"

"Yeah?"

"Will you kiss me?"

He directed me against a wall and lowered his head to press his mouth against mine. My lips parted immediately so that his tongue could sweep in and take

152

control. I should have understood him from his kisses alone. They were never timid, never shy. He was a dominant man who could lead me anywhere he wanted. I'd been his first, had walked him through a moment of shyness, but now that something else in him had come to the surface, he would never be shy again.

His hands were tight over my breasts, his thumbs teasing the nipples as a moan rolled over my lips that he swallowed. Reaching for him, I dragged my fingertips down his strong chest, lower so that I could unbutton his pants. I wanted him more than I'd wanted anything in my life.

Rowan kicked off his boots without releasing our kiss, his body flinching once I had his pants pushed down and could wrap my hands over the hard length of him.

"God, Rainey," he whispered. "Do you have any clue what you do to me?"

My eyes flicked open to meet his. "Show me."

He came alive in that moment, making short work of my pants as he shoved them to my ankles and explored between my legs with one hand. Lifting me with the other arm, he walked me to my bed, dropped me on the mattress, yanked my pants and panties off my ankles and dropped them to the ground.

Kicking his pants off, he reached behind to pull off his shirt, his body naked before my eyes. He was beautiful, too. So beautiful I couldn't look away.

I told him so and he grinned as he dropped to his knees in front of me. "Spread your legs."

"Rowan-"

"I said spread them, Rainey." Eyes meeting mine, he canted his head to the side. "Don't make me say it again."

Smiling shyly, I parted my legs for him, a shiver coursing over me to be so exposed to his eyes. He slid a finger inside me as he watched the motion of his hand, fascinated by my body. "Lie back. Let me love you while you enjoy it."

Doing as he said, I nearly came apart when he kissed his way up my thigh, his fingers still moving inside me as he closed his mouth over my clit to lick slow circles before sucking. My hands went to his head, my hips moving on their own as he worked me into a pleasurable knot, increasing his speed as moans poured from my lips and my body arched.

Stars burst behind my eyes as I climaxed, waves of incredible pleasure rolling over me again and again and again.

When I finished, he lifted my body up to lay me flat over the bed, crawling on top while holding his chest above me with his arms. His lips glistened from what he'd just done and I sprang up to kiss him, my arms wrapping over his shoulders to tug him down on top of me.

His mouth pulled away and pressed to my ear, his breath a wave of heat against my neck. "I'll love you forever, Rainey. Protect you. Take care of you. There's nowhere you can go where I won't find you."

Lifting his head to look down at me, he said, "You and me forever. Do you understand that? Fuck everybody else. They don't matter. They never did. Just you and me, okay?"

Even though I nodded my head in agreement, I knew this couldn't be. Tonight would pass. The days would wander forward and I would tell him to go back to Megan while I returned to being the girl who fucked for drugs.

But, for tonight, I would let him think whatever he wanted. I would give him that.

Positioning himself between my legs, he notched the tip of his cock between my legs and pushed up on his arms while I wrapped my legs around his waist. Before pushing inside, he grabbed my chin and made sure I was looking at him. My mouth opened on a moan as his hips thrust forward, sinking himself inside.

"Forever," he whispered, pulling out just enough to thrust forward again.

Rowan's head dropped down to take a nipple into his mouth, his pace picking up. My muscles locked around him as our bodies moved in time to one another. Grabbing my butt, he lifted my hips higher, his strokes harder, faster.

I orgasmed again while he was still going, the virgin boy I'd once known gone. Pushing back so he was on his knees, he lifted me up to straddle him, my chest crushed against his as his hands directed my hips to move at the rhythm he wanted.

Rowan kissed with such desperation that it forced the breath from my lungs, one hand on my hip while the other wrapped in my hair. I moved for him, above him, taking him as hard and deep as he needed.

He pulled out to come, but kept kissing me, laying me back on the bed, his weight on top of me. Breaking this kiss, he buried his face in my neck, our chests beating together, tears welling in my eyes once again because I knew I was lying to him when I promised, "Forever."

CHAPTER FIFTEEN

Justin - Present

Her hand moved between her legs when she talked about Rowan. I'm not sure she knew what she was doing. She was lost in that memory, so far away that when she pulled her leg up to the couch, when her shirt rode up so that her panties were exposed, when she traced her finger over the lace at the crook of her thigh, Rainey had no idea I was sitting there watching her.

Yes, I reacted. Professionalism completely gone, I sat and listened to Rainey describe sex with the boy she loved while a dead body floated in the bathroom next to them - watching her hand move over her body the entire time. Transfixed by that hand and where it was going.

My mind had checked out apparently. My willpower dissolving. Rainey Day had reeled me in just like every other man who knew her. Whether she knew that or not was the question.

As soon as she opened her eyes, I focused my attention on my notepad. The girl had just confessed to a murder and I was fighting everything inside me not to become erect.

"I know what I just told you, Doc. You don't have to point it out. I know I confessed to killing somebody."

Clearing my throat, I refused to look her direction. "It sounded like Rowan killed David."

"Yeah," she answered, "but I helped. There's a fancy term for that-"

"Accessory."

Snapping her fingers. "That's it. I knew you were smart enough to remember it. I was an accessory. I

156

knew Rowan murdered David and I didn't say a word about it. I woke up to my mother screaming the next morning and stumbled out of my room to pretend I had no idea what happened."

Growing quiet, she was completely oblivious to the show she was giving me from across the room, her modesty as absent as my willpower.

"You can tell on me, Doc. Report it to the detectives. It's fine with me. Because if I had to do it all over again, I would. David deserved what happened to him. And quite frankly, my mom deserved better than a piece of shit boyfriend who imagined her daughter while he was having sex with her. Even you have to admit that's twisted."

Silently, I agreed with her. I was glad David was dead. Would have shaken Rowan's hand and congratulated him for the effort if he was alive for me to do so. I had a duty to report this information. If anything, it proved Rainey had the potential to cover up a murder. But given the circumstances of David's death, I didn't believe she was capable of bludgeoning four people to death without mercy. David's death had shocked her. That much I knew.

"I'm not going to report this. As far as I'm concerned, Rowan killed David, and Rowan is not here to answer for it."

Glancing up at her, I was careful to keep my eyes on her face. "I'll keep your secret as long as you can promise me I won't hear of any other murders you took part in for the rest of this story."

Her eyes darkened, shadows chasing across her face. With a soft voice, she answered, "I don't make promises, Justin. I can't."

"Why not?"

"Because Rowan made me promises he couldn't keep. When he died, he broke all of them."

Her provocative posture folded over itself. Gone was the Rainey attempting to seduce, and in her place was a woman shattering apart, her arms holding her body, tears streaming down her face. She bent over as her shoulders shook with silent sobs. It was heart-wrenching to see her in such pain. While crying she continued to talk, continued to admit to all the horrible ways she looked at herself.

"That boy - no, man - Rowan was no boy by the time he died. So, that *man* did everything he could for me and I just kept on hurting him because I couldn't let him love me. He died thinking I didn't care about him. All he wanted was for me to respect myself, to care about my life as much as he did, and I wouldn't stop striking out at him, pushing him away and letting him believe I didn't want him."

Closing my eyes, I sat tense in my seat, fighting an internal battle as to what I should do. She was in so much pain at that moment. Bawling. Her body shaking so bad that it looked like she could break.

I set my pen and pad aside to walk into her bathroom and grab tissues for her to use. My eyes scanned right to the bathtub and I shivered. All I could see was David's dead body floating in water with his eyes wide open.

Steeling my spine, I returned to the living room and sat on the couch next to Rainey, silently arguing with myself about being so close to her. Touching her shoulder, I watched her straighten up, her eyes stained red from crying.

"Here, I brought you a tissue."

It was stupid of me to sit there with her, but I wanted to comfort the poor woman. She was so fragile at that moment, completely crushed by a past she could never change.

Having never been so close to her, I noticed she smelled like lavender. Perhaps it was her shampoo, or a perfume she wore, but the scent was pleasant - delicate like her.

"Thank you," she said, plucking the tissue from my fingers before dabbing at her eyes. "I'm sorry, I'm trying not to think about what happened to Rowan. But we're coming up to that night - the night he died and it's tearing me apart. Absolutely shredding me to think about it. He was so good, you know? So damn good that everybody was nothing but garbage when compared to him."

Rubbing the back of my neck, I watched her pull herself together.

"Rainey, I know I keep saying it, but I really am sorry all this happened to you. Life isn't fair. It's brutal. And while some people seem to have all the luck, others, like you, struggle. Despite everything, you survived. I think if Rowan were here, he would be happy to know that you're still fighting. That you haven't given up."

She nodded her head and peered up at me from beneath tear-wet lashes, her face so damn innocent that it was difficult to remember she'd helped a man kill someone. Right on the couch where I was sitting, in fact.

I tried to shake away the thought.

"Despite your past, you're still young. You can make something of your life. There are programs to help you go to school, to learn a trade. To get out of this neighborhood you hate so much. I know you feel lost with Rowan gone, but think about him and fight harder. Do what he would have wanted you to do with your life. Be something for him as well as yourself."

"I am," she answered. "Except for the party, that mistake I was making with Michael, I've been trying to be better. After all the Connors were dead, I realized I needed to straighten up. If I don't, I'll end up just like them. Just like my mom."

Rainey wilted, and I wrapped my hands over her shoulders. It broke so many professional rules, I refused to mentally list them in my thoughts. "You can do this. You're strong enough to survive."

Before I could stop her, Rainey leaned forward and crushed her body against mine in a tight hug. The lavender scent was stronger, her hair tickling my cheek from where her head was lying against my shoulder. I froze, my arms limp at my sides, but I lifted them to wrap around her.

While she was calming down, her body trembling as the heartache bled out of her, I was trying my best not to notice how her breasts felt crushed against my chest. Just like every other man in her life, I was the bastard who couldn't ignore how my body reacted to her presence.

Right here on this couch, where her mother's boyfriend had fucked her while demanding she call him Daddy, and also the same place she'd helped Rowan stage David's murder.

What the fuck was wrong with me?

Breaking her hold, I stood from the couch and backed away. She glanced up at me confused. "Are you okay? Did I upset you?"

"No, Rainey-" *I'm just a fucking pervert who is struggling with seriously inappropriate thoughts.* "I just noticed the time and think it's best we cut this short today. You've had an emotional moment and it would be best if we picked this back up tomorrow morning."

"O-okay. If you say so."

I practically leapt in the direction of my things, gathering them together before racing for the front door. Moving so quickly, I didn't bother looking across the street to see Rainey's audience, just jumped in my car, pulled out while leaving a cloud of dirt in my path and hit the gas as I drove down her street.

By the time I returned to my apartment, my hands were shaking and I was cursing myself for ever having agreed to this case. How was I to know it would be so difficult? How was I to guess that the woman I'd interview would be as tempting as she was?

There was no way to know any of that, and yet there I was, absolutely convinced that I could have done something to prevent this reaction.

In desperate need of a distraction, I changed into shorts and a t-shirt, strapped my iPod to my bicep and went for a jog. The wind against my face was good for me, the powerful movement of my body helping ease sore muscles. I quickened my pace every time Rainey Day was in my thoughts, punishing myself until my legs burned and my lungs were on fire. None of it mattered. By the time I crawled up my stairs and returned home, that damn woman was still front and center in my head, images of her fingertip stroking up her thigh, of the flash of blue panties that kept drawing my eye when she moved.

Rainey had no shame, and it appeared neither did I.

Still, I wouldn't give in to the need to exorcise the desire from my body. Taking a cool shower to rinse the sweat from my skin, I was studiously keeping my hands from my cock, even if it stood erect. It was uncomfortable, but I managed, and within another half hour, I'd cooked and eaten dinner.

Normally, I'm not the type to watch television, but that night I needed something to keep my mind off the case. Unfortunately, almost every movie and television show is guaranteed to contain some scene with sex. I'd flip to watch one, groan when the obligatory scene appeared, then flip to another. Over and over again until I found myself watching reruns of Sesame Street because I knew it would be safe.

At least, I thought it would be. Apparently the word for the day was rainy, images of raindrops pattering windows in sync with doleful singing puppets upset that they couldn't go outside and play.

"Damn it!" I turned it off and headed for bed, finally losing the battle with myself when my hand shoved down my shorts and I pumped the shaft with thoughts of a blue eyed brunette in my head.

The liquid heat of my release on my hand felt like a betrayal, a reminder that despite my professionalism, despite my training, despite everything I thought set me apart from weaker men, I was no better than my base impulses.

Freud would have a field day with my behavior in that moment, his Austrian accent clear in my head, condemning everything I struggled with as some deep seated, repressed and dark desire for violent sexual conquest.

Perhaps Rainey was tempting solely because she was so easy to manipulate and control. Not to mention the fact that her body was built for sin.

Clenching my hand, I shot out of bed, cleaned up and crawled back beneath the covers terrified that my dreams that night would involve blue panties, dead floating bodies and a brunette woman whispering *Daddy*.

Thankfully, that wasn't the case. I didn't dream at all, somehow managing to get a few hours of uninterrupted sleep before the sun rose again and I was in my car pulling up to Rainey's house. She stood in the doorway waiting for me, her body covered by a pink and white sundress that hung down to just above her knees.

Wanting to keep the topic of conversation as safe as possible, I followed Rainey into the living room, taking my usual seat, while focusing on anything but her. Immediately I launched into questions about the party and the friends who were murdered.

It didn't escape my notice that I considered the discussion of four bludgeoned young adults with their skulls cracked open lying among blood splattered walls as 'safe'.

Safe for me, maybe, but not for other people.

"Let's get back to discussing the party: You've mentioned how you know Angel and Megan, however, we have yet to discuss how you knew Michael and Preston. I'd like you to tell me where you knew them from."

My voice was clipped and distant, a clinical approach to a woman who was crawling under my skin with tiny skittering fingernails. When our eyes met as I glanced up, Rainey was staring at me with her crooked lips pinned together in such a way I would have sworn she was trying not to laugh.

"Something bothering you, Doc?"

A sharp cut of my head to the left in negation. "No, I just want to stay on topic today. How did you know those two boys?"

Her brow arched, her stare curious, but she shook her head and leaned back against her seat, ready to divulge the information I needed.

"Well," she drawled, her husky voice as sensual as could be, "it's a good thing we've reached that part of the story, I guess. I met Michael and Preston a few days after David was dead."

Jotting down a note, I looked up at her without concern for what she might say next. I should have known better than to think Rainey didn't have a few more surprises up her sleeve. "How did you know them, Rainey?"

She lit a cigarette, smiled and asked, "Have you ever heard the term 'running a train', Doc? Because that's how I met Michael and Preston."

My heart sank into my stomach.

Son of a fucking bitch...

CHAPTER SIXTEEN

Rainey - Past

Mom had a hard time after David died. She was crushed, unable to function like she normally did, her ability to get up in the afternoons was pretty much absent and she lost one of her jobs because of it. Life was going downhill for her fast and there was very little I could do to help her.

Not that I didn't try. I cooked dinner and held her when she cried. I stayed home more because I was too afraid of leaving her alone. Something inside her had died right along with David and I wasn't special enough - important enough - for her to keep going.

After a week, she began locking herself in her room at night, not caring whether I was there or not. The rules she'd put in place for me while David was alive were gone. I was free to roam again. Hell, I probably could have brought the entire Connor family over and had sex with them in the living room and she wouldn't have cared. It was that bad.

Still, I tried, and for two weeks I lied to Rowan and told him she wouldn't let me go over to his house and had forbidden him from coming to mine. That lie wasn't as much for my mom as it was for him. I kept telling him to go back to Megan, to seek out a new life, to get out of Clayton Heights and become something because I refused to be the girl that ruined him.

Rowan had potential, more than any of us. And because I could see the truth of what was inside him, I couldn't bear the weight of keeping him from seeing it himself.

The first week, he resisted. He kept knocking on my window and coming to the front door. I sent him away every damn time, crying after watching him cross the yard and return to his house.

Rowan went back to his girlfriend by the end of the second week. His car was gone most of the time and after a few days of that, I felt comfortable to go over to my neighbors' house again.

Mom wasn't the only person struggling. I had nightmares of David's death, would wake up in a cold sweat after seeing his dead eyes looking up from beneath the surface of the water. Every so often I dreamed the police came to Rowan's house and arrested him for what we had done.

Obviously, it never happened, but I was still afraid it could. It's why I had to push him away. Because of me, he'd committed a crime, one that would lock him away for the rest of his life, and it would all be my fault.

During the third week, I tried to stay home as much as possible, but I would find myself watching out the window for Rowan to drive away and then run next door to get high. By that point, it was mainly Joel and Jacob I went to.

Paul was dealing in heavier drugs that even I had no desire to get into. In a way, I was beginning to have a little more respect for myself. I wasn't sure what had changed or why I was avoiding Paul as much as I was, but there was something not quite right with being with him. Mainly, it had to do with Rowan. Whenever I saw his father, it felt like more of a betrayal, like I was stabbing a knife into Rowan's back and twisting it just to be around Paul.

A month had passed and except for my mom continuing to spiral downhill, life had returned to normal. Rowan was happy with Megan, we still said hello in passing, but he wasn't constantly trying to corner me and beg me to be his girl. It hurt a little, the distance in his eyes when he looked at me, but I reminded myself it was best for him.

I loved Rowan. With everything inside of me, I loved the innocent boy he once was and the man he was becoming. And for that, I knew the only thing I could do to show him that love was to stay away from him so he could seek out a better life.

"Hey, Rainey. Are you going to be around tonight?"

Sitting on the couch in the Connors' living room, I twisted around to find Joel standing behind the recliner. Over the years, he'd somehow become even more pretty, his dirty blonde hair longer so that it framed his face, his brown eyes flecked with both green and gold. He had a bone structure in his face that would have done well if he went into modeling. But Joel wasn't the model type. Beneath all that prettiness, he was as rough and rugged as the rest of the men in this house.

"I can be. Why?"

"We're having a small party and I invited some friends over. Just thought I'd invite you, too."

With my legs crossed in front of me, I played with the frayed bottom hem of my jeans. It was early afternoon, everybody in the house just now waking up. Everybody but Rowan, that was. He'd driven off an hour ago, which is why I had come over.

Next door, my mom's car was still in the driveway, which meant she'd missed work again. I was going to have to start working to make up for the money she lost. I didn't mind. I was twenty. It was time for me to do something with my life besides sleep around and get high.

"Sounds like fun. I'll stick around."

Joel smiled. "I woke up with wood this morning. Want to come back to my room, smoke a joint, and take care of it for me?"

Shrugging a shoulder, I stood from the couch and followed him back. It wasn't like I was there to watch television. I could do that at home.

While we were walking through the hall someone knocked on the front door. Joel looked at me funny and brushed past me to go answer it, but Paul came out of his room and said the door was for him. We didn't think much of it, so we continued back to Joel's room, closing the door behind us.

Sitting on his bed, Joel went about rolling a joint while I stood against a wall looking at all the posters he'd hung up of half naked women.

"Like what you see?"

"Huh?" Pulling my gaze from a blond woman holding her top up like she was keeping it from falling off, I stared at him.

"Those women," he answered. "Do you like looking at them?"

"They're pretty, I guess."

He stopped twisting the paper in his hand, grinned up at me. "Have you ever been with a woman, Rainey?"

I shook my head. "No. I've never had reason to."

Joel went back to what he was doing. "I was thinking that maybe I could get you and Angel together some time. I wouldn't mind watching you two fuck while I smoke a joint or something. It would be hot as hell."

His eyes tipped up. "It would just be me watching of course, because I'm not letting some other guy see Angel naked. Speaking of which," he put the joint to his lips and lit the tip, "why do you still have clothes on? Didn't you come back here for a reason?"

"I didn't know what you wanted me to do. If I'm just sucking you, I don't see a reason to take off my pants."

His voice was strained from holding in a drag. "I'd like to fuck you this morning. Bury my face in those tits." He blew out. "I'd like to see Angel playing with them. Although she'd probably get jealous. Hers aren't as nice."

Taking off my clothes while he watched, I walked over to his bed.

"Lie on your back." Handing me the joint, he said, "Smoke this."

With my fingers pinching the joint, I took a few hits while he stripped down and climbed between my legs. It was mechanical now, our fucking, matter of fact in a way that made it sad. A means to an end, really. For him, not me. I didn't get off unless it was Rowan in the bed. He was the only person who made me feel something.

Joel held my hips down while he thrust inside, grunts falling over his lips as I took a few more puffs of the joint and lay there. As usual, he played with my chest, rolling his face in it, licking and sucking. I was beginning to think he had mommy issues he hadn't yet worked through.

His hips were still moving, hands still locked on my body when he looked at me and asked, "What's going on between you and Rowan?"

The question surprised me, my head rolling over the pillow, our eyes locking. "Why do you ask?"

Hips moving faster, Joel's jaw clenched as he finished off to pull out and come on my chest. Staring down at the mess like it was an art exhibit, he smiled.

Yep, mommy issues...

"No reason. Well, yeah, there's a reason. The kid has been aggravated lately. Any time your name is brought up, he acts like he wants to beat all our asses. Haven't you fucked him already?"

Joel stood from the bed, grabbed a towel to clean himself and tossed it to me to do the same. Wiping off his mess, I bit the inside of my cheek. Why did he have to bring up Rowan? I was doing a damn good job of pretending he was happy and that things had gone back to the way they'd always been.

"I've had sex with him. A couple times, actually. Plus, he's with Megan. I'm not sure why he's aggravated when you bring me up."

The truth was, I knew exactly why Rowan would get upset, but I wouldn't tell Joel. He would only end up telling Jacob and Frankie and they would use that information to make Rowan's life hell.

Rolling another joint to give to me, Joel shook his head. "Doesn't make sense to me. Megan's hot, her family is loaded, and she's not a slut like you. I'm not sure why Rowan gets all pissy when your name is brought up."

It stung, every damn word he said hitting me like a bullet. But it was all true. "I keep telling him to stay with her. She's good for him."

"Like I said: I don't get it." He tossed me the joint and tipped his chin to his door, an invitation for me to get dressed and leave. After pulling my clothes on, I had my hand on the knob ready to walk out when he said, "Be sure to stick around for the party tonight. I told my friends about you."

Sighing heavily, I knew in my gut what he intended. "How many?"

"Two."

"And what do I get out of it?"

"Don't worry, Rainey. I'll take care of you. I always do. I promised these guys a party and I intend to deliver."

Stepping into the hall, I shut his door and leaned back against it, my eyes drifting left to stare at Rowan's bedroom door. I missed him so much it hurt, but I knew better than to act on it. Keeping our distance was the best thing for Rowan. Megan was the best thing for him. Yet knowing that didn't make the pain any easier.

I flopped down on the couch in the living room and turned the television back on. It did nothing to mask the sound of Paul fucking someone in his room. Now I understood how Rowan felt to sit here while I was in there. You could hear everything. The grunts and moans, the slap of skin, Paul telling his guest to get dressed and get out while he measured out a bag for her of whatever it was he was selling.

His bedroom door opened behind me and when I turned to see the woman he was walking to the door, my heart dropped into my stomach, slamming down so hard I felt like I would throw up.

"Mom?"

She looked horrible; hair a mess, eyes bruised with half moon circles, cheeks sunken in from refusing to eat very much since David died. Refusing to meet my eyes, she hurried out of the house, Paul closing the door quietly behind her. From the window, I watched her walk through the two yards and up to our house, my jaw hanging open as rage filtered though me.

"What the fuck, Paul? That was my mom!"

He glanced at me, his chest bare, belly rounded and soft because he'd gained weight in the two, almost three, years I'd known him. Paul cocked a brow. The bastard hadn't even bothered to buckle his belt.

"We're all adults, Rainey. Get the fuck over it. I'm not even sure why you're complaining. Didn't you just get done fucking my son? It's not my fault those punks don't last as long as me."

"That's not why I'm upset. She's my mom!"

"Listen, kid. If Joel didn't get you off and you need some relief, I have no problem going again. Just march your pretty little ass into my bedroom and I'll take care of you. Otherwise, shut the fuck up. Your mom needed something and I gave it to her. No big deal."

Pushing to my feet, I glared at him. "That's sick!"

He shrugged a shoulder. "How is it any different than what you've been doing? The world is sick, kid. It is what it is. Now smoke a damn joint and calm down. If that doesn't help, there's some alcohol in the kitchen. You need to get over yourself."

Kicking his door open, he disappeared into his room, shutting it behind him with a hard slam. I stood in the living room, my hands fisting. Not wanting to be in the house, but also not wanting to go home, I stalked into the kitchen and grabbed a bottle of vodka, the glass cool against my palm as I retreated to the only place that comforted me anymore.

Rowan's room was quiet. It smelled like him. Hurrying across the floor, I climbed beneath his covers and bundled them over me. I must have finished off at least a third of the bottle before I fell asleep. It was stupid to be in there. Dangerous. But I was hurting so bad, I didn't think of the consequences. I just wanted to hide.

I woke up to Rowan's knuckles brushing softly along my jaw, his blue eyes staring down at me with heartache behind them. Outside, the sun was setting. I'd slept most of the day away.

"You've been avoiding me."

My voice was lazy, deeper because I hadn't quite woken fully. "For good reason."

"That's impossible. There's no reason out there good enough for you to shove me away."

I was still so tired, my heart hurt, a hammer beating the inside of my skull to remember what had sent me fleeing into his room in the first place. "Paul is fucking my mom."

Eyes closing, Rowan sighed. "Yeah, I know. He has been for a week now. Which is why I know all the lies you told me about not being allowed over here are bullshit. Scoot over."

"Why?"

"Scoot, Rainey. Don't make me move you myself."

Rowan crawled onto the mattress to spoon me from behind, his strong arms wrapping around me, holding me tight to his warm body. Burying his face in my neck, he planted a soft kiss on my skin.

"I'd say I'm sorry about your mom, but I'm not. What you're feeling right now is what you've made me feel for years."

Anger coiled deep in my belly. "What's that supposed to mean? She's my mom"

"And you're my girl, but I've had to watch you fuck my dad and my brothers." Voice deep against my ear, Rowan didn't sound like himself. He was pissed off,

173

hurt, cold like the night he'd killed David. I tried to push away from him, but he tugged me back, his arms steel bands around me.

"You're not going anywhere, Rainey. You're going to listen to what I have to say for once." He laughed, the sound soft, yet bitter. "That's just like you. I mention how I feel and you run off as fast as you can. You have no problem hurting me, but you'll be damned to sit around and witness it. Just close your eyes, Rainey. Pretend that you haven't ripped my heart from my chest and crushed it between your fingers. That's what you always do."

"Rowan-"

His hand pressed over my mouth, his breath hot against my neck. He trembled against me, so filled with heartache and rage that there was no telling what he would do.

"Don't say my name. Just do what you do best and pretend I'm Jacob, or Frankie, or Joel."

Reaching down, he unbuttoned my pants. I attempted to push away from him again, but he let go of my mouth to lock an arm around my chest.

"What's wrong, Rainey? You don't like it when I use you for the only thing you *think* you're good for?"

Shoving my pants and panties down to my thighs, he worked behind me to remove his. I was still fighting to get away, but he wouldn't let me go. "I don't see what the fucking problem is. I'll toss you a fucking twenty for this, okay? Is that the going rate?"

"Rowan, stop." Tears flooded my eyes. I didn't understand what was wrong, but this wasn't *him*. Not Rowan. He wouldn't do this.

His hand gripped my breast from over my shirt, squeezing so hard that I yelped into the pillow.

"Funny, that's the sound you make when you fuck my dad." He notched the tip of his cock at my body. "Tell me no, Rainey. Go ahead and tell me you don't want this. That you're better than this."

He was daring me to say it. The tip pushing inside me as a threat. As if that would be enough to make me admit he was always right. Even though I was still crying, I shook my head, my voice weak. "I'm not. Twenty is fine, Rowan."

"Damn it, tell me you're better than this, Rainey!"

I bit my lip, absolutely refusing.

His forehead landed in my hair, his hips thrusting forward and back, over and over again as we lay there trembling, our hearts breaking together because there was no walking back from this. Rowan was using me. Just like Jacob. Just like Joel. Just like Paul and Frankie. He was taking what I was offering without either of us claiming it was love.

I'd broken him. For him to do this, for Rowan of all people to do to me what men had always done, it meant I'd finally crushed what was once innocent and sweet inside him.

While he fucked me, he talked. I don't think he was expecting much of an answer, his words were simply a confession he needed me to hear while he shredded what we had always been despite every complication and screwed up circumstance.

"I haven't slept with Megan yet. Haven't been able to. All I can think about is who you're with and what you're doing with them. She's wants me, Rainey. Has pretty much begged me to do to her what I'm doing to you right now."

Tightening his arms around me, his hips picked up in pace, his breath beating against my neck because even though he hated me at that moment, he still loved how it felt to be inside me. I did that to him. Me and nobody else.

"Maybe -fuck," he pushed deeper, his words broken up by the climax getting close. "Maybe I should finally stop waiting around for you to stop being such a fucking slut-"

My eyes clenched shut, tears rolling down my cheeks.

"-and just be with a girl who can keep her damn legs together."

Harder and faster, he moved. His release close. I knew. I'd been with so many men, I could tell you how many minutes or even seconds they would last. Their breath picks up, sweat beading at their temples and on their chest, their muscles flexing as they chase that orgasm like it's running from them at top speed. Rowan was chasing it now.

"Maybe I've been a stupid kid this entire time thinking that you could be anything more than what you are: a toy for men to fuck."

He came without pulling out. I tried to wiggle away from him, tried to move so he wouldn't finish inside me, but he locked his arm at the last second, pushing so deep that I couldn't get away.

"Rowan, what have you done?"

Releasing me suddenly, he sat up on the side of the bed, his face buried in his hands. Unsure what to say, I waited for him to speak first. Rowan was silent for what felt like hours, his body still, his broad shoulders tight.

Sitting up, I touched him and he shot to his feet, pulled his pants up his legs and buttoned them.

"Rowan?"

176

He turned to me and reached in his back pocket to yank out his wallet. The twenty dollar bill floated down to the mattress at my feet, the face on the front of it staring up at me with accusation.

"That's how it works, right? I get mine and pay you for it?" Eyes stained red, he glared at me, a tear tracking down his cheek, shimmering within the soft sunlight that filtered in through his curtains. "What do I do now? Tell you to get out? Your job here is done?"

Pulling my legs to my chest, I wrapped my arms around my shins, my pants still hooked around my ankles.

"Is that how it works, Rainey?"

Bottom lip quivering, I nodded. "Yeah, Rowan. That's how it works. That's how it will always work. Don't you get that? Look what I've done to you! This isn't you. You're better than this. I've taken something good and destroyed it. Yes, you should be with Megan. She's a decent girl who loves you."

"You love me," he shouted, no doubt loud enough for everyone in the house to hear.

I shouted right back. "I'm ruining you. This life, this screwed up, complicated, disgusting life is not the one you should be living. I just want you to become someone else. To go away and do all the wonderful things I know you're capable of doing. Go to school. Make something of yourself. Marry Megan and have lots of pretty babies. Stop looking at me as if I'm the person you want. Go find another life, Rowan, and don't do it for me. Do it for yourself."

Stabbing his fingers through his hair, he crossed the room and opened his door. "Get out."

"Rowan."

"Get the fuck out! I'm done with you."

177

With blurry eyes and tear soaked cheeks, I pushed to my feet and pulled up my pants. Walking past the bed, I had almost reached the door when he growled, "You forgot your payment."

My soul bled out onto the carpet at my feet, leaving me empty and hollow.

"It was on the house," I whispered, brushing past him to walk out into the hall. Jacob and Joel both peered out of their rooms, most likely drawn by the argument they'd heard through the thin walls. To their credit, neither of them said a word as I passed en route to the living room.

Rowan left the house ten minutes later, the car starting just before the tires peeled down the road.

I didn't think the day could get much worse.

Joel dropped down next to me, the couch cushion dipping, and passed me a joint.

While I took a drag, he commented, "I told you he's been pissy lately. Thought maybe he was angry we were hitting it and he wasn't."

Glancing at me, he took the joint back and inhaled, holding the breath while he said, "If you ask me, Rowan is stupid for falling in love. We all knew what you were the minute we met you."

A cloud rolled over his lips and he passed it back. "Not saying that like it's a bad thing. It's just the truth, you know?"

Oddly, I found it kind of sweet that Joel had followed me out here to talk. Sweet for him, at least. "Yeah, I know."

"You still up for partying tonight? Sounds like you could use some fun."

Nodding, I relaxed against the couch. "Yeah, I'll probably need to take a shower first. Rowan, he-"

"Do what you must."

The day bled into the night slowly. After showering and crying my eyes out some more, I spent the hours alternating between watching television and taking naps. Jacob and Joel left me alone for the most part. Paul left a few hours after Rowan, and Frankie was gone, probably in jail for another fight. I never asked about him. He didn't matter.

Around seven, people showed up at the house. Joel turned on some music, started passing drinks around, lit a few joints while men and women milled about in the kitchen, living room and bedrooms. I stayed on the couch for the most part, watching the party occur around me, not really talking to anyone other than a few people who introduced themselves.

It had to be close to nine when Joel dropped down on one side of me, Jacob on the other, and two other guys I didn't know stood awkwardly in front of us. I was drunk by this point, all the events of the day crushing in on me while I drank straight from a bottle of vodka that Joel had tossed to me earlier.

"How are you feeling, Rainey?"

Leaning against Joel's chest, I smiled. "I think I'm numb."

He massaged my shoulders. "Hopefully not too numb. These are my friends I wanted to introduce you to, Michael and Preston. They've been down on their luck in the lady department lately and I told them you might be able to help them out."

The two guys smiled down at me, one taller than the other. Michael had brown hair and brown eyes, his shoulders thick with muscle, his waist narrow. I imagined he could be a football player for as big as he was.

Preston, on the other hand, was short and round. I thought I recognized him from school, but couldn't be sure. He had reddish blond hair and his pale skin was ruddy. He wasn't what most people would consider attractive, but when had I ever cared about that?

"You ever heard of running a train, Rainey?"

Shaking my head, I drank from my bottle and answered, "No."

"It's where a bunch of guys take turns on one girl. I was thinking the five of us could have some fun. Jacob and I both will pay you for it. Give you cash and drugs. What do you say?"

What did I always say? This was my life now, the girl in the neighborhood who had a hell of a time keeping her pants on. My life would never change. "How much money?"

"A hundred bucks, plus we'll throw in an ounce of pot. That should keep you pretty stoned for the next week or so."

The two boys leered down at me, Michael's shoulders shaking with silent laughter.

I shrugged a shoulder. "Why not? What do you need me to do?"

"Just go in my room, strip down and get on the bed. Then we'll wander in there one at a time to get what we want. When we're done, you're done."

Seeing double because of the weed and booze, it took me several attempts to stand from the couch. Joel stood up to help steady me, walking with his arm around my waist to lead me to his room. Jacob, Michael and Preston poured in behind them.

Joel helped me get undressed, someone in the room whistling when he removed my shirt. *What did I tell you about her? Hell yeah, man, that's what I'm talking about.*

180

Their conversation floated in and out of my awareness. I was so messed up, but knew I would have done this sober. My reputation and self-worth were already as low as they could get. Rowan hated me. My mom was losing her damn mind. My entire world was falling apart. Might as well take it lying on my back.

Leading me to his bed, Joel whispered against my ear, "Are you well enough to hold yourself up on hands and knees?"

I nodded and he helped me get into a position where I was facing the three men near the door. They were all blurry, which helped in a way.

"Who's up first?"

"Let Preston go at her. This poor bastard hasn't gotten any in over a year."

"Those tits, though. God damn."

None of it felt real, which was fine by me. I didn't want it to be real. I just wanted to go back to a time where Rowan loved me, where he looked at me like I hung the moon.

How selfish was that? He finally moved on like I told him to, but all I wanted was for him to come running back.

The blurs moved around, one approaching me while the other three stood by the open door. He climbed behind me and shoved down his pants, his hands gripping my hips as he shoved inside, grunting with each quick stroke. He wasn't very good at it, his rhythm jerky and uncoordinated. He wouldn't last long.

"Woot! Get it, man! Look at her chest bounce. Do it harder, Preston. She can take it."

This is where I was in life. Just like Rowan had said. A toy that men fucked. A party favor. An

181

entertainment and nothing else. Preston finished pretty quick. In truth, I'd barely felt him, he was that small. Poor guy. No wonder he never got any.

A towel flew across the room and landed beside me. "Clean up your mess when you're done."

While Preston did that, the other three stood talking, other people passing the open door, pausing, shaking their heads and laughing. Someone high fived another and kept going down the hall.

"Michael, you're up."

Just like the first, Michael got behind me. He actually tried to play with my clit as if that would turn me on. It was too bad for him that the only person who could get me going was out with his girlfriend, having sex with her for the first time. I hoped he loved her. I hoped I was right and she loved him. I hoped I'd taught him well enough that he rocked her world while rolling around beneath the covers.

My body was bouncing again. More hoots and hollers, except this time, a female voice rose up above it all, two people standing in the doorway looking past the guys waiting for their turn.

"Holy shit! What a slut!" Her tinkling laughter caught my attention even more and I blinked my eyes several times to clear my vision.

Rowan and a girl I assumed was Megan stood at the door watching me, Michael still gripping my hips and slamming his body behind mine.

My eyes met Rowan's begging him not to agree with her. Rage rolled behind his gaze, so pure that I could feel the burning heat of it from across the room.

"Yeah," he answered her, wrapping his arm over her shoulder, "Rainey's nothing but a stupid whore my brothers hire. Don't worry about her. We should just hang out in my room."

I had to duck my head to keep everyone from seeing me cry. The tears wouldn't stop pouring.

Something snapped in me, whether it was my pride, my heart, my soul, I wasn't sure, but hearing him say that was the last straw. "Get off me."

My voice was so low, that Michael didn't hear me at first.

"Get the fuck off me!"

"Hey! What's wrong?"

Who knows how I managed to shove him off with how drunk I was, but after accomplishing that, I stumbled off the bed and dove for my clothes.

"Rainey, babe, what's wrong? I thought we were having fun." Joel's voice filled the room, but I ignored him. After pulling on my clothes, I shoved past them into the hall, stumbling my way out of the house and across my yard.

Throwing the door open, all I wanted to do was hug my mom so she could lie to me and tell me it would be all right.

"Mom?"

I must have bumped into every wall as I stumbled past. Mom wasn't in the living room or the kitchen, so I went to her room in search of her. Stepping inside it, I didn't see her on the bed, but when I looked past the mattress, I saw her hair on the floor. "Mom?"

Dropping to the ground, I crawled around the foot of her bed to find her splayed over the carpet, a pile of vomit by her mouth, her eyes open and a needle sticking out of her arm.

"Mom!" Crawling closer, I shook her shoulder, felt for a pulse, but I was too messed up to know what I was doing. "Mom, wake up."

Panic surged through me, a jolt of adrenaline that sobered me up enough to understand what I was seeing. "Oh my God. Mom!"

She didn't respond, her body lying so still that I knew, but didn't want to believe. "No. Oh, no no no."

Pushing to my feet, I ran from my house. It was instinct to run to Rowan, to burst through the front door of his house, shove past all the people and run down the hall. I was crying again, but ignored everybody who tried to talk to me. I had to get to Rowan.

Throwing his door open, I almost fell to my knees to see him in bed with Megan. She was lying on her back and he was on top of her, the blanket covering their bodies. Rowan looked over at me, anger drawing his eyebrows together. "What the fuck, Rainey? Get out!"

"Rowan, I need help."

It was a whisper, I don't think he heard me.

"Get out!"

I forced strength into my voice. "Rowan, I need your help. Please."

"What the fuck is her problem?" Megan glared at me from beneath him.

"Rowan, I think my mom is dead."

Everything stopped for a split second. The noise of the party disappeared. Megan disappeared. Everything disappeared into the background except for Rowan and I staring at each other without speaking.

Rowan and Rainey, forever.

The thought hit me as hard as a speeding train while the world around us snapped back and my hand tightened over his doorknob.

He jumped up from the bed, grabbed his pants and ignored Megan's stream of curse words and questions. Leaving her behind, he raced toward me, taking me by the shoulders to lead me out of the house and across my yard. His voice was soft as he spoke to me, but I couldn't hear a damn word he said. Nothing was making sense at that point.

I showed him back to my mom's room and leaned against a wall as he kneeled down to check on her. When he lifted his eyes to me, I knew I was right.

She was gone.

From whatever Paul had given her, my mother was just gone.

"Rainey." Pushing to his feet, Rowan grabbed me and pulled me into a tight hug, his entire body somehow sheltering mine. I buried my face in his shoulder and cried so hard, I was choking on the sobs.

"Rainey, we need to call the police. We need to report this."

"I know."

"Come on."

What happened after that was a blur. All I remembered while we waited for the police and medical people to document the scene and pull the body from the house was Rowan sitting next to me.

He never returned to Megan and he never let me go. I answered a lot of questions, but couldn't recall a single one by the time the house cleared out and we were alone.

Still holding me, he whispered, "It's okay, Rainey. I've got you. I'll always have you."

185

Rowan took me to the bathroom and stripped off my clothes. I didn't say anything - couldn't say anything - as he drew me a hot bath and helped me into the water. While he used a washcloth to clean my skin, I stared helplessly at a wall. My entire world had just imploded.

My mom was gone.

I was alone.

After cleaning me up, Rowan wrapped me in a towel, carried me to my bedroom and helped me into a nightshirt and underwear. He lay beside me that night holding me and whispering all the things he would do to make me better.

It occurred to me that I'd ruined the first time he'd had sex with Megan, had most likely driven a wedge between them because I'd left him with no choice but to choose me over her.

That day was one of the worst things I'd ever experienced, and as I lay there in the warm arms of a person I'd grown to love, I had no idea that in a few shorts weeks, everything would only get worse.

CHAPTER SEVENTEEN

Justin - Present

While Rainey described for me one of the absolute worst days of her life, a song played in my head, the theme to Sesame Street to be exact, the dichotomy of such a happy tune against the backdrop of her horrible memories freezing me in place, scrambling my thoughts while I tried to gather myself together enough to counsel her regarding the trauma she'd endured.

This wasn't a moment where a doctor would ask his patient how that memory made her feel. It was deeper than that, a precipice upon which the session could tip over, sending us both sliding into a depressive cavern with no possible way of climbing back.

That one day alone would have broken anybody. It didn't matter how strong they were, how emotionally balanced. Surviving the heartache, the humiliation, the trauma of finding her mother dead on the floor, Rainey had proven how fierce her strength really was.

Quite frankly, had I experienced even one week of her life, I would have found myself strapped to a bed in a Thorazine haze once the doctors and nurses had wrestled me into a mental facility.

This woman had lived hard.

Had become hard.

Had fought tooth and nail to continue scrabbling forward while everything around her was falling apart.

Based on what she told me, it would only continue to get worse. I wasn't sure I was prepared for it.

In no way did I excuse Rainey for how her actions and decisions had played a role in what was done to her, but she was young, disastrously so, her intellect questionable and her motives still not clear enough for me to comprehend where her story was ultimately heading.

Tapping my pen against my notepad, I watched her lying over the couch. She took that pose in the moments she was reliving a memory that haunted her.

"How did you act toward Paul after your mother died? Did you continue going over to his house?"

It wasn't the best question, nothing that would dig into her psyche to pull all of her secrets to the surface, but it's what I asked while I attempted to settle my thoughts.

I didn't get turned on again, at least. Okay, maybe just a little bit when she described the train being run. *Damn it.* I wasn't just going to Hell, I was driving the truck there myself.

"Not as often, but not because of what happened with my mom."

"You were avoiding Rowan again, weren't you?"

Rainey's legs were bent with her feet on the couch, fingertips softly scraping over her thighs as the skirt of her sundress fell down. She touched the mark on her arm again, absent minded, so lost in thought that I wondered if she remembered I was sitting in the room.

"That and getting a job. My mom was dead. The bills needed to be paid. So I had to do something. They hired me at the convenience store on the corner. I wasn't great at the job, but I muddled through."

"Did Rowan go back to Megan? What happened with you two after the night your mom died?"

"Yeah," she breathed, "he went back to her. I guess she understood why he'd jumped up when he did. She's a sweet girl, like I said. And she loved him."

Nodding, I watched her closely, wondering when she would return to this conversation. Rainey had a way of connecting intimately to a person through speech and eye contact alone. But in moments like this, I knew she was drifting off, lost to the memories that plagued her.

"Are we getting close to the night of the party, Rainey? The one that occurred a week ago?"

Hands gripping her thighs, she squeezed so hard, the skin around her fingers turned white. "No. We're at the point I've wanted to avoid talking about. The night that Rowan died."

"We can skip it if you want. If it has nothing to do with your friends' deaths, then I'm not sure we need to discuss it."

"It has everything to do with their deaths."

Curious about her comment, I paused to allow her to fill in the blanks. She sat up, her eyes finally meeting mine as her head tilted slightly to the left. I'd never seen her so composed and calm.

Unable to stand the silence any longer, I asked, "What is it you're trying to tell me, Rainey? Have you remembered more about the night they died? Do you know who killed them?"

"I caused his death. Have I told you that? I think I have."

Her hands scrubbed down her thighs, her dress pooled at her hips, the front unbuttoned. I hadn't even noticed her doing that. So lost in her story, I wasn't paying attention to her movements the entire time.

With the front open, only the inner swells of her breasts were exposed to my view. Yet, it was her face that drew my attention. Lips slightly parted, eyes cast to the right, Rainey's face was almost angelic, her pale skin glowing beneath the low light of the room. Beyond the bruises that marred her jaw and the orb of her eye, she was truly exquisite in her beauty.

"You told me, although, I'm not sure I agree that you carry the blame. You weren't driving the car that killed him."

Blue eyes peeking up, the color popping against her dark eyelashes, Rainey grinned, an expression more solemn than happy. "Did I tell you what I was doing when he died?"

No, but I assume it's going to be bad...

"You haven't told me about that night, no."

"I was watching his girlfriend give head to Jacob while Joel was doing me from behind."

I took a breath, held it, released it slowly. "His girlfriend, as in Megan?"

Rainey nodded.

"Didn't you say she was a sweet girl?"

"She was. But something happened that night. I think she was angry. Trying to get even with him or something. Megan had been drinking and she wasn't so messed up that she didn't know what she was doing, but I let it happen. I didn't try to talk her out of it. Didn't try to stop her. I think I wanted her to do something that dragged her as low as me."

Rainey blinked. "Why would I want that?"

Sadly, the answer was plain and obvious. It hung between us as if Rainey could reach forward and pluck it from the air. She couldn't face it, so I made a suggestion that would open her eyes to see what had been right there in front of her the entire time.

"Perhaps because, deep down, you were in love with Rowan. I know you kept telling him to find a new life, to move on without you, so to say, but I don't think you wanted that. You were telling him what you thought was right to tell him, but not necessarily true."

"Rowan and Rainey forever," she smiled, the expression not reaching her eyes. "Yet while he died - as he burned in a car not more than a few blocks from here - I was watching his girlfriend cheat on him while I was having sex with his brother. He was burning and I was getting off."

The comment surprised me, my brows lifting up my forehead. "I thought you said you only orgasmed while with Rowan."

Dangerous territory, Justin...

A bark of laughter shook her shoulders, her eyes pinning mine. "I didn't get off because of anything Jacob was doing, Doc. I got off because I knew that when Rowan found out what Megan had done, the two of them would be over."

Aaaaand we've set a new low bar for fucked up.

It was back and forth with Rainey. Constantly and eternally.

Rubbing at the bridge of my nose, I crossed an ankle over a knee and sighed heavily. "Are you ready to talk about that night, Rainey?"

I assumed once we passed this hurdle, we could finally get to the details of the night her friends died.

Nodding, she answered, "Yeah, I think I am."

CHAPTER EIGHTEEN

Rainey - Past

It was difficult after mom died. She was already struggling to pay the bills at the time of her death, not that I even knew what most of those bills were. Catching up and keeping everything together was next to impossible.

Rowan attempted to help me figure it out. He was intelligent like that, was responsible with money. He had a good head on his shoulders that set him apart from the rest of the fucked up people where we lived.

That was one of his most impressive qualities: Rowan, despite all the drugs, the partying, the sex and the crime, never fell victim to it. Sure, he experimented, and yes, he killed someone, but he never became like everybody around him. Somehow he managed to blend in while remaining separate, like a butterfly mingling among moths; more beautiful, more powerful, yet somehow still more delicate.

It took a few weeks for us to figure out where everything stood. As it was, I couldn't afford to bury mom, so I released her body to the city. They told me she would be cremated and her remains would be scattered in a pauper's grave. It didn't feel right that she wouldn't have a headstone or some kind of marker that told the world she'd once existed. I liked to think when they spread her ashes, some of them escaped into the wind, that bits and pieces of her reached the sky, tore through the atmosphere to settle amongst the stars.

She deserved the fairy tale and all she'd been given was a nightmare. With her gone, I had to continue the story, just keep trudging along with the hope that one day, I didn't end up dying alone like she did.

People shouldn't die alone. They should be surrounded by family and loved ones, they should be held and reminded that their lives had meaning. The universe is rarely so kind.

"You clock out in fifteen minutes, Rainey. Do you need one of us to walk you home?"

I turned to see Mr. Crews stroll forward. An older man, most likely in his eighties, he'd owned the convenience store for over forty years. Up until recently, he'd always been a friendly face behind the counter, but time had slowed him down, his wife demanding that he reserve what was left of it for his family.

To replace himself, he'd hired four residents of Clayton Heights, myself included, and assigned me the morning shift for fear that anything late at night would endanger me walking back and forth. Technically, I could use my mom's car, but without a valid license, I was afraid of driving it and getting pulled over.

"It's only two, and it's a bright, beautiful day outside. I think I can manage on my own, Mr. Crews. Thanks for the offer, though."

He grinned a toothless smile, his double chin wobbling, his cheeks stained a dusty red. "A pretty girl like you needs to be careful in this area. There's no telling what the men around here will think. They'll try to take advantage of you. Always be careful, Rainey. Not all men are bad, but there are a lot of nasty ones hanging out just trying to hurt nice girls."

Nice... If only he knew the truth. Most of the truly bad ones in this area lived right next door and each had touched, licked, sucked or fucked every part of me. I was safe from what he worried could happen.

"I'll be careful. I promise."

Ten minutes later, Jeff walked in, a younger kid, maybe sixteen or seventeen. I wondered if he was in the same grade as Rowan, but never worked up the courage to ask. School had just let out, which meant Rowan would be on his way home to jog, get a shower and pick up Megan for their date. Every Friday night, like clockwork.

"Hey, Rainey."

Jeff was cute as a button, but although he was near the same age as Rowan, he didn't appear as old. Perhaps circumstances age us more than the years do. The harder the life, the faster you grow.

After switching out the till, I clocked out while Jeff took over. Waving as I left, I stepped out into the daylight. It was a cold day, snow was coming, but not so soon that the sun had a problem warming my skin. I should have brought a jacket, should have worn pants instead of shorts. The temperatures were dropping fast.

Above my head, the trees swayed in a soft breeze, the birds in the branches singing. I felt peaceful strolling past the rows of chain link fencing, my fingers trailing over the metal, my mind lost in a fog of what I planned to do with the rest of my life.

I wondered if it was true for everyone that you never feel like a true adult until the day your parents die. Several weeks ago, I was still a kid with a million years ahead of me to figure things out. But now I was all I had, a woman who had to grow the hell up and come up with a plan. The store paid decent enough to keep me going, but eventually I'd have to figure out something better.

"Rainey! Hey!" A sharp whistle followed the sound of my name and I turned to see Joel jogging across the road toward me. He caught up, his long legs bounding beneath him, his hair a mess around his face. Throwing an arm over my shoulder, he tugged me against him for a hug.

I had to admit that, even though Joel always had ulterior motives, he treated me decent, never putting me down just for the enjoyment of being a jerk. "We're having a party tonight, beautiful, you in?"

Having avoided their house as much as possible over the last few weeks (except for those times I needed an escape so badly, I was willing to brave seeing Paul or Rowan in passing) I wasn't sure going to a party was the best idea. "I don't know-"

"Listen, what happened to your mom sucks. I get that. And I feel really shitty that dad sold her the junk that took her out, but you can't stop living your life because bad things happen."

"It's not just that, Joel. It's Rowan. He's got a good thing going with Megan and every time I go around there, I end up screwing things up for him."

"He loves you," Joel commented matter of fact. "So what? That's his problem, not yours. Woman, I would have fallen in love, too, if I didn't have Angel to keep me distracted. You give good tail. Know what I mean? We should have known better than to let you be his first time. Now he's all puppy dog eyes when he looks at you, but again, not your problem."

"Joel-"

"Which is why I want you at this party tonight. I have a business deal to work out with you. A little birdy told me you're hard up for cash. And me and a couple of buddies just happen to be hard up. Seems to me we could work out an arrangement where everybody walks away happy. Well, we'll be happy. You'll probably limp a little, but hey, you'll be two hundred dollars richer for it."

As we were nearing our houses, Rowan drove by, slowing as he approached, his head ducking down so he could look at us through the passenger side window. Joel smiled and waved, which only pissed Rowan off. His tires gave a small squeal over the payment as he hit the gas to drive the rest of the way home.

"See? That right there is why it's not a good idea."

"Screw him. He's got Megan. He should be happy hitting that and not worrying about you. His girl has a tight little body on her and makes these little squeaky noises when they fuck. *Oh, Rowan, yes, give it to me harder. Oh! Oh! Oh!* Half the time I expect her to start singing opera when she comes. But whatever, that's his thing and has nothing to do with us."

Glaring at him, I tried to ignore the way my heart ached to know Rowan and Megan's sex life had taken off. Guess that early departure from their first time didn't bother her enough not to try again. It made me sick.

He was right, though. I needed the money. "What time do you want me over there?"

"Come early. Get drunk. You're more fun when you're stumbling. I'll even toss in free joints."

"What time, Joel?"

"Seven."

A sigh blew from my lungs. "I'll see you then."

He flashed me a beaming grin. "This is why I love you." Reaching, he squeezed my breast and I slapped his hand away, separating myself from his arm so I could walk up my driveway.

"See you tonight, Rainey. Don't bother with clothes. Unless of course it's some sexy leather number with holes in all the right places."

Shaking my head, I let myself into my house to find Rowan sitting on my couch waiting for me. I hadn't even noticed he'd walked to my house instead of his.

"What was that all about?"

Setting my keys on a side table, I took a seat in the chair facing him. "What was what?"

"Don't play stupid, Rainey. It might work with other people, but it doesn't work with me. What were you talking to Joel about?"

Rowan had let his hair grow out, the ends dusting his shoulders, the front brushed back. I wanted to run my fingers through it. "He invited me to a party tonight."

Cursing under his breath, he darted his eyes to my window, the blue made brighter by the subdued sunlight. "How much are they paying you?"

"I don't think that's any of your-"

"How much?" Gaze meeting mine, his jaw was tight, the dark stubble causing his cheeks to appear more sunken than they were.

"Two hundred."

"I'll give it to you to stay home."

Rowan had been on edge for weeks around me, but to suddenly lash out was surprising. "Why do you even have that much money on you?"

"Don't worry about that. Just take it and stay your ass home."

"I'm not taking your money."

His grin was feral, angry. "Why? Is my cash not as good as Joel's?"

"No, but I haven't earned-"

"Then fuck me for it! I don't care what I have to do to make you take it. I don't want you at that party tonight. Two hundred? Either your rates have gone up or Joel is planning on you sleeping with a lot of guys. I can't stand watching it, Rainey!"

I wouldn't respond to his rage. I'd learned my lesson on that. Keeping my voice calm, I reminded him, "We're not together, Rowan. You're with Megan. I've said that a thousand times. What I choose to do with my body is my decision."

He pushed to his feet as if he planned to lunge across at me, stopping suddenly, his hand fisting and relaxing again. Turning, he strode to my front window to stare out over the tall weeds in the yard, his voice too calm for what he had to be feeling. "Has it ever occurred to you that I don't want you at my house?"

Something Joel had said came to mind, and like the idiot I was, I repeated it. "It's not my fault you fell in love with me, Rowan. I warned you not to."

"Warned me?" He laughed. "Yeah, you warned me all right with your damn body all over mine without expecting a damn thing for it. Do you realize I'm the only one?"

"What?"

Twisting just enough to glare at me, Rowan's mouth pulled into a smirk, his eyes blazing. "I'm the only one you fucked without getting paid for it. Either with drugs or money, it doesn't matter. No. You wanted *me*, just me."

Quieting for a moment, he glanced away. "I turn eighteen in two days. We can leave here, Rainey. I have a plan and I have the money to keep us going for a while."

"How?"

"How isn't important. I can take care of you, just like I promised. I can love you and protect you. And it's like I've always said, Rainey, I'll find you."

Rowan and Rainey forever...

All those promises, as if they were chiseled into his heart on the day he made them, the day I'd first taken him to his room to show him what it meant to love a woman.

"Rowan, come here."

His hand fisted against the window, eyes closing. He was resisting me as much as he was begging me to promise him everything in return.

"Come here," I insisted, my voice soft, as comforting as I could make it. He liked it when I spoke softly. *Like a lullaby,* he'd once said.

Cursing beneath his breath, he pushed away from the window and walked to me, immediately lowering himself to his knees at my feet. Head bowed, he couldn't look at me, the posture reminding me of a man who had lost the will to fight.

Broken...

There was no other way to describe what I'd done to him. Like a bull in a China shop, I'd run him through, my horns stabbing his heart while my hooves stomped and crushed every bit of strength and goodness he had in him. And here I was doing it again, my stampede not quite through.

I ran my fingers through his hair. Like silk, it twined over my skin, so soft. His shoulders trembled at the exact second I touched him.

It was like taming a wild animal. You know it has the ability to tear you to shreds with sharp claws and gnashing teeth, but it makes you feel powerful for its love and obedience.

Rowan made me feel powerful. He made me believe I was worth more than what I'd become.

It was too bad that my story would never be worth the paper it was written on. Nobody cares about girls like me. We're lost to the shadows, tossed aside and forgotten about by a world that only wishes to see beauty, intelligence and fortune.

"Look at me."

The world might not care to see me, but Rowan did, his eyes lifting as his neck craned back. Shimmering blue, those eyes had seen me since the day we first met. Only me, his Rainey Summer Day, the girl who'd ruined him the minute she moved next door.

"I want to love you," I said, "and in so many ways, I do. But it's because I love you that I have to push you away. You may not understand that now. Someday, you will. I'll only hurt you. I'll drag you down into the mud with me because my choices are too heavy. I choose to do what I do at your house. I choose to have sex with men for what I can get out of them. That has always been my choice. I'll do it again tonight. Right there in front of you. And I'll collect my money while your heart breaks apart if you choose to wallow in the muck with me by watching."

"I'll be there tonight," he said through clenched teeth. "So will Megan. So will Angel."

Surprise shot my brows up my forehead.

Rowan smiled, the expression bitter. "Oh? Joel didn't tell you that part? He doesn't intend to be with you himself, he's acting like your damn pimp."

200

"I don't know what to say about that."

"Say no."

Shaking my head, I brushed away the hair that had fallen over his face. "I'll still go. I'll still be there tonight."

His fingertips swept up the backs of my calves. A shiver coursed through me at his touch. Every time I promised myself that it would be the last with him, I'm drawn in again. "Rowan, touching me is dangerous."

Hands locking just beneath my knees, Rowan pushed my legs apart far enough to kiss the inside of my thigh. "I don't care," he said against my skin.

On a whisper, "You know I won't say no. I'll make love to you right here and now, but then tonight, I'll be taking men back to a bedroom to earn the money Joel promised me. Can you handle that?"

"No."

"Then stop touching me."

"No."

His hands crept up the tops of my thighs, higher until he was ripping at the button of my shorts. "I need this, Rainey. I need you."

In a way, I needed him, too. "Go sit on the couch, baby, let me make it better."

Blue eyes lifting to mine, he reached to cup my cheek. I met his stare, completely open to him. There were no lies between us, no deceit. Just us.

Pushing to his feet, Rowan grabbed my hand and led me across the room to the couch. Sitting down, he stripped off his shirt and unbuttoned his pants, shoving his jeans and underwear down to his ankles. He was already hard. Always ready when it came to me.

Following his lead, I pulled my shirt off, slipped my panties and shorts down my legs and kicked them

201

away, loving the way he worshipped me with eyes that swore he'd never seen anything more beautiful.

Cupping my ass as I straddled him, Rowan watched the point where our bodies came together, one of my hands on his shoulder while my other held him in place as I sank down, taking every inch of him slowly.

His head fell back, my name rolling over his lips on a prayer. Leaning forward, I pressed a kiss over his heart, dragged my lips up his neck and along the line of his strong jaw. He turned his face at the last second, catching my mouth with his. Our tongues danced as I began to move. Our breath mingling. Our bodies always a perfect fit.

Gripping the cheeks of my ass, he guided me into the rhythm he wanted, completely lost to the act.

I wrapped my arms over his shoulders and crushed my chest to his, burying my face against his neck as our bodies moved together.

"Rainey," he whispered, hands tight over me, still moving me just the way he wanted. "I'll never get enough of this. Of you."

I told myself it would be the last time, not understanding that I was tempting fate with the thought.

We both got off on that couch, our orgasms timed, our bodies in tune. And when we were done, I held on to him for several minutes knowing that I would crush him in the course of several hours, knowing that once I let go, I would return to being the slut I'd always been.

Rowan knew it, too, begging me one last time to stay home before leaving my house.

The sun set while I was getting dressed to walk next door, music already filtering across my yard as people arrived to my neighbors' house. Looking in a mirror, I ran my hands down the tight black dress I'd borrowed from my mother's closet. The back dipped down almost to my ass, the front open between my breasts to reveal the inner curves.

Slipping on a pair of heels, I wore my hair down, the ends brushing the small of my back. I was ready to earn some cash.

The temperature outside had plummeted fast. Already ice was coating the grass and I regretted not grabbing a jacket. Hurrying over, I slipped and damn near landed on my ass in their driveway.

As soon as I walked inside Rowan's house, tension wrapped around me. Just as Rowan had said, Megan and Angel sat on one of the couches, their eyes locking to me in unison.

"Oh, great, the prostitute is here." Angel's eyes narrowed, her lips pulling up into a sneer. "Or are you a stripper tonight, Rainey? Either way, I guess the party can get started now. Everybody line up."

Rolling my shoulders back, I ignored her. But then Megan started in, surprising me. "Last time I saw her, everyone was running a train on her ass. Then she came after Rowan crying about her mommy being dead."

"Hey! What the fuck, Megan?"

Rowan stood at the end of the hallway. He'd walked in just in time to overhear his girlfriend's comment.

"It's fine, Rowan-"

"No, it's not." Glaring at Megan, Rowan's anger was overshadowed by a few men standing in the kitchen, their voices rising up in hoots and hollers to notice me. I guessed Joel had told them my purpose for being there.

"Hell, fucking yeah, baby. Go ahead and take it off."

203

I needed a drink...or ten. Already this night was bullshit.

Walking past Rowan, I didn't dare meet eyes with him. I was there for a purpose, one I would fulfill because I needed the money. Smiling sweetly as I walked into the kitchen, I took the bottle of alcohol Joel handed me and drank deeply from it, the guys around me ogling and whispering their praise of my chest and ass. I didn't recognize any of them. Besides Joel and Jacob, there were four standing around.

Behind me, Rowan was arguing with Megan and Angel. I tried not to pay attention. I had a job to do.

The heavy beat of the music helped drown out their words, and I stepped up next to Jacob. "Let's do this."

He smiled and handed me a joint. "Careful with that," he warned. It's laced with something special."

"Seriously, Rowan, look at her. She's a fucking whore..."

Still, they argued, and I would only prove the two women right. Jacob wasn't lying about the weed being laced. Instantly, I felt loose, my eyes slightly out of focus, the beat of my heart a drum in my head.

Jacob leaned over. "You feeling that yet?"

"Yeah," I nodded, at least I think I did. I felt warm all over, my body tingling.

"Take another hit, Rainey. I rolled this up especially for you. You'll need it."

"Say another word about her and I swear I'll..."

"Shut the fuck up in there, will you?" Joel walked to the living room to break up the argument. Rowan's voice was on edge. We all knew he was capable of bringing this party to its knees if he became angry enough.

"Hey, hey, hey, ladies and gentlemen. There's no reason to fight..."

The room spun as Joel attempted to calm everyone down.

"You ready?" Jacob's voice whispered against my ear.

"Yeah." Peering up, I looked between the four strange men watching me, their eyes filled with need.

"Who's first?" Jacob called out. "You, whatever the fuck your name is, take her back. Second door on the right."

Even Jacob didn't know who these guys were. That worried me. But money was money, and I'd be too busy to hear Rowan and Joel going at it in the living room. That had to count for something.

A warm hand grabbed mine, pulled me down the hall and into Jacob's bedroom.

This is where it all started for me three years ago. I'd agreed to have sex with one guy for one joint, and as the days rolled on, I found myself in a moment where I was fucking strangers for cash.

I wasn't sure how it all had happened.

The guy was talking to me, but I wasn't paying much attention to what he had to say. I was too worried about the argument in the living room. Too worried about what Rowan would do.

He pushed me down on the bed, pulled my dress off me and began playing with my breasts. I closed my eyes, unable to look at him. He kept talking, but I didn't care what he had to say. It would all be over soon enough and I could go home.

The man never bothered to take my heels off. I think he preferred I keep wearing them. He spread my legs, pulled me to the edge of the bed and thrust inside my body, holding me by gripping my hips. My head fell back, my eyes closed as I floated along on the wind. Whatever Jacob had given me was strong.

"Take it bitch, all of it..."

His hips kept moving and I floated back to the day I first met Rowan. His eyes had been so big and blue, his smile friendly. He'd wanted so badly to seem older than he was.

...do whatever I want. Can't I?..."

The man flipped me over, notching himself at my ass. He wasn't gentle about it. Not as careful as Paul, but not as rough as Frankie. I'd be able to walk.

"Fuck, yes..."

I would hate myself in the morning. My fingers curled into Jacob's blanket, my body bucking forward, the bed squeaking beneath me. Ten seconds. This man would be done in ten.

"Fuck!"

He finished. I could have started a stopwatch and been exactly right. Next up. Another stranger.

Using a towel, he cleaned me up. That was the rule, after all. I heard the man zip up his pants and leave, heard another come in the room and shut the door. Rolling over the mattress, I sat up and looked at him bleary eyed.

"Play with your tits while you suck me."

Whatever the customer wanted, right? I took him into my mouth as he pumped the shaft, my hands molding and squeezing my boobs.

From outside, voices grew louder. Glass breaking, a heavy thud followed by shouting. The man stopped what he was doing and turned toward the door.

Joel came in. "Party's over, man."

"What? I wasn't finished."

"Tuck your shit in your pants and get the fuck out. My brother damn near killed your friend for bragging about what's going on back here like a fucking dumbass. Get the fuck out."

Rowan...

The stranger left the room and Joel grabbed my dress from the floor. "Rainey, babe, you've caused some problems tonight. Angel just left. I think she broke up with me, and Rowan is losing his shit over you. Your puppy can't handle this. Do you hear me?"

My head rolled over my shoulders, I was so out of it.

"Son of a bitch. What did Jacob give you?"

Joel lifted my arms one at a time to pull the dress over me. After I was decent, he wrapped my arm over his shoulder and lifted me up. My ankles rolled over my heels.

"Rainey, kick off your shoes. You can't walk in those right now."

I did as he said so he could walk me out of the room and into the living room. It was a bad idea. Rowan took one look at me and it only made him angrier. Everyone had cleared out except for Megan who was crying on the couch.

Setting me down on the recliner, Joel moved away so Rowan could look at me. His knuckles had blood on them, his finger pressed beneath my chin so he could tip my head up.

"What did you two give her?"

"Dude, it's fine."

Megan continued to cry.

Another man walked out from the hallway. I turned to look at him. Didn't recognize him as one of the four.

"Rowan, can you give me a lift home? My work just called. I forgot I was supposed to go in tonight."

Stepping away from me, Rowan grabbed his keys. He was too angry to drive. I knew that.

"They're going to smell alcohol on me..."

"I have an extra toothbrush..."

Both Rowan and the guy walked away. I needed to stop them. Stop Rowan.

"Joel," I think I said his name.

"You're a bitch, you know that?"

My head lobbed right. Megan was staring at me, tears streaming down her cheeks. "None of this would have happened if you could keep your damn legs closed."

"What happened?"

The front door slammed closed and Megan began to cry harder, burying her face in her hands."

I closed my eyes, willing the room to stay still for just a second, just long enough for me to catch up. Eventually, it did, I could feel my hands again. My toes. I opened my eyes.

"Joel!"

"Rainey."

He was in the kitchen behind me. Pushing up from the chair, I stumbled in. "You have to keep Rowan from driving."

Joel's brows tugged together. "Damn, you are out of it. He left almost an hour ago."

"Who was the guy with him?"

Shrugging, "Hell if I know. One of his friends. Never met the kid before." He paused, stared at me. "You feeling okay?"

I was worried, but other than that, I was coming around.

"The party's not over, Rainey. Come with me."

I'm not sure how I missed what was happening on the couch when I first woke up, but when Joel walked with me into the living room I saw Megan straddling Jacob's lap, his hands on her ass while she kissed his neck.

"What the-"

"Shhhh," Joel wrapped his arms around me from behind, both of us standing at the recliner. "Megan's been all up on Jacob for the last twenty minutes. I think she's done with your pup."

I should have told her to stop, should have said something, but I knew this would be the end of her and Rowan.

I turn eighteen in two days. We can leave here, Rainey. I have a plan and I have the money to keep us going for a while...

Was it possible? Was Rowan really able to get me out of here?

Joel's hands moved over my dress, slipping inside the front opening to cup my breasts. "You still want that money?"

Nodding, I watched Megan slide down from Jacob's lap to kneel between his legs. She unbuttoned his pants, pulled him free, a sloppy smile on her face before her mouth wrapped over him and her head bobbed over his lap.

Jacob grinned and took a drag, his free hand twisting into her hair.

I should have stopped her.

My skirt was lifted up to my hips. "Hold on to the back of the chair, Rainey."

Joel was inside me then, his hips moving against me in almost perfect timing to the bobbing of Megan's head.

209

Five minutes may have passed, the room silent except for the wet sound of Megan's mouth and the slap of skin of Joel pumping behind me.

A loud noise occurred outside, like a gunshot or a bomb. Within a minute, the distant horizon lit up with a red glow, like fire across the sky.

All of our heads turned to the window.

It was Joel who spoke first. "What the fuck?"

He kept moving inside me while I watched the glow. Jacob directed Megan back to what she was doing. "Never a dull damn moment in this neighborhood."

Another twenty seconds

I knew Joel would be finishing then.

Like a stopwatch, I could time how long it would take him to come.

CHAPTER NINETEEN

Justin - Present

It was in that moment that I understood the mask Rainey was wearing. To meet her for the first time, you would believe her weak, would pity her lack of intelligence, would want to shelter her under your wing because surely a woman as victimized as her would only be swept away by the cruelties of this world if somebody wasn't there to save her.

Yet, listening to her tell her tale, watching her body language as she recounted every horrifying detail, you could see beneath the delicate surface to the steel residing just beneath her skin.

She was beautiful. Utterly and terrifyingly so. Beguiling, so damn circuitous that Rainey spoke circles around me, her consciousness wandering over meandering trails, leading to where, I wasn't sure. But still, I followed her words, snatching them from behind her, the breadcrumbs she dropped on her path.

Rowan had been right to compare her voice to a lullaby. The deep tone comforting, the husky rasp seductive, the smooth flow of words all blending into one another until mesmerizing. You become trapped, shocked into a stupor, that part of yourself pulled away while your eyes watched without understanding what they were seeing.

By the time, she'd finished telling me her recollection of the night that Rowan died, I was gazing across the room at a pair of hypnotic blue eyes, full lips moving over every heart-wrenching word that brought her memories to life.

I wanted to comfort her. Shelter her. Rip her from a world that had treated her poorly so that her stupid choices would punish her no longer.

"How are you doing over there, Doc? You look like you want to cry."

Cry or beat the shit out of someone, I wasn't sure. It was too bad every single one of those bastards were dead. I would have loved putting them in the ground myself.

"How do you live with yourself, Rainey? How do you continue forward after everything that has happened?"

Horrible questions coming from a psychologist. It was my job to remind her she could keep going. My job to teach her how to cope with her past and look forward to a future that might somehow be brighter. In that, I was failing.

Her finger traced down her neck, her eyes catching mine as her lips pulled up at the corners. "I guess I have to think that things can't get worse than they already have been. Rock bottom is the lowest a person can go, right? Well, I was born there."

Softly, she added, "There's nowhere else to go but up."

Her hand shook as she lifted a glass of water, her lips wrapping over the rim. She wasn't as strong as I thought. The glass slipped, water splashing the front of her dress, the skirt and the cushion beneath it. "Shit."

"I'll get you something to clean that up."

Setting my pen and notepad aside, I grabbed some paper towels from the kitchen and brought them to Rainey. As she dabbed at her dress and the cushion, I sat down beside her. "It's not your fault Rowan died. I

212

know you think that, but after hearing what happened that night, I don't agree."

Fanning the top of her dress, Rainey couldn't contain the tears that slipped down her cheeks. "If I had just stayed home, if I'd just listened to him and not gone along with Joel, Rowan wouldn't have been on the road that night."

"It was his friend, Rainey. It sounded like the man he drove home was someone who knew him and was there by his invitation. Regardless of what you were doing, Rowan may have driven him home regardless. Would have wrecked regardless."

"Yeah, but he wouldn't have been as angry. People drive like maniacs when they're mad."

Reaching forward, I brushed the hair from her face that had stuck to the skin from her tears. I didn't think about what I was doing; it was simply instinct to touch her, to comfort a woman who blamed herself for a circumstance that was outside of her control.

She leaned into the touch, her shimmering eyes lifting to look at me. "I caused it, Justin. Don't you understand that? Don't you see?"

Her skin was so soft against my palm, warm, inviting. She was a tiny bird that had fallen from the nest, so insanely vulnerable and lost that I wondered if she would ever find her way again.

I wasn't thinking. I was acting on an impulse that closed the world out and locked me into a moment alone with this beautiful girl.

"Justin?"

My name on her lips was endearing, dark eyelashes fanning her pale skin when she closed her eyes and opened them again.

Another blink, innocence masking every promiscuous bone inside her. If I didn't pull my hand away now, I would be breaking down every professional boundary designed to keep mistakes like this from happening.

"Do you think it's possible for me to change? To be better than I am?"

My palm was still against her cheek, thumb sweeping her cheekbone as she leaned further into the touch. The front of her dress stuck to her skin leaving nothing to the imagination, the skirt pooling at the crook of her hips. Just a little bit higher and I would be able to see -

"Justin?"

My gaze dragged up, a shake of my head. "Yeah, I think you can."

It was too late. She'd noticed, her lips parting just enough that I could see the glimmer of her teeth. Voice a whisper, "Do you think I could be the type of girl you would want?"

The question should have launched me from the couch, should have pressed my back against the opposite wall, should have sent me scrambling for the door. Too deep. I was in way too fucking deep.

She leaned forward and my eyes dropped to her chest again. I wasn't thinking, wasn't responding in the way I should. It was intoxicating, this moment, for how wrong it truly was.

Rainey's lips brushed mine, my hand falling away, arms dead at my sides. I should have been pushing her back, should have been telling her to stop. Instead, my body stilled as she nipped at my bottom lip with her teeth and slanted her full mouth over mine.

"Rainey," I warned, but there was no strength to it. Merely a breath as she pressed her chest to mine and straddled my lap.

Her hands cupped my face, lips parting, tongue tracing along the crease of my mouth with tempting fluttering touches. Still, I hadn't moved my hands from beside me because the moment I did -

My lips parted and her tongue slid over mine, her hips rolling so fucking slowly that every muscle in my body became tight.

Professional boundaries be damned.

The front of my shirt was wet from being pressed to her dress. I didn't want to think about what was occurring in my pants. She knew though, her body rubbing against it, a slow screw above my clothes.

Push her away...

The thought was there, right there, directly in the front of my thoughts. Finally, bringing my hands up to do just that, I gripped her waist. She moaned into my mouth, the sound intoxicating.

The instant her lips broke from mine so she could press kisses along my jaw, I managed to speak. My voice deep, gritty, broken. "We shouldn't be doing this."

Mouth against my ear. "I shouldn't have done a lot of things." Pure wickedness, that sound. Breathless, husky, raw.

Hands sliding down, my fingers clenched over her writhing hips. Slow, so insanely slow, she moved.

"Rainey..."

Sliding my palms down her thighs, I was balanced on a precipice. I could stop this right now. Walk away. Grab my things. Leave.

She buried her fingers in my hair, her mouth finding mine again, my hands clamping down on her skin as if to halt the movement of her hips.

Our kiss deepened, hands dragging back up her thighs until they locked over the crease of her hips. She moved above me, dancing to some slow music I couldn't hear. My fingertips edged beneath her skirt, the temptation mere inches from where I held her, the scalloped edges of her panties a line leading up. I followed them, willing myself to stop, willing myself to-

Her moan was a siren's call, pure pleasure in that sound, anticipation for my fingers to explore between her legs, to move over just a few more inches. *Fuck...she's soaked...*

I tugged my hands away, grabbed her by the waist and forced her back to the cushion of the couch, my own body shoving to my feet and jumping several feet away. Eyes clenched, I tried to ignore the hammering of my heart, the discomfort of my pants, how labored my breath had become.

"Justin?"

"We can't do this, Rainey. I'm sorry, but we can't." My voice sounded pained, blood rushing in my head like rolling thunder.

She was quiet for a minute. I refused to look at her. Unable to handle tears or a rejected expression, I kept my eyes closed, willing my body to calm down. This could not happen. The thought only made me want it more.

"It's me, isn't it? Because of everything I've done? There's no walking back from my choices, is there?"

While that should have been true, while her lifestyle should have bothered me, that wasn't the problem forefront in my mind.

"I'm interviewing you as a subject in a murder investigation. We can't have sexual relations."

Opening my eyes, I found her staring at me, confusion furrowing her brow.

"Even if I was a victim?"

"Even then. Especially then. I refuse to victimize you further."

A shy smile. "I don't know what you consider victimizing a person, but that's not what we just did. At least, not the way I see it. I like you."

Which is why I needed to get the hell out of there. Take a cold shower. Go over my notes and figure out my plan to end this interview. "We should break for the day, Rainey. We can start again tomorrow."

Exhaustion stalked me, bone-deep dread breathing down my neck, sneaking up on me in all corners of my mind whispering *something isn't right, the pieces aren't fitting together*. I blamed it on the story, on a series of events that shouldn't have been real.

In many ways, Rainey had popped the bubble of my ordinary and sheltered life, lifted the veil and revealed to me a world that was cruel and terrifying. Perhaps that was the reason for my fascination. Perhaps that's how this girl had wrapped herself around my thoughts, a virus infecting every waking moment, chasing me into restless sleep.

Something wasn't adding up.

"I should go, Rainey. I'll see you tomorrow."

Silence as I gathered my things, my path to the front door almost complete when Rainey called out, "Hey, Doc?"

Head bowed, I struggled with whether to continue walking forward, or acknowledge that she'd spoken. Deep breath. I turned. Met her eyes. Regretting both the fact that I had to turn her away and that I hadn't done it fast enough. Her web had been woven and I was the fly dangling on the last delicate string.

"Will my being a victim continue making me one for the rest of my life?"

"I don't understand what you're asking me."

For the first time since I'd met her, Rainey's face was a blank mask, indecipherable, her thoughts all her own. "You said we couldn't do what we were doing because I'm a victim. But doesn't that victimize me further? Isn't it just another road block preventing me from moving on?"

A deep sigh blew over my lips. "I'd be taking advantage of you if I'd allowed that to go further."

Her lips curled at the corners. "Nobody has taken advantage of me, Dr. Redding. I can promise you that."

Brows knitting between my eyes, I inclined my head. "Good night, Rainey."

It was a relief to escape the house, the cool afternoon air washing over me, clearing my head when the last few hours had been foggy. Wanting to run, I controlled my pace between her front door and the car. With my door open, I tossed the notepad on the passenger seat when a hand slammed down on the hood beside my head.

A gun could have been shot next to my ear and it wouldn't have been louder.

"Jesus!" I startled and turned, my pulse picking up, my feet instantly stepping away.

The man from across the street, the same one who'd been watching Rainey for two days, stood staring at me with a smirk on his face.

"Is she open for business again?" He tipped his chin toward the house.

"I'm sorry?" Too shaken by his close proximity and the manner in which he'd grabbed my attention, I didn't quite catch what he'd said.

"Rainey. Word is she gives it up for a little bit of cash. I figured since the neighbors are gone, she might be in need of some money. Isn't that why you've been here every day?"

He grinned, tilted his head. "I mean, all day? She lets you go that long? Normally it's one pop and you're out with most chicks, but if she's willing to give a few hours, sounds worth it to me. I can sit back and watch a movie while she bobs the knob, you know? Watch some football while she's bent over in front of me."

His smile was lascivious, an arrogant curl to the corners that turned my stomach as much as it drilled anger up my spine.

Taking a second to look at him, I noted the dirty jeans, the ragged black t-shirt, the weeks worth of dark stubble shadowing his cheeks and jaw. Beyond his mouth, I couldn't see much of his face; the bill of his cap was pulled too low.

"How much are you paying her? Think twenty will get my dick wet?"

With a stroke of a thumb over his bottom lip, he leaned against my car, preventing me from shutting the door.

My jaw was tight with fury, not just for what he'd said about Rainey, but also for his blocking my ability

219

to leave. "That's not why I'm here. And, no, she isn't doing anything for money as far as I'm aware."

"Oh yeah?" Another sliding grin. "That's funny because anybody can see directly into her house with her front curtains pulled open. And I just happened to be walking by and saw her all up on your shit. Hips rolling, her mouth on yours."

I glanced behind me. The man wasn't lying. You could see her entire living room.

"She looked like she was into it. Know what I mean? Just thought she could be into me, too."

Scanning me up and down, he laughed softly. "Might rock her world, actually. If you're my competition." He grabbed his crotch and my hand fisted.

It didn't make me feel better to size him up. He had two inches of height on me, his shoulders rigid with muscle, his biceps testing the width of his short sleeves. He was in as good of shape as me, if not better.

Voice low, "You should come around late at night. She never closes those curtains and when it's dark out, she has the lights on, but that's it. Woman loves being naked, but who can blame her, right? With a body like that, I'd be naked all the time, too."

His admission caught my attention, although I'm not sure he understood what he was saying. "You must watch her a lot."

The question was: Did he watch her enough to follow her other places?

It occurred to me I could be conversing with a murderer, a guy who looked strong enough to have beaten four kids to death. Add to that his disgusting mentality, and I thought it possible bludgeoning four people wouldn't have bothered him too much at all.

Not if he could get to Rainey. Sex with her would be the ultimate prize and why kill her if there was a chance he could get it again?

"It's hard not to watch her. You've seen her. You know I'm right." His voice deepened more as he spoke, idle curiosity transitioning into a tone that did little to disguise a familiarity with violence. The warning wasn't lost on me.

Every instinct told me to get the hell away from him, but I had Rainey to think about. Not to mention a case to help solve. "You didn't tell me your name."

"On purpose," he said on a laugh. "My name isn't important. All I want to know is what are my chances of walking up to that door with some cash in hand and being let inside to spend it?"

None, as far as I was concerned. "I was actually just dropping some things in my car and heading back up. Tonight won't be a good one to stop by." Stepping forward, I reached to close my door. "You mind?"

He glanced at where he was blocking my door from shutting, smiled and stepped aside just enough to allow me to close it.

"You don't need to get all upset, brother. I just thought you might be willing to help me out."

Shutting the door, I hit the button to lock it. I didn't like leaving my notes and the file in open view on the passenger seat with him in such close proximity, but I was more concerned with watching over Rainey until he left her property.

"Have a good day," I said, giving him a sharp nod of my head before walking up the dirt path to her porch. Rainey must not have been watching, she didn't open the door as I was coming up the steps. Knocking, I waited, Rainey's eyes widening with surprise to see I'd returned.

"Did you forget something?"

"Just let me inside, please, I'll tell you why I'm here in a minute."

She stepped aside and allowed me in, closing the door quietly behind us. "Is everything okay?"

Without answering her, I walked immediately into the living to shut the curtains. The man was no longer leaning against my car, his long stride fluid as he crossed the street to the opposite sidewalk. Taking one last look at the house, he left, rounding a corner and moving out of view.

"Rainey, you need to keep your curtains closed." I turned to find her standing inches from me, confusion behind her wide, blue eyes.

"What happened?"

"There was a man at my car asking me if you had sex for money. He told me he's watched you at night. Has anyone come to your door lately that you didn't know? Or do you know him? It's the same man from the other day."

She shrugged her shoulder, the front of her dress still unbuttoned down the center of her breasts. "A lot of people watch my house, Justin. I told you that. They're curious."

"Do you know that particular man?"

Another shrug. "Possibly knew him from next door, but I met a lot of people over there. The family were dealers. People came in and out all the time."

Pinching at the bridge of my nose, I breathed heavily. "Rainey, you were just in a house where four of your friends were murdered. Someone may think you know their face. Can identify them. You need to be

222

more careful. That man told me he watches your windows at night because you walk around naked."

"So?"

My eyes clenched shut, opened again. "So, that could make a person want to harm you. Do you understand that?

She blinked, her expression unchanged after hearing someone could possibly do her harm.

"Listen, I'm going to have the detective send a police car to watch your house -"

"That's not a good idea, Doc. Not in Clayton Heights."

Frustration overtook me, "You need-"

"What I need is to get out of this place. But not because I'm in danger. Sending the cops won't do any good except make me a target for people who don't want them here. Don't you get that?"

"Rainey-"

"Hey." Stepping closer, she pressed her palm to my chest, craning her neck to look up at me. "Thank you for being concerned for me. That means a lot because not a lot of people have cared to worry about me in my life. But I know how to survive in this neighborhood, Justin, you have to believe me in that. I'm safe here. It's never been strangers that have hurt me. Always people I already knew. So, while we're finishing this, I'll keep my curtains closed and my doors locked, but don't send the police in. They're not welcome here unless there's a body to be dragged out."

The heat of her hand sank beneath my shirt, my muscles tighter in reaction to her close proximity. It astonished me how protective I felt for her, how this woman, in only a few short days, had somehow breached every protocol I had in place. She was dangerous in so many ways.

"Fine, but I'm not leaving immediately, not with that man hanging around."

A mischievous grin curled her lips. "What would you like to do while we wait?"

I sighed, grabbed her hand and pulled it away from my chest. "Why don't we talk about what happened after Rowan died?"

Shadows rolled behind her eyes. "We can do that."

I took my usual seat and waited for her to take hers on the couch. Legs folded in front of her, she toyed with the bottom hem of her dress where it splashed over her thighs.

It felt strange not to have my pen and pad to take notes, but I would jot down any information I felt was important after leaving.

"Did you continue going over to your neighbors' house after Rowan died?"

Nodding her head, she brushed her fingers over the mark again. I wondered if I asked her about it now, would she tell me? What was the five?

"Yeah, Doc, I went over there. With Rowan gone, everything started spiraling down."

"And why's that?"

She grinned, the expression tight. "Because I thought there was no one left to watch over me."

CHAPTER TWENTY

Rainey - Past

Life is cruel. I've known that since the moment I had any understanding of myself, knew that I'd been born into a situation where my mother struggled and my father hadn't stuck around long enough to see my birth.

Often, as a child, I would watch the other little kids at school run around in their nice clothes and answer all the questions the teacher could ask when calling on them. They'd raise their hands, so proud to be able to learn.

Meanwhile, I was the girl in the back of the class. My clothes were usually too small for me, but my mom couldn't afford new ones. When she did buy more, she always bought them a few sizes too big so I'd have time to grow into them. By the time they fit right, they already had stains and holes.

I was never the kid who raised her hand, waving frantically, to show off with everything I'd learned. I didn't have a mom home at night to help me with homework, and most of the time I was keeping busy dodging her poor choices in boyfriends. Life for me had started out at the bottom and somehow managed to continue finding new lows for me to sink to.

It was like quicksand. No matter how hard I struggled, the situation only became worse. I had no choice but to remain still and go along with it, to allow circumstance to drag me down as far as it could take me. I kept thinking it couldn't possibly get lower.

It always did.

Rowan's remains were spread in a public grave much like my mom's. I had no way of visiting him except in my thoughts. Thinking up insane stories in my head, I pretended he was somehow still there watching over me, that even though I couldn't feel his arms, they were wrapped around me with the same fierce love he'd shown me in life.

In truth, I had no idea what I'd done those first few months after learning he'd died. I hated myself, I knew that, and the hatred left me stuck in a fog from which I wasn't sure I'd ever crawl out.

Drugs. Alcohol. Sex. I became lost to it, each day leaving work to chase the freedom of oblivion, to punish myself by finally giving in to the knowledge that I wasn't worth the air I was breathing.

Nobody blamed me for Rowan's death, but I did. Nobody wanted to think that if we hadn't behaved so badly that night, he might still be alive. Nobody wanted to talk about it, especially his brothers. They just wanted to keep rolling on as if Rowan had never existed in the first place.

"Are you planning on moving into this room or something? You spend all your time here."

My eyes flicked open at the sound of Joel's voice, my vision blurry from dried tears, the pillow beneath my head crumpled from the way in which I hugged it.

Every day I crawled in Rowan's bed so I could breathe him in, the scent still strong despite the eight months that had passed.

It was comforting to be in there, even if a layer of dust had settled on the surfaces of the tables and bureau, even if nothing had moved out of place since the night he died. I think I was pretending that one day I would wake up to feel his knuckles brush down my face, to open my eyes and discover it had all been a bad dream.

"I'm just sleeping. Didn't get much last night and I had to be at work early this morning."

Joel stepped into the room, shut the door behind him and sat on the edge of the bed. Out of the entire family, he was the one who'd taken Rowan's death the hardest. Both of us sought comfort in being stoned out of our minds. It was easier than remembering the sound of the car crashing, of recalling what we had been doing when fire lit up the sky.

"You need to start moving past this, Rainey. He's not coming back. What happened to him - well, it wasn't fair. He was a good kid. Better than the rest of the assholes in this place, but torturing yourself won't fix things."

Curling tighter into the blanket, I breathed in Rowan's scent. It was fading more each day, being replaced with my own. "It makes me feel better to be in here. Like I'm still close to him, you know?"

"You fell in love with him, too." Joel shook his head, a sad smile stretching his lips. "I wouldn't have guessed it a few months ago, but I see it now. You cared for him a lot more than you let on."

Teasing me, he flicked my leg from above the blanket. "Maybe you're not as much of a slut as we all thought you were."

My voice was a grumble. "Very funny, Joel. Shouldn't you be out with Angel since you two are all hot and heavy again?"

He grinned, his eyes twinkling with an idea I was sure I didn't want to hear. "Actually, that is why I came in here looking for you. Angel is coming over tonight. We have the house all to ourselves. Dad is on a run.

Jacob's nailing some chick in Chicago for the weekend and Frankie is out with friends for the night."

"Oh? Do you need me to leave? I can go home."

Shaking his head, his smile stretched wider. "That's not what I had in mind. I wanted you to hang around. Party with us."

My brows tugged together. "Angel hates me."

"That's because she doesn't know you. Except for what she knows about you banging just about everybody in the house, she's never given you a chance to introduce yourself. You're a cool girl, Rainey, and I think you and Angel could be friends."

Highly doubting it, I reminded him, "You cheat on her almost every day with me, Joel. She suspects that, which is why she hates me."

"Most likely because she's not included."

Rolling my eyes, I buried my face in the pillow, knowing exactly what he was suggesting. "Joel," my voice was muffled. "She'll never go for it."

Scooting up the bed, he laid down facing me. "I tend to think she will."

I peered over at him, pulling my face from the pillow. "What's in it for me?"

Tsking, he shook his head. "Can't it ever just be about the experience?"

It was about the experience once. But only with Rowan. "What's in it for me?"

"Hundred bucks and an ounce? Does that work?"

Uninterested in being with a woman, the amount he offered didn't cut it. I wasn't sure what he wanted me to do with her and I knew he'd pay a lot more to fulfill one of his ridiculous fantasies. "Three hundred."

Joel's brows shot up his forehead. "That's robbery!"

"Three hundred or I'm not doing it. That girl will probably try to claw my eyes out. We'll call it hazard pay."

Laughter rolled over his lips. Three hundred wasn't too much to ask. Joel and I both knew it. He made a killing dealing drugs. "Fine. Three hundred. But none of that quiet Rainey shit you always do. I want moans and hair pulling and to know that you're really into it."

Groaning, I buried my head in the pillow again. "Fine. Get out. Let me know when she gets here and you want me to do whatever."

Joel left the room, the quiet soothing me into sleep for a few more hours.

It was dark out by the time he came back, the door sliding open, his voice soft when he called my name. "Pssst. Hey, Rainey. Wake up."

Outside, thunder rolled across the sky, a storm shaking the house as rain battered the windows. Lightning cracked down, the sky lit for a few seconds, the glow brightening Joel's face.

My first thought was that he looked funny. His eyes were too round, his jaw tense, hands fisting and releasing again before he rubbed them down his thighs. "You okay, Joel?"

"Yeah. Get your ass in my room." Even his voice sounded funny, clipped and sharp. Normally he sounded friendly, but not tonight. His biceps kept bunching, legs unable to remain still.

"Joel, what's wrong with you?"

"Nothing, just get your ass in my room!"

Pushing up from the bed, I almost told him to forget about it. "What are you on?"

"Does it matter? Angel wants to fuck and you said you'd get in on it. Three hundred, remember?"

"I don't know."

"Dammit, Rainey." Lunging forward, he grabbed me by the arm and dragged me from the bed. His grip was too tight, the force of it causing me to wince. He led me into his room. Angel was naked from the waist up, her body swaying to the beat of the music booming from his speakers. She appeared just as messed up as him.

"Take this," Joel said, nudging my elbow with his. I looked down to see a white pill in his palm. He could barely keep his hand still.

"What is it?"

"Just take it."

I shook my head. "Not unless I know what it is." Shrugging, he pocketed the pill.

"Suit yourself."

Angel hadn't noticed us standing there, she was too out of it.

"Babe! Hey!" Joel crossed the room to wrap his arms around her, their bodies swaying together. Whispering against Angel's ear, he reached down to cup her butt. I couldn't hear what he was saying, but she smiled without opening her eyes.

Joel led her to the bed, laying her down on the mattress to kiss her. Angel was grinding against him, all into it. I still didn't think she saw me.

He looked up, waved me over. "Take off your top."

"Does she even know I'm here?"

Glaring up at me, his pupils were large mirrors. Almost all of the iris was hidden, his eyes pure black. "What does it matter? Take off your top."

"I don't know about this, Joel."

"Do it!"

Flinching in response to his voice, I sighed and stripped off my shirt. He stood from the bed and shoved me down to sit near her. Moving to sit next to her head, he lifted her torso onto his lap, holding her up against his chest. "Angel, babe. Rainey's here to have some fun with us. Open your eyes."

Eyelids fluttering, she could barely keep them open, her pupils as large as Joel's. She grinned, the expression sloppy. "Rainey," she slurred my name, "My best friend ever."

My eyebrow crooked. Something was definitely wrong with her.

"Babe, lean forward and play with her tits. Rainey likes that."

He half shoved her, half held her up, Angel's eyes closed again as her hands cupped my breasts. Joel shoved her forward even more. "Suck on one."

Face colliding against my chest, Angel rolled her head to attempt to take my nipple into her mouth. She couldn't see straight to find it.

I was willing to do a lot of things for money. Sex was sex and I'd long ago split with the idea that it meant anything more than two bodies moving together, but this wasn't right. It didn't matter how much Joel was paying me, or what little I valued being with another person, I wasn't going to take advantage of someone who didn't know what they were doing.

Glancing at Joel, I noticed he already had his dick in his hands, furiously pumping.

If he wanted to have sex with her like this, that was on him, but I wanted nothing to do with it.

"The deal's off, Joel."

Standing from the bed, I grabbed my shirt and pulled it on. As I was walking from the room, I heard him yell after me.

"What the fuck, Rainey? Get back here!"

"I'm not doing this, Joel. It's wrong."

Nope. Not going to happen. Angel already hated me enough. I wasn't going to give her one more reason. It was odd to think I had limits. Usually I was up for anything if the price was right, but what Joel wanted was wrong. He was so hard up to get Angel and me together that he'd drugged her out of her mind just to see it happen.

He screamed my name again. I kept going, not giving much of a damn what he wanted. I'd reached many lows in my life, but I wasn't going near that one.

Opening the front door, I groaned to step out into the pouring rain, the bottoms of my jeans getting soaked from large puddles and mud squishing up through my toes. I'd left my sandals in Rowan's room where I'd taken them off to crawl into bed.

I was halfway through my yard when lightning streaked across the sky, followed by the roll of thunder, the noise so loud it sounded like a train was bearing down on me, a steady thud thud thud-

That wasn't thunder. I glanced over my shoulder to see Joel running at full speed, his face twisted in rage, his body slamming mine to the ground before I had the chance to react.

"You fucking bitch! Do you think you're too good for me or something?" The slap of his palm against my cheek spun my head right, the sound competing with the crack of lightning above us.

"Joel!" He was too large for me to push away, too fucked up on whatever drug he'd taken to be reasoned with. Tears sprang from my eyes to mix with the rain, my head slamming left when he backhanded me.

"Stupid fucking cunt!"

Flipping me over, he shoved my face into the mud, his fingers gripping my hair with such force that strands snapped from my scalp. I tried to open my mouth to scream, but the mud rushed up, choking me.

He pulled my pants down, still screaming about how I was just a two-bit whore, no better than him, no better than anybody. I could barely breathe, the mud too thick, the rain pounding down on us so loud I doubted anybody in the neighboring houses could hear us.

When he shoved inside me, he held my head down, slamming me from behind like I was being punished for having just a hint of morals or integrity. I hated him in that moment, another switch being flipped that made me hate all the Connor men.

Every single fucking one of them, except Rowan.

Why do the good people always die young? I didn't understand why this world seemed to punish the shining lights while allowing the shadows to linger eternally. I wondered if perhaps the soul of the good burned as brightly as stars, the world unable to contain such fire, so it devised different ways to extinguish them.

It depressed me to think for as bad as I'd been, I'd live my horrible existence forever. I wasn't a star, wouldn't burn out like Rowan had.

Finished with me, Joel kept yelling at my back, but released my hair, my head rolling to the side so I could spit out the mud and take a breath. As if what he'd done wasn't bad enough, he pushed up to his feet and kicked me between the legs.

"You dumb bitch! Stay the fuck away from my house!"

233

The pain of that kick flattened me over the ground, my mouth gaping open on a silent scream as thunder rolled over my head.

He left me there in my front yard with my pants around my thighs, not giving a damn that I could barely walk after what he'd done.

I crawled to my porch using the strength of my arms. Sliding up the cement steps, I ignored the scrape of them against my skin, ignored the pain still radiating through my body as I pushed up just enough to reach the handle of my door.

Managing to get inside, I curled up into a tight ball, a streak of mud trailing behind me as I held myself and cried.

CHAPTER TWENTY-ONE

Justin - Present

If Rainey told me she continued going to that house and having sex with Joel after what he'd done, I had every intention of recommending her to be committed. It wasn't that the story shocked me, I'd heard worse, knew violence came in every form, but to return to a man who would treat her so poorly indicated Rainey had issues so destructive that she couldn't be trusted to look out for herself.

"Joel died that night," she admitted, her eyes meeting mine without remorse. "He was found naked in an alley toward the front of the neighborhood stabbed over two dozen times. The man who found him said his death was brutal. Blood everywhere despite the heavy rain."

He deserved it...

I bit my cheek to refrain from speaking the thought aloud. "I think you know what I'm about to say."

"You're sorry?" She grinned, shook her head. "Yeah, I am too. That shouldn't have happened. Joel wasn't that bad of a guy, but whatever they'd taken that night was more than he could handle. Angel was grieving for a long time after he died. I never told her what he did that night, to her or me. I didn't want it to be the last memory she had of him."

Two down. The Connor men were dropping like flies.

"Do you have any idea what may have happened to him?"

Her fingers fluttered over the scar on her arm, drawing my attention. "I have no idea. The next morning, I woke up to a bunch of police cars outside their house. I thought Joel got busted for dealing or something. They came to my house as well after Angel told them she thought I had something to do with it. I guess she knew I was sleeping in Rowan's room, but didn't remember Joel bringing me in to have sex with her. I didn't tell the cops what he did to me. It didn't matter."

Eyes focused on the five tally marks, I couldn't help but wonder what she was hiding. "You didn't answer my question. Not entirely. Can you think of anybody who would have killed Joel? Don't you find it odd that he died only a few hours after what he did to you?"

Rainey shrugged, her eyes refusing to meet mine. "Who knows with how fucked up he was? I thought maybe he walked out into the neighborhood, naked - who the hell knows with what he was on? He may have made it all the way to the front and started a fight with someone. Even Angel didn't know what they'd taken that night."

It was getting late and I wanted to report to Grenshaw before heading home. "I need to go, Rainey, but I'll be back in the morning. Do me a favor and make sure you lock your doors and keep your curtains closed."

Nodding, she didn't bother standing to walk me to the door. I paused before turning the corner, stared at her. Blue eyes peeked up at me. "What?"

"It's a bit difficult to lock the door behind me while sitting on the couch."

"Oh!" A smile, her body shoving up and her feet racing over the floor. "Sorry. I was thinking."

"About?"

"Nothing important." She opened the door, "Have a good night, Justin. I'll see you in the morning."

It made me feel a little better to see the streets and sidewalks empty when I left, to hear the click of a deadbolt behind me as I walked down her steps. At least she had enough sense to take my warning seriously and protect herself from those who would do her harm.

Due to the late hour, I arrived at the station after the sun had set, the stars above me bringing to mind what Rainey had said about good people. It was sad to think she didn't count herself among them, that she believed her circumstances would never change.

She feared being a victim would only prevent her from moving forward in life to experience anything more than what life had already given her.

The usual receptionist was gone, her replacement reading a magazine without noticing I'd walked in. A younger man with tawny hair, he startled when I spoke. "Good evening. Is Detective Grenshaw available?"

Without answering, he picked up the phone, stabbed a button with a grudging finger and said, "The shrink is here to see you."

It appeared everybody knew who I was regardless of whether I'd met them or not.

After he hung up the phone, he glanced at me with curious brown eyes. "This about the Day girl?"

I cocked a brow. *Why else would I be here?*

"Heard she might have been involved in the death of those other four, at least that's what they're saying around here."

Nodding my head, I refused to answer. It concerned me that Grenshaw may have discovered additional information without telling me. I didn't believe Rainey was a killer, but then I couldn't discount her either. There was still so much to know.

Grenshaw opened the front door, his blue tie pulled loose, the front of his pants struggling to hold up his gut. Waving me back, he didn't say a word. Once we'd settled in the room, I took my seat and glanced at him. "Have you learned something new?"

"Jumping right to it, aren't you?" He dropped his weight into a seat, shoulders wilted with exhaustion. "Why do you think I have something additional to tell you?"

"Your receptionist mentioned you're looking at Rainey as having been involved."

Grenshaw scrubbed a hand down his face. "Yeah, about that. I need to remind the guys to keep their traps shut while in the break room inhaling snacks."

Pausing he shook his head. "No, I haven't found anything else. It's just the circumstances, you know? Your questions about the Connor family rang some bells in my head and I started looking into their deaths more. The timeline is strange. All of them dying so close in time to each other. It's like every couple of months another one went down. Then these kids. Not to mention Rainey's mother and her boyfriend. Either this girl has shit luck or something else is going on."

I wouldn't betray Rainey's involvement in David's death, but I could fill Grenshaw in on at least one small detail. "Rowan killed David, the mother's boyfriend. Rainey admitted it to me during the interview."

His brows shot up. "And she didn't tell us this? What else is she hiding?"

"She didn't know until after Rowan told her." It was a lie, but one I was willing to swallow. "And after what

238

David did to her, I'm not inclined to hold it against Rowan for what he did. You would have done the same if she were someone you cared about."

He nodded. "Yeah, you have me there."

Relaxing back in my seat, I thought of the man outside her house, my mind racing over the possibility that Rainey had a violent admirer close to home.

"I was approached today outside of Rainey's house by a man who was a touch too interested in what she had to offer."

"What do you mean?"

"He wanted to know if she was a prostitute, how much she charged. The guy wouldn't give me a name, but mentioned he watches her house. Apparently, she has a bad habit of walking around without clothes while the curtains are open."

Grenshaw grabbed an errant rubber band from the table and played it around his fingers. "Doesn't surprise me with her history in that neighborhood."

"Are you aware that on the night Joel Connor died, he'd attacked Rainey in her front yard earlier that evening? He forced sex on her and injured her so badly she had to crawl to get back inside her house."

"Son of a bitch," his eyes met mine. "What hasn't been done to that woman?"

He wasn't wrong to ask the question, but that wasn't my point. "What if this guy has been watching her for a long time? Perhaps he saw what happened that night and took care of the problem?"

The rubber band worked around his fingers faster, the skin turning white from the strain. "Are you suggesting she has a secret admirer who's killing the people who hurt her?"

It was a flicker of a thought, there and then gone again. An impossibility. Or was it? Rowan had killed David for touching her, had promised to kill all of them for having hurt her. Was it possible?

"Let me ask you this: I know Rowan's remains were cremated and scattered in a communal grave, but what was the state of his body following the car accident that killed him? Was he identifiable?"

Grenshaw stilled, his eyes holding mine while his thoughts worked quickly to catch what I was implying. "You don't think the kid staged his own death-"

"Anything's possible."

"How does that even make sense? Why stage his death, avoid her for a handful of months and then act as some unseen avenger taking out everyone who hurts her? Why not just stay in her life and get her away from that crap?"

Drumming my fingers on the table, I glanced at the white board where the five possible reasons for her scars stared back at me. She'd touched that mark when she spoke of Joel's death. Was she counting down their deaths?

"Rowan attempted to get her away. Had promised to take care of her, but she refused. She kept pushing him away and telling him to go on without her."

Sighing, I stabbed my hand though my hair, frustration riding me. "It's insane, I know. But is it possible?"

Dropping the rubber band, Grenshaw grabbed the laptop from the table, flipped the cover and typed, his chubby fingers flying over the keys.

"According to the medical examiner's report, Rowan's body was badly burned, his physical features unrecognizable, the body in a pugilistic posture."

240

Glancing up, "That's best described as a boxer's pose, hands fisted, arms and knees bent. It's caused from the contraction of muscle due to the fire."

I nodded, waved him on.

"Says here, the impact of the face with the steering wheel knocked out the majority of his teeth and there was internal burning of the lungs. The examiner opined he survived the initial impact, and it would have taken anywhere between three to five minutes for him to die from the fire."

His eyes continued scanning. "Due to lack of dental records, identification couldn't be made via the teeth they found in the car. Ah. They identified him through DNA. It was definitely Rowan."

My palm pressed flat against the table. "It was worth a shot."

"A long shot," he agreed, "but not bad thinking. Weirder shit has happened."

"I still wonder about this guy outside her house. I told her you could send a police car by every so often to look around, but she warned me against it. Said it would make her a target in that neighborhood."

"She's not lying. Clayton Heights is rough and they don't appreciate our presence. If she became the cause of it, her neighbors wouldn't be too pleased."

None of this was easy. "So, we're left with a girl who potentially knows something about a murderer still on the loose and we have no way of keeping an eye on her while a strange man stalks her house. Excellent."

Grenshaw stared at me silently, his eyes assessing. "You care about her."

"I worry for her," I answered, although his statement was uncomfortably close to the truth.

Silence and then, "Be careful, Justin. We still don't know the depth of her involvement. She hasn't been ruled out."

My mind kept spinning over the idea that someone was watching her, and in some fucked up way, protecting her. "You told me Paul and Jacob were shot to death in a drug deal gone wrong. Do we have any details on that case? Anything beyond the drugs? Was Rainey there the night it happened?"

Another flurry of keystrokes, Grenshaw's eyes scanning the information. I could see the blue lettering reflected in his gaze.

"Paul and Jacob Connor were shot in their home. According to some witnesses, they'd thrown a party that night," he grew quiet, eyes moving furiously over the information.

"Ah, hell, one witness admitted they had a girl they claimed to have abducted there that night. She was tied up in a back bedroom. They were allowing guys to do what they wanted to her for the right price. Fuck, you don't think-"

"That it was Rainey? It's highly probable. Whether she was allowing it or not is questionable." With her, it could go either way. "Where was the girl when their bodies were found?"

"No clue. Frankie found them when he got home and said there was nobody else there."

Thinking of her scar again, I tapped my hand on the table and stood up. "I should go. I continue her interview early in the morning."

I spent the remainder of the evening thinking about the case, about the potential Rainey had attracted a threat far worse than the family that once lived next door to her, about the possibility of whether Rainey was capable of taking part in the murders of her friends, but mostly about the moment she'd kissed me and straddled my lap.

I cared about her. Grenshaw wasn't wrong. Even more dangerous, I wanted her, although my attraction to her didn't make sense. It was physical, of course, that fact couldn't be denied, but there was something else. A desire to shelter her maybe? To take her from that life and watch her blossom into what she could become without the weight of Clayton Heights holding her down.

Rainey couldn't be involved, or could she? Yes, she'd taken part in David's murder, but after what he'd done to her on that couch...

The same couch where they began his murder. The same couch where she last had sex with Rowan...

I was beginning to hate that couch. Wanted to drag it outside, smash it apart and burn it to the ground.

It was the first thing I saw when walking into her living the following morning, our same routine followed: her waiting at the door for me when I walked up the dirt path to her porch.

Taking a moment to arrange my notepad and file, I clicked my pen and glanced up at Rainey. "Did you have a good night?"

She nodded, smiled, her hands wringing over each other in her lap. Today she wore a simple T-shirt with cotton shorts. Nothing flirtatious or revealing. I was equally as disappointed as I was relieved.

"You look nervous. Did something happen last night that I should know about? That man didn't come by -"

"No. Nothing like that," she answered, her eyes not meeting mine. "I just wanted to apologize for kissing you. I know it was inappropriate."

243

I didn't want to go there, to even begin thinking about what had almost occurred between us. The case was too important. Finishing this...

"Forget it happened, Rainey. I have."

Eyes closing, she was stung by the comment, not understanding that it was one I had to make to keep from tossing my notepad aside and crossing the room to make the same mistake again. I clicked my pen a second time.

"We left off on the night Joel died. According to my timeline, that was only a year, give or take, prior to the most recent murders. From what I know, Jacob and Paul were the next to die. Do you want to skip ahead in time and talk about them, or is there something I should know that occurred before that?"

Shaking her head, "No. Everything kept going as usual until that night."

"You kept sleeping with Jacob for drugs? Even after what Joel did?"

It was beguiling, her logic. But it was the life she lived. Nothing would change her past. The only possible change that could occur now was her future.

"Yes," her voice became a whisper. "And Paul."

Damn it, Rainey...

"Even after what happened with your mom?"

"Even after," she admitted. "Without Rowan, and after everything that happened-I don't know. I was lost, I guess. Beat down."

"You felt defeated?"

Her eyes met mine. "Yes."

It was understandable. Forgivable.

"Okay, Rainey. Tell me about the night Paul and Jacob died."

CHAPTER TWENTY-TWO

Rainey - Past

All our lives we're told to go high. Reach for the sky. Climb those ladders. Scale those walls. Jump over hurdles.

The theme is on every poster I saw in school. In every inspirational movie, or even uplifting commercials which didn't have much to do with the product being sold. Like we're supposed to sprout wings or something. As if it's easy. As if, with just a little bit of faith, or strength, or a stroke of luck, we all can lift ourselves up and become something.

But what about those of who can't? Those weighed down by circumstance? Those who have been beaten by misfortune, chained by poverty, stomped by the pounding feet of everybody else who's trying to achieve, or simply buried beneath the muck of the fortunate who have no problem in taking advantage?

What about those of us who have given up?

We can't fly, our wings are too shredded. We can't climb, every rung on our ladder has been split in two. We can't scale those walls because the ropes we've been given are frayed or severed. We can't jump hurdles when there's not enough distance in front of us to run.

What we can do is go low, find new ways to keep going, even the odds a little bit by figuring out how to sneak around barriers, and I'll be damned to listen to anyone judging me for the choices I made to survive.

Instead of flying, I'll crawl.

Instead of climbing the ladder, I'll squeeze through the lowest rungs.

Instead of scaling walls, you better believe I'll dig a tunnel under them.

And instead of jumping a hurdle, I'll just knock the damn thing down.

That was the only means to continue on, because those were the only options given to me when I'd been born scraping the bottom.

You could feel sorry for me. Laugh at me. Call me stupid or a slut. It didn't matter to me because I was still breathing. I was still marching on despite knowing there wasn't a light at the end of my tunnel. I continued forward even if the entire time I was blind.

I was never leaving Clayton Heights. That much was obvious. So rather than fighting against it with the idea of becoming better, I dove down beneath the water and settled myself in the muck. Rather than fighting against what was happening, I'd thrown my hands up in surrender and enjoyed the feeling of giving up.

"Rainey! Get your fine ass over here woman. Jacob and I want to talk to you about something."

Walking up the front path to my porch, I turned my head to see Paul crouching down by his motorcycle, tools in hand as he tuned it following a recent run. I was exhausted from work, my till had come out thirty dollars short again, and Mr. Crews was at his wit's end with my inability to count money.

Every time it happened, the money was taken out of my paycheck. After a while, it added up. I was behind on rent. Behind on the power bill, and had just enough food in my house to eat for one more day. There was nothing I could do to keep things going if I didn't go along with whatever favors Jacob and Paul asked of me for what little money they were willing to throw me for it.

Hating that I couldn't tell him to fuck off and leave me alone, I turned instead, walked over the weeds that were as tall as my knees and passed around the chain link fence into his yard. "Hey, Paul. Did you want to go in your room or something?"

Sleeping with him, letting him do the things to me that I knew damn well he'd done to my mother, left a bitter taste in my mouth. In many ways, he'd taken from me, hadn't felt bad about, and then waltzed right in to show me I would still bend over when he flashed some money in my face.

Jacob was the same way. Both of them always tossing it in my face that I had no way out of this mess, so I might as well lie back and enjoy it.

"I have some friends coming in from out of town tonight. Thought you might want to entertain them for me."

Paul squinted his eyes against the sun at my back, his hands stained with grease and his shirt off revealing the additional weight he'd packed on. I hated having him behind me. Sweat would trickle down on my back as he took what he wanted. He no longer gave enough of a damn to pretend like he wanted to make sure I liked it as well. We'd crossed that bridge a long time ago before he doused it in gasoline and lit a match.

"What do you want me to do? Dance for them? Walk around naked like a damn buffet? Run a train?"

Sadly, I'd done all of those things already, had succumbed to the knowledge that I was nothing better than a party favor.

"Got a different idea in mind," he answered, yanking the wrench over a bolt before dropping it on the ground and wiping his hands on a cloth.

"Some of the guys here tonight will know who you are, a few around the neighborhood, but many won't. I thought we could hustle them, make them believe they're getting something they're not." He peered up at me again. "You won't be the one hustling, if you're worried about that. All you'll need to do is lie there and take it as usual. What do you say?"

"How many?"

"Does it really fucking matter, Rainey?"

Not liking the way he barked the question, I rolled my shoulders and grit my teeth. "How much?"

"Five hundred. And we'll give you something so you won't give a shit what's happening while you're back there. You'll be flying and you might actually enjoy yourself for once."

I hadn't enjoyed anything since Rowan. Not one damn thing. Not one damn day. But five hundred could at least get the bills caught up. "Fine. When do you need me over there?"

"Around six so we can get you set up."

"And all I have to do is stay in a room?"

His brown eyes locked to mine. "You know the drill, Rainey. Only difference is that this time you'll be tied up."

"What?"

"Take it or leave it, kid. There will be a hood over your face, too. So no complaining about that. It's all part of the hustle."

"Why can't I just take them back there like usual?"

"Because it's more fun when they think you can't say no. Men are sick, understand? Some of worse than others. You know that. Hell, you've been living next door to it for years. Stop acting so damn surprised."

"Paul!"

From the opposite sidewalk, a man came jogging over, his hand waving in the air and a baseball cap pulled low covering his face. He slowed down when approaching us, making sure to look me over before turning his attention to the man kneeling next to me.

"Hey, I was hoping I could score a bag off you."

Paul stood to his feet and waved the guy over. Before walking off, he reminded me, "Be here at six. We'll take it from there."

The two disappeared inside and I went home to take a long bath, tears rolling over my cheeks to think about just how far I'd fallen.

Six rolled around quickly and I walked into the Connor house to find everybody standing in the kitchen talking to the same guy who'd come over earlier. He nodded his head in my direction, his body hunched over the island countertop braced on his elbows, talking to Paul and Jacob. Despite being inside, he hadn't bothered to take off his hat.

Paul called out to me, "Go in my room, Rainey. I'll be in there in a second."

Doing as I was told, I turned left to walk into his bedroom, took a seat on the bed to wait. I could hear laughter coming from the kitchen, the slap of hands as they were saying goodbye to their guest and then the door opened as Paul and Jacob walked into the room.

"Take it off, woman, then scoot your pretty ass up the bed. Jacob's going to tie your hands to the headboard before helping you get in the mood. It's like I said, all I need you to do is lie there and look pretty. Got me?"

My brow tugged together in confusion. "I thought you said I'd have a hood over my head."

"Nobody's interested in your face. Not tonight anyway. Your body is pretty enough. Now strip and scoot."

Shaking my head, I slipped off my clothes, pushed up to the head of the bed and sat there while Jacob tied my hands to the headboard.

While we were doing that, Paul rolled up a few joints, leaving them on the top of the bureau. Turning, he met eyes with Jacob. "Those are for her. One every couple of hours and she'll be good to go. Might as well help her smoke one now because people should start showing up soon."

He tossed one our direction, Jacob snatching from the air and sticking it to my lips as Paul left the room. His shoulders shook with laughter as he lit the end and had me take a drag. "I can't believe you're doing this."

I shrugged as much as I could with my hands bound. "Money's money, right?"

Almost instantly, my body started to relax, the bed beneath me feeling more like a cloud than a mattress. Paul had laced the joint with something. Whatever it was took effect while I continued pulling a drag every time Jacob pressed the joint to my lips. "Still, Rainey, even you have to admit this is low."

"What do you care?" I asked.

"I don't. I'm just saying. If you're going to lay here without even knowing who you're going to fuck, that's pretty bad. Just thought I'd leave you with that thought before covering your head. Dad is telling these guys that it's whatever goes. And you have no way of stopping them. You can cry and scream all you want. He has no plans of untying you until it's over."

My head was suddenly foggy, my body relaxing down against the bed. It felt like a heavy blanket covered me, my arms hanging limp from the ropes tied at my wrists and my legs not responding despite how I tried to move them.

"I can quit when I want," I slurred with my eyes closed and my head falling back.

"No, Rainey, you can't. But, hey," he stood up from the bed, the mattress moving when his weight was lifted. "At least you won't remember much of what happened. I doubt you'll have very little idea of what's going on. Enjoy your ride. I'll come back and help you smoke another in a few hours."

The entire room went dark as he slipped a hood over my head, absolute silence after he walked from the room and closed the door. Sadly, none of it mattered. With whatever they'd given me, I was so far gone that my mind was wandering from dream to dream, visions of happier times in my head, one smiling face shining within them all.

It had been over a year since the night Rowan died, and still I could see him as clearly as if he was standing in front of me, big blue eyes crinkled at the corners while his lips pulled into a beaming grin. He was beautiful. Too beautiful for words. Too beautiful for me.

While I floated through memories, people must have arrived at the house. Music thumped on the opposite side of the wall, the regular sounds of a party with rambling voices and the clink of beer bottles. Outside the rumble of motorcycle engines filtered into my thoughts, yet none of it mattered to me given the state I was in.

The door opened. At least, I think it did. A masculine voice cutting through the music, suddenly loud before muting again. The heavy fall of boots against the ground. Hands explored up my legs. A belt unbuckled and hit the ground. The mattress dipped at my feet, weight and body heat above me. My legs were being spread.

"You're better than this, Rainey..."

I could hear Rowan speaking against my ear, smell the crisp scent of spearmint on his breath as he handed me a breath mint and shook his head.

No, I'm not, I thought as hands gripped over my breasts, the man saying something, his thick belly pressed to mine. The rough texture of stubble against my skin as he sucked the tip of my breast into his mouth. My hands tugged at the ropes and he laughed. "You're not going anywhere, sweetheart, just relax. Behave and I'll let you enjoy this."

I highly doubted that would happen, but he didn't have to worry about me fighting back. I was here by my choice. Ha. Joke's on him, I guess.

The bed dipped between my legs more, his grubby hands gripping my hips to lift me up, his dick jabbing between my legs because the idiot apparently had shitty aim.

"Rainey, I'm serious. You should have a guy that cares about you. That sees you as more than a girl to use and toss aside. But you don't make people see you that way. You let them hurt you. It has to stop..."

Rowan had been so sweet back then. Barely sixteen, his face still baby soft and his body so damn skinny. He still had hope in his eyes when he was that young. The belief that I would become better than what I was.

252

The man pushed inside me, his fingers gripping down, grunts falling over his lips. I couldn't really feel much. I wasn't there entirely, my mind drifting off to feel a boy lift me from the ground, his arms tight around my waist.

"What's got you in such a good mood?"

"A girl."

"Oh yeah? Who is she?"

She should have been me. Rowan, if he'd lived, would have been nineteen now. I wondered if he could have actually gotten me away from here. If I'd just said yes to leaving with him, would I have been happy wherever we went?

The man finished. Another one entered. More of the same. *Yeah, bitch. Take it. You know you want it. Stop fighting and I'll make you like it.* It's like these assholes were reading from a script. I didn't think I was fighting. Maybe they liked to pretend I was because it made them feel superior somehow.

"I'll love you forever, Rainey. Protect you. Take care of you. There's nowhere you can go where I won't find you. Rowan and Rainey, forever."

"Promise?"

"Promise."

People shouldn't make promises they can't keep.

That man finished. Next up. By that time, I think I was crying. Not because of what was happening to me, but because I couldn't stop drifting back into memories.

The night wore on, Jacob coming in once or twice to remove the hood and force me to smoke another joint. My thoughts became more jumbled with each one. I don't think he knew I didn't need them.

I didn't even notice the men coming in any more, just the loud yelling, gun shots, glass breaking and

253

more yelling, Paul's voice rising up before another shot. Silence. A door opening. The sound of heavy steps. I was being untied, the hood pulled off my head. I couldn't even open my eyes until my clothes were back on and I was being carried somewhere.

My head fell back and I remember seeing Paul on the kitchen floor, a dark puddle around him. Jacob was sleeping by the front door, which I thought was odd.

In and out. Pain in my arm, like being cut open. And then a pillow beneath my head. A door closing.

The night must have been over. I could finally rest.

CHAPTER TWENTY-THREE

Justin - Present

There were so many questions I wanted to ask that choosing the first was difficult. From end to beginning or beginning to end? The chronology wasn't important to me, but to Rainey, it would be.

Although her mind wandered, it still had a specific route, a snail's crawl through time, beginning at the bottom and circling lower until we both sat in the muck together.

"A witness claimed they had an abducted girl that night. Were allowing men to pay to spend time with her."

"Fuck me, you mean?" A tilt of her head, a ghost of a smile. "I think by this point in the story, polite words aren't needed. We both know what I was. Hell, maybe what I still am."

"My point is to confirm you were there by choice that night."

Nodding, she picked at a frayed string on her shirt, shame and regret written clearly in her expression, surprising me to see it.

"There are several details of that story I'd like to discuss. The first being the man you described at the beginning."

Millions of men wear ball caps in this country, and I was sure a majority of the men in this neighborhood were among them, but still, if it was possible that the man from her recollection and the one I spoke to in front of her house were one in the same, it could answer so many questions.

"Is he the same man we've seen across the street? The one who approached me yesterday?"

"How am I supposed to know?" She answered with a weak shrug. "There are a ton of men around here who wear hats."

I jotted the information down regardless. "Did the police speak to you at all about the night Paul and Jacob died? Did they question you about whether you were there?"

Her eyes met mine. "Why would they? It's not like they came to me to report that Rowan was dead. And the only reason they questioned me about Joel was because Angel pointed them in my direction."

"Frankie didn't mention-"

"Frankie didn't give a damn that his entire family was gone, Doc. He wasn't that type of person. As far as he saw it, he had the house to himself after they all died. He could take up as the neighborhood dealer and make a ton of money for it. Hell, I wouldn't have been shocked to learn Frankie was the one that shot them."

"Rainey, you just told me a man carried you out and took you to your house. Doesn't that make you wonder if he was the man who shot them?"

She stilled, her eyes wandering to the window as her fingers fluttered over the mark on her arm. The unintentional movement reminded me of another question.

"You mentioned when he brought you to your house, you felt something cutting your arm. Is that where you got the mark you're touching at this moment?"

Eyes closing for several seconds, Rainey opened them to return her attention to me. "I woke up with these cuts, yes. They were bandaged, but not stitched or anything. So that's why they scarred, I think."

"What do they mean, Rainey?"

Brow knitting, she became defensive, her demeanor shifting from a scared woman to anger. "How was I supposed to know? I didn't even know who carried me to my house. I was too fucked up. No, I didn't know if that man shot Jacob and Paul, and no, I didn't talk to the police. What was I supposed to say to them? *'Oh, hey, I was doing drugs next door and fucking strange men when two people were killed?'* I don't think so, Justin. Only a stupid person would say that. They'd start looking at me like I had something to do with it."

Did she have something to do with it?

The question echoed in my mind, Grenshaw's warning about Rainey filtering in to mingle with my uncertainty.

As it stood, there was no person alive who could attest to Rainey's true demeanor at the time of the events. The only known live witness was Rainey herself.

"Why are you so upset, Rainey?"

Tears were streaming down her cheeks, her pale face beaming an angry crimson. Her body language was closed off, her eyes darting around the room with the refusal to meet mine.

"You act as if I wanted any of this to happen. You also accused me of being a stupid victim. I'm not stupid, Justin. Never have been. If anything, I'm a victim of circumstance, sure, but not a victim when it comes to what I did with any of the Connor family. I did what I had to do to survive. You're a smart guy. I'm sure you were raised in a nice house by nice parents. You got to go to school and now you have a career that pays you enough to support yourself. That's good for you, but it doesn't mean we all had the same good fortune. You have no idea how hard it is to live my life. None at all. So rather than sitting here judging me, why don't you just take your fancy pen and paper and get the hell out?"

Before I could respond, she stood from the couch and stalked into the kitchen out of sight. A heavy breath poured over my lips, one filled with regret for having upset her, exhaustion for the story she told that still hadn't provided me with a single answer as to how her friends died in the most recent attack.

Setting my pen and notepad aside, I followed after her, my steps much slower than hers. "Rainey?"

She leaned against the counter, face buried in her hands. From where I stood, I could see her shoulders shaking, could hear the soft sobs that wracked her chest.

I stepped closer, unsure how she would react to my presence. "Are you okay?"

"No, I'm not okay," she spoke against her palms. Pulling her face away, she stared at me with red rimmed eyes. "I thought you were here to help me. After what those cops did, after the things they said to me, I thought that maybe you were sent as an apology. I don't know how to tell this story, I don't understand it myself, but that's not why you're here, is it? Did they send you to drive the nails in deeper? To make me feel worse?"

Confusion saddled me. "What are you talking about?"

I'd walked closer as she spoke, my gaze shifting down to her as I took a mirrored position against the opposite counter. The edge bit into my hips, but I ignored the discomfort.

"Those cops, Grenshaw and the other guy. They practically laughed at me while I explained my story. They egged me on by asking me detailed questions about what I did with the Connor family. They didn't care to know the truth, they just wanted to hear me talk about how it made me feel to sleep with so many people. Like I was some dumb whore. Like I was lying to cover stuff up."

Surprise lifted my brows before anger narrowed my eyes. I hadn't watched the full interview, had no idea what she was talking about, but I would correct that mistake tonight. "I didn't know they'd treated you that way. I would apologize on their behalf, but I'm too angry if what you're telling me is true."

"It's not your place to apologize for them." There was more to that statement she didn't say, a thought she kept to herself. I could hear it in her voice, see it in the way she looked away before finishing the sentence.

"And what should I be apologizing for? What have I done?"

Rainey laughed, a sad bark of sound that shook her shoulders as she slapped away a tear. "I'm not sure that you have a reason. You rejected me, Doc, told me I was a victim, but if that's how you really feel, then it is what it is. I can't do anything about that."

Hands gripping the counter at my sides, I crossed an ankle over the other. "I didn't reject you for being a victim."

"Oh, yeah?" Blue eyes met mine. "Did you do it because of my past? Because of what I've done?"

In truth, I wasn't rejecting her. Not fully, at least. If I could change our circumstances and make it possible for us to explore what might happen between us, I would. She was a beautiful girl, there was no denying that. Something about her spoke to me - called to every male instinct I had. It was through sheer force of will that I refrained from reaching out to touch her.

"Not because of that, either. It's because you are involved in a murder investigation, one I've been hired to help conduct."

"So, you think I had something to do with it, right? That I was strong enough to do what was done to my friends all by myself?"

Wrapping her arms around her midsection, she laughed. "I'm not that strong and I'm not that smart. Not to take out an entire family and then turn around to beat four more people to death."

No, she wasn't. In that she wasn't lying. "Who do you think carried you out of their house and carved that mark onto your arm? It has to mean something."

Shrugging, Rainey averted her eyes, the sunlight streaming in through the windows, highlighting the wet trails where her tears had fallen.

"What do you think of me, Justin? No bullshitting me or saying what's polite. What do you really think? Do you think I'm capable of hurting another person?"

She looked so small in that moment, unsure of herself, frightened. If I had to guess based solely on what stood in front of me, my answer would have been no.

"Not from what you've told me, no."

Nodding, she scratched her neck, the movement of her arm tugging the bottom hem of her shirt up just enough to see the skin of her abdomen.

"Do you think I'm not good enough for you?" She whispered, her gaze colliding with mine, daring me to be honest. "Has life done that to me? Made me less than worthy of a person like you?"

"No. I think you've made mistakes. I think your past is-" Sighing, I raked my hand through my hair attempting to formulate a nice way of saying it. "I think it's convoluted and distressing."

Canting her head, she grinned. "Convo what?"

Grinning back at her, I said, "Messy and upsetting. But it's your past, Rainey. You can change it."

"How am I supposed to do that if people like you won't give me the chance?"

"It's not that I don't want to-"

Fuck! If I could just close this damn case, I would show her exactly how much I wanted her. Ever since meeting her, she's been the only thing on my mind. Rainey had pushed me beyond professional boundaries in my mind and she wasn't helping the matter by looking at me with longing now.

Lips curled at the corners, she blinked her eyes. "So, what you're saying is that you would like to know somebody like me?"

Know? I'd like to toss her on that counter and strip her damn clothes off, but that would make me as bad as all the other men who'd seen her as nothing more than a body to fuck.

Her question was dangerous. Denying it would set her back on course to believing she wasn't worth my time. Admitting it would give her reason to try.

Unfortunately, my silence only opened the door for her to step forward and close the distance between us.

"Justin?"

Our chests pressed together, her neck craning to look up at me as she reached to touch my cheek. Releasing my death grip on the counter, I grabbed her hips to push her away, but her fingertip traced my bottom lip, making it damn near impossible.

"How many times have we've been right here, Doc? So close, yet so far away?" She smiled, the movement of her lips drawing my focus, her eyes wide with desire. It would be so easy to just let go, to lean down and taste that mouth, to allow my hands to explore and appreciate all her feminine curves.

"The case-" My voice was pure grit, my body tight through every muscle. Rainey didn't appear to care about what prevented us from knowing each other, all she cared about was pressing forward.

Pulling my head down by cupping my cheeks, she pushed up on her toes to brush her lips across mine. My hands remained on her hips, fingers loose, a refusal against what I knew I wanted.

Logic collided against desire, my mind racing with all the reasons I should stop this before it went further, yet my body wouldn't cooperate. I stood still, allowing her to flick her tongue along the crease of my mouth, the scent of lavender floating across my senses as the taste of mint invaded my mouth. She was kissing me fully now, her chest tight against mine, my hands gripping her hips now that I'd surrendered to the moment.

Still, something nagged at me, a factor in this equation that wasn't right. Mint?

I broke the kiss. "Did you quit smoking?"

When had that happened and why hadn't I noticed?

"Two days ago, Doc. Keep up."

She was half laughing over the answer, her blue eyes locked to mine. "I told you I can quit stuff when I want. It's not my fault you didn't believe me."

Rainey didn't give me time to answer; she simply wrapped one hand around the back of my head and pulled me to her, her other hand sliding down to grip mine and rip it from her hip, directing it up to cup her breast over her shirt.

Damn it. My body reacted before my brain could catch up. I molded the weight of her against my palm, my cock hard as soon as a moan slipped from her lips to vibrate against mine.

Knowing I should stop what was happening, I lost control instead, releasing her so I could run that same hand up beneath her shirt to feel skin against skin. The feel of her was everything I imagined it would be. Firm, yet soft. Young, so damn young.

Crushing the weight against my palm and flicking my thumb over the hard nipple was everything I shouldn't have been doing as she kissed me with a needy sweep of her tongue, her hips pressed against mine.

Speaking against my mouth as I continued touching her in ways that went against my better judgment, she rubbed her hand over the front of my pants. "You want me, Justin. I've known that. Just let go to it."

I thought I was, but this girl moved a hell of a lot faster, only because she wasn't restrained by right or wrong, wasn't bound by professionalism.

A twinkle in her eyes and I was undone, my ability to stop what was occurring between us fully surrendering to lust.

"I'll take care of you," she promised on a husky whisper, the sound of her voice running through me as violently as my need to explore every inch of her body.

With a ghost of a smile curling her lips, Rainey sank down to her knees in front of me, her fingers working

263

at the button and zipper of my slacks, the words *stop, no, this is a seriously bad idea* trapped at the back of my throat.

I could only manage a nonsensical grunt when she pulled me free and wrapped her hand over the hard shaft, my eyes peering down to find her glancing up at me. Without breaking eye contact, she wrapped her lips over the tip and flicked out with her tongue.

"Fuck..."

My head fell back as my hips bucked, the wet warmth of her mouth slowly taking me in, inch by excruciating inch.

Without thought, my hand went to her head, my fingers twining within her dark hair as she bobbed and licked, sucked and worked me into a knot of desire and need.

There was no stopping this, not now when we'd reached a point of no return. Her mouth was pure magic, the stroke of her hand driving me until I grit my teeth on a climax that swept over me without apology.

Rainey pushed to her feet, her hand still toying with what was left of my erection, her mischievous eyes meeting mine with victory written into the blue color. "Tell me you didn't want that."

"I didn't- We shouldn't have- This can't-"

It was impossible to finish even one of the statements, despite how true they were.

Pressing against me, Rainey ran her hand up my abdomen and chest, over my shoulder and behind my head to pull my mouth down to hers. I could taste myself on her.

"Rainey, I need to finish this case before that happens again."

Her lips were trailing light kisses along my jaw. Nipping at my earlobe, she laughed, the sound soft and so utterly intoxicating that I stilled to hear it, adherence to my job warring with the demand that I take her right here against the counter without giving a damn what would come of it.

"Other things can happen then. There are more ways to enjoy each other than just one."

A shudder tore through my body, my erection coming alive in the feminine hand that kept touching and stroking, teasing me with a light scrape of fingernails before wrapping the strength of her fingers over me again.

Gripping the front of my shirt, Rainey slanted her mouth over mine, her tongue fluttering across my lips before dipping inside to taste me.

I was losing this battle, losing the ability to remember why I should say no.

Releasing me entirely, she stepped away as her eyes locked to mine, her gaze bright and excited while mine was hooded with the need to take what she was offering without fear of consequence.

"It can be our little secret, Doc." She pulled her shirt over her head, revealing her body to me without shyness or hesitation. My gaze dropped to the fullness of her breasts, my mouth watering with the need to bite and taste.

"Touch me, Justin. Stop pretending like you don't want this."

Stepping forward would be awkward given that my slacks were around my ankles. I could pull them up, fasten them and walk away, or I could kick my shoes off, step out of the slacks and give in to the sensual torture of seeing this woman half dressed and begging for me to show her what I wanted.

The second option won out, and by the time I'd freed myself of the clothing, I stepped forward to wrap one hand in her hair to kiss her while my other hand palmed her breast. She moaned into my mouth, her back arching into my touch.

"You're doing this on purpose," I accused, not caring that my words were skating so close to the truth.

Backing Rainey against the opposite counter top, I dropped my hand to her shorts and shoved them down her hips. My fingers explored between her legs to find she was so fucking wet and ready. "You're killing me. You know that?"

She grinned against my mouth. "Shut up and do what you've been wanting to do for days now."

Slipping my fingers inside her, I watched with fascination at the way her mouth opened on a moan, at her eyes clenching shut and opening again in raw invitation.

There was no way I could stop this. We'd gone too far to turn back.

Lifting her to the counter, I dipped my head to take a nipple into my mouth, my hand shaping the other breast as she hung her arms over my shoulders watching me enjoy her.

I was hard again, my body throbbing with the need to know what it was like to be inside her.

Lifting my head to kiss her one last time, I asked, "Are you sure about this, Rainey? Are you sure you want this?"

"I haven't said no, have I?"

She hadn't said no to a lot of things, but that didn't mean she wanted it.

"Rainey, do you want this with me?"

Her fingers idly played with my hair, the tips dragging down my neck, seducing me further. "Yes."

That was all I needed to hear. Gripping her hips, I pulled her to the edge of the counter, notched my cock between her legs and thrust inside her body with one hard, long movement. She breathed out, her head falling back, her chest pushing forward as her back arched.

I was possessed, every thrust inside her shoving us both forward and back, her tits bouncing with the movement, every bit of integrity I had left bleeding away as I grabbed her by the back of the head and took her mouth with mine.

There was no walking back from this mistake...and yes, that is exactly what it would be when I left this house and had a moment to take a breath to think about what I had done. But, for now, I became lost in the sensation of her, lost to the soft mewls and moans that crawled up her throat to escape her lips, lost to the sight of her when she broke our kiss to lie over the countertop, her back arching , her hands gripping the sides as I continued using her body to please mine.

Fucking hell, this girl was addictive, every move she made drawing my eye, her breasts bouncing with every thrust, her legs wrapping around my waist holding me tight to her body while I fought the urge to come.

I wanted to watch her get off, wanted to hear what she sounded like when reaching a climax, but the sight of her was too much, the feel of her...

"Fuck!" I pulled out, my release pulsing wet and heavy into my hand.

Never in my life had I been a two-pump chump, but this girl made it impossible to hold out.

"I'm sorry," I said, breaking free of her legs to run to the sink and wash my hand.

"For?" Sitting up, Rainey blinked in my direction, completely comfortable in her skin.

"Not getting you off."

Her lips tipped into a grin. "Maybe next time." With the high of finally having her wearing down, anxiety for what I'd done crept in. "I need to finish this case, Rainey." Eyes meeting hers, I explained, "This interview needs to end so I can submit my report."

Voice quiet, she asked, "What are you going to tell them?"

"The truth."

"And that is?"

Drying my hands on a dishtowel, I picked up her clothes from the floor and handed them to her. "I need to know what happened the night your friends died, Rainey."

She slipped on her shirt, talking as she did so. "I haven't reached that point of the story yet."

"Then skip ahead. Just tell me what you know. Did you kill them?"

"No." Hopping down from the counter, she pulled on her underwear and shorts. "I didn't kill them."

It was all I needed to know.

Grabbing my pants, I got dressed and was tying my shoes when I told her, "I need to go. I think I can finish this report tonight and turn it in."

"Does that mean the interview is over? I haven't finished telling you-"

Turning, I kissed her into silence, not caring about what happened the night of the fire. That was all that was left for her to tell me before the night her friends were murdered. "Yeah, the interview is over. I need to finish this report. It's important."

Nodding, she followed me into the living room, quietly watching as I gathered my things. Rainey walked me to her front door after that, craning her neck to look up at me as I stepped out onto the porch. "Thank you, Justin. For everything."

Leaning down, I kissed her, a quick peck on the lips that I wished could be more. "I'll make sure they know everything. You didn't do this, Rainey, and I'll include that in my report."

Turning to leave, I noticed the same man across the street again, my temper rising at the sight of him. "Rainey, be sure to lock your door."

She did as I asked, the deadbolt latching as I ran down the steps to my car. Opening the door, I turned and made sure that son of a bitch knew I was watching him. He strolled away slowly, turning a corner to get out of view.

If anything, I had more concern about the man stalking her than anything else. I would include him in my report, and then when this was all finished, I would move Rainey out of here to get her away from the danger he presented.

CHAPTER TWENTY-FOUR

Justin - Present

Mistakes, we all make them.

Some are the result of poor decision making. Others the consequence of bad judgment calls. Most people don't recognize the mistake while it's being made. They are a bomb waiting to detonate, a speeding train with the conductor asleep behind the wheel, they are potential not yet realized until the act of making them is done.

Yet, my mistake had been a conscious decision. I had no excuse for my actions, no ability to claim I didn't understand what was being done. I'd known through every step of the act, from before touching Rainey for the first time, through the moment of finally tasting her, and all the way through the moment where I left her house to return home, the consequences of what we'd done staring me directly in the face.

No longer was I an objective reporter. No longer could I honestly claim that the opinions in my report were unclouded of my feelings for the subject being interviewed. I hadn't just crossed a line that was drawn in the sand, I'm tumbled over a boundary as formidable as a twenty foot wall, scaled it without concern for what I was doing and jumped with arms outspread not caring that my reputation and integrity would be stripped away for having fallen.

Now, I sat at the table in my dining room with my laptop open and ready for what I had to type, my fingers frozen over the keys, a blue glow illuminating my face like a spotlight of accusation shining up at me.

Pursuant to my professional license, typing this report and submitting it as a documented analytical opinion with subjective influence was criminal. But I would do it regardless...for her.

Relaxing back in my seat, I scrubbed my hands over my face, a heavy sigh blowing across my lips. There were so many unanswered questions still lingering in my thoughts, so may fears as to what could happen to Rainey if she never left Clayton Heights.

She'd managed to survive in that place for five years, but I suspected the only reason was because of her simple and submissive nature. What would have happened to her if she'd said no to that family instead of yes?

Everything about this case bothered me, but it was the outside influences, the external factors that bothered me the most.

Did I believe Rainey was capable of killing four people in such a violent manner?

That was the ultimate question and one I could answer honestly as no. Someone else had killed her friends, and judging by the story she told me, judging by a man who had more interest in her than was comfortable, I thought there was a distinct possibility that either someone followed Rainey that night, or someone had followed Preston after a deal gone bad.

It was the only question I was asked to answer, all the other details unimportant to my role in this case.

Would Grenshaw pin the deaths on her regardless?

It was another question that lingered.

Beside my computer was the file folder Grenshaw had given me. Inside that folder was the disc of her first interview with the detectives. Had they toyed with her as if she were nothing more than entertainment?

Pulling the disc from the folder, I took a few hours to watch the interview, and like Rainey had said, both detectives treated her as if she were amusing, but not credible. She told parts of the same story to them that she told me, however their reaction was ridicule.

"Before you tell me anything, I have to ask this: Were you walking funny when you left her house?"

Grenshaw's first words to me following my initial meeting with her were telling. Rather than listening to what she was trying to say to him, he'd simply seen her as a sexual object, someone to be dismissed as nothing more than a promiscuous woman.

If anything, this solidified my need to protect her. Yes, turning in the report was wrong. Certifying myself as a neutral reporter and unbiased was criminal. But, if not me, who would be on Rainey's side?

She had no one left. No one, but me.

It took me several hours to draft the report, a few more to review it and tweak the final changes. The finished product ran through the gamut of Rainey's experiences, the end notes suggesting that there were multiple unidentified individuals that were more likely to be responsible for the murders than the woman I interviewed.

In truth, the mark on Rainey's arm continued to bother me. What did it mean and why would someone carve it into her skin? Was it a brand of ownership perhaps? A sick minded individual's message to someone else who would see it.

Why five? None of it made sense.

I could have spent the rest of the night contemplating its meaning, but instead, I did my best to get some sleep, arriving early the next morning at the police precinct to deliver my final report.

Grenshaw was in his office when I arrived, his eyes bleary from the late hours he'd been working, his suit jacket wrinkled where it was tossed across a table. With the cuffs of his shirt sleeves rolled up to his forearms, he leaned back heavily in his seat with his feet propped up on the surface of his desk. I felt like I'd interrupted a nap, or possibly woken him up from a night spent sleeping in the same place where he worked.

"Give me the summary, Justin. Was it her?"

Shaking my head, I mirrored his relaxed posture, but crossed an ankle over my knee rather than propping my feet on his desk.

"I don't believe she's capable of having committed these crimes. Every person around her that has died had problems of their own. They had enemies, competitors, issues that went beyond their association with Rainey. As to the night of the most recent murders, there is the potential that the deaths had something to do with whatever made Preston angry. There's also a question about this man that appears to be stalking Rainey. She admitted to me that she was at the Connor house the night Jacob and Paul died, that someone carried her from their house and took her home."

He grumbled, "Yet another fact she failed to tell us."

"Did you interview her in that matter?"

Squeezing the bridge of his nose, Grenshaw clenched his eyes shut, wracking his brain for the answers. "I'm not certain, but I don't think we did."

"Then how would she have been able to tell you?"

His response was a roll of his shoulders, his hands folding over his stomach. "So, what do you think, Justin? That somebody else did this?"

"That's not my call to make. I was hired to evaluate Rainey. She's a terrible witness to what happened the night her friends died, but she has been forthcoming as to how she knew them and why she was at the party that night. Even if the details she gave painted her in a horrible light."

Displeased with my assessment, Grenshaw pulled his feet from the desk, his chair groaning as he leaned forward to brace himself on his forearms. Eyes meeting mine, he shrugged. "This is another unsolved case."

I wasn't happy with how easily he was giving up. "Follow the lead on Preston's activities as a dealer. I'd also suggest you find out who the man in Rainey's neighborhood is that is watching her. You might have your answer in one of those two places."

"Yeah, man. I hear you. It's a little more complicated than patrolling Clayton Heights, though. The minute he sees cop cars in there, he'll know something is up. They watch those streets like hawks. Even undercovers don't go undetected. If something is out of the ordinary, they all know."

Rainey had warned me of the same thing the first day I arrived for the interview. I didn't envy Grenshaw for his job and the difficulties of solving these cases.

"I should go," I said, standing from my seat. "Good luck with all of this."

Grenshaw waved me off after thanking me for the part I'd played. Happy to have the case behind me, I drove to Rainey's house next. It was important that I let her know the interview was over, and I wanted to settle her concerns that she was being looked at as a suspect. As to everything else, I wasn't sure what to say or do.

Getting in so deep with her was stupid on my part, but I was willing to help her if she would let me.

274

Rainey needed someone strong in her life, someone who had the means to help her escape Clayton Heights. I hadn't known her long enough to be sure what I wanted between us, but I knew I wanted something.

Did I love her? No.

Could I? That's what I wanted to discover.

Ignoring the way my heart slammed into my throat as soon as I pulled into her driveway, I got out of the car to walk up her dirt drive, a sigh blowing over my lips when I knocked on the door.

She didn't answer immediately, but then she didn't expect me like the other days I'd come by. Knocking again, I looked across the street to see if people were watching. As usual, there were a few wary gazes staring back.

The door opened and I turned to find Rainey wrapped in a towel, her shoulders bare, her legs naked. It angered me and scared me for her at the same time.

"Rainey, you had no idea it was me at the door. Didn't it occur to you to get dressed before answering? This," I said, running my finger down the center fold of the towel, "is dangerous."

Her blue eyes held surprise, widening just a bit at what I'd said. "I thought the interview was over."

My cock jumped at the thought of what I'd find beneath the towel. "It is. I came by to tell you I submitted my final report and you don't have to worry about Grenshaw eyeing you as a suspect anymore. You can put all of this behind you and move forward like you've wanted."

Rather than stepping aside to let me into the house, Rainey blocked the door, holding it open just enough for me to see her.

"Are you going to let me in?"

Casting a quick glance over her shoulder, she returned her eyes to mine. "It's not a good time right now."

Suspicion flooded me. "Why not?"

She didn't need to answer me. Whoever she had inside her house let me know all I needed.

"Rainey! Damn it, woman, get back here. I'm sitting here with my cock in my hand."

It was a punch to the chest, the knowledge that despite what I'd thought we'd shared, she'd already jumped in bed with somebody else. Apology shone in her eyes, her body fidgeting in place. She knew just by looking at me that I wasn't happy to hear another man's voice.

"I'm sorry," she whispered, "and I'm grateful that you helped me out like you did, but I still need to pay my bills. I told you before that you don't understand what it's like being me. I do what I have to do so I can get by-"

How the fuck could she do this? "That's the other reason I'm here, Rainey. I want to help you get away from this place. You don't have to do this shit anymore. Just tell that asshole to leave and we can talk. I want to help you."

The door flew open, Rainey jumping in place as a man came into view next to her. Lifting my eyes, I stilled to see it was the same asshole who had confronted me at my car. All he wore was a pair of jeans hanging loose on his hips, his bare chest heavily muscled, his eyes narrowed on me.

"Go back to the couch, Rainey. I'll deal with this for you."

276

Casting me one last apologetic look, Rainey walked away, her *customer* smirking at me from over the threshold to her house.

He grinned with one arm braced against the door, the other hanging loose at his side. There was a bandage on his left forearm, but beneath that was corded muscle. "Apparently twenty bucks gets you a lot with this girl. You know what I mean?"

All I felt was fury. Seeing it in my face only made him smile wider.

"Hate to tell you this, man, but Rainey's schedule is full today. I suggest you get lost. If you're really hard up, there's some second rate pussy two streets down. House number 1530. Just knock on the door. She'll know why you're there."

With that, he closed the door in my face, his laughter deep on the opposite side. I heard Rainey squeal a few seconds later, my feet frozen to the spot where I stood.

Finally finding the ability to walk away, I sat in my car for a few minutes, disbelief saturating every cell in my body.

The drive home gave me plenty of time to think about what had occurred, my first instinct was to forget I'd ever known her; my second was to turn around and drag that son of bitch out of her house and claim Rainey as mine.

By the time I got home, I was livid.

Deciding to run, I changed into shorts and a shirt, strapped my iPod to my bicep and pounded four miles in under an hour. The exercise helped bleed some of the anger and tension out of my body, but it did nothing to clear my head.

277

A cold shower did nothing to help, and while lying in bed that night, I couldn't fall asleep because of my thoughts of her.

This wasn't right. This wasn't how all of this should end.

I'd be damned to let her go back to a life that would eventually kill her.

Throwing myself out of bed, I made a decision to confront Rainey and make her see there were more options available to her than Clayton Heights.

Not giving a damn about the time, I jumped in my car and made the drive over.

She would decide this tonight whether she wanted to or not.

My only hope was that she was smart enough to see that leaving it all behind and moving forward with me was the best choice she could make.

CHAPTER TWENTY-FIVE

Rainey - Present

Sex for drugs. Sex for money. Sex for favors, or handouts or both. It's what I'd learned to do in life to get by. I wasn't born with a genius brain, hadn't been gifted with much talent, but what I was given was a body that drew the eye and the knowledge of how to use it.

The not-so-subtle sway of my hips makes a man leer at my ass. The teasing bounce of my tits makes his fingers curl and his palms tingle to mold them against his skin. Everything I do is meant to attract them, from the innocent widening of my eyes to the curl of my lip over my teeth. It's an image I'd mastered years ago. One that serves me well and pays the bills.

Most of the time, I didn't feel guilty for making a man see one thing while I thought another. With Justin I had, only because he was kind. He hadn't deserved the way I'd used him, hadn't known he was being pulled in for one simple purpose with every intention of being shoved away once I got what I'd wanted.

The look on his face when he caught me with another man this morning was enough to freeze me in place. Besides Rowan, it was the first time I'd seen somebody hurt to know what I'd given him wasn't for him alone.

Yet, if he knew why, I think he'd thank me for the favor. I wasn't just shoving him away by sleeping with another man, I was saving his life.

In truth, I could have saved us days in that interview by just sticking to the story of the night four people died. I don't know why the other details were so important for me to tell. Maybe I was seeking understanding, absolution, or both. Maybe I'm just looking for one person to hear how everything had crumbled apart so they could know what happened for death to be deserved.

I'd been angry for so long. Lost. Miserable. Chomping at the bit for something good to come around. Something that would save me. Something that would make me sane again. But as the days passed and the hopelessness infected me, my mind wandered down dark trails, the world around me shattering as I tried to make sense of how I'd arrived in such a lonely and fucked up place.

I think I wanted Justin to know so he could justify my decisions...so he could tell me that, despite it all, every one of those people had deserved to die.

Who the hell was I kidding? If they knew the truth, most people would cringe away in disgust, would shout from the rooftops that I deserved to rot. I was one big, living and breathing secret, the thoughts in me festering, the knowledge in my heart horrifying.

Most people can't look past the bodies to see the reasons *why*.

It had been difficult for me, at first. I won't lie and claim it was easy.

From the minute we're born, we're told that taking another life is wrong, we're told we're sick if we enjoy it. I'm not sure if enjoy is the word I would use to describe how I felt, but I didn't regret their deaths either. Every single one of them had to die if starting over could ever be an option.

Justin hadn't allowed me to finish my story. He still didn't know, and for that reason, he'd been hurt when I opened the door, his heart had shattered beneath the weight of the knowledge that even after giving myself to him on a silver platter, I would turn to another for the same thing without feeling an ounce of remorse.

There was no way he could understand the truth of what I had become, no way he could accept how the pieces fit together to lead to what had been done.

He would never give me the absolution I sought, would never understand that to live a life in the gutters, you had to ensure your teeth were always sharp.

I'd thought myself insane for so long that hearing someone on the outside tell me it was justified and normal was all I'd hoped for when I started him on a timeline that began five long years ago.

The blood on my hands would never be washed off, its crimson color painting my nails, its heat forever warming my pale skin. And if given the option of turning back and walking away from what I knew was to come, I would shake my head and smile pretty as I stood amongst the violence and asked for it all over again.

Love does that to you, doesn't it? I'd been driven mad by circumstance, beaten down by heartache, and reborn when every person who'd ever hurt me was stabbed or shot, burned or bludgeoned, their bodies and ashes delivered to the ground.

It was over now. My life was no longer sinking beneath deep waters until I was choking on the losses I'd suffered. Retribution has cleared a path, the embers of the fires finally drifting off into the night to twinkle like stars. I knew where I'd been and where I was going, my heart beating a steady rhythm because life could begin again.

The sun had set hours ago. I needed to get a bath and eat something so my stomach would stop growling. The past week had tied me in knots, the memories of the past five years making it difficult to get through the day without my heart aching for how hard the road had been.

I was a survivor. I knew that and clung to the belief. Not a victim as Justin had claimed, not a weak woman who had allowed people to use her. It may seem that way to an outside observer, but really, I'd always known how to get what I wanted.

Steam billowed from the shower as I stripped down to nothing. I'd pulled the curtain aside and was stepping in when I heard someone pounding on the front door, desperate to get in.

Turning, I cocked a brow wondering who the hell would be here at such a late hour.

With a huff of breath, I wrapped a towel around me, my feet bare as I padded through the house to open the door. Justin stared back at me, the light from inside illuminating his anxious eyes.

"Justin? What are you-"

He shoved me inside, his pupils so wide they looked full black. Slamming the door behind him, his chest heaved as if he'd run to my house instead of driven. Glancing at my towel, his gaze lifted to mine, a sheen of red dusting his cheeks.

"I'm not letting you do this."

"Do what? Get a bath? Because that's what I was about to do."

I had to crane my neck to look at him. He matched my every step, remaining so close to me that our breath was colliding in a warm cloud between us, his chest rubbing against mine.

282

"Why did you let that guy into your house today? How could you do something so fucking stupid? You have no idea if he's the man who killed your friends, no clue if he plans to do the same thing to you."

My heart fell into my stomach, regret filtering through me for what I'd done. The lies I had to tell in order to walk away from those murders without revealing the truth of my involvement.

"It's how I make a living, Justin. And if he was planning on killing me, he had every opportunity this afternoon. Yet, here I am, alive and well."

My concern was that if Justin didn't leave soon, the same wouldn't be said about him. He was the last issue that needed to be resolved, a loose thread that needed snipping, but I couldn't bring myself to let it happen.

He'd tried to help me in the only way he knew how, and I'd taken advantage of him to make sure he submitted a report clearing me of wrongdoing.

People think I'm stupid, and in many ways, they're right. But when it came to manipulating people to get what I wanted, I was a master of moving the game pieces, offering myself up like some poor, dumb girl, too weak and too scared to do anything about it.

"So, after everything, you just fucked him? It didn't matter to you that we'd had sex the day before? Didn't matter that I was coming back for you with the apparently stupid belief you wanted a relationship with me? Did sex with me mean anything to you? Or was I just another means to an end?"

With a river of questions, he kept backing me farther into the house, my attempt at retreat useless. "Slow down so I can answer you."

My back hit a wall and he towered over me, his eyes boring into mine like he wanted to strip away my skin and bones to pick through my thoughts.

Taking a breath, he closed his eyes, opening them again when he said, "Fine. You're right. I'll slow down, Rainey, but you have to understand why I'm upset. It feels like you intentionally slept with me to get me to submit that report. That, once again, you used your body to get your way."

He wasn't wrong, but how was I supposed to admit that to him? When I first met Justin, I'd hoped that he wouldn't be able to see past our differences, that he would give in and fuck my body, but then turn around and leave like any normal man would do.

I was a fucking mess. I knew that. I'd learned to accept it. But instead of running for the hills like I'd hoped he would do, he came back wanting more.

Just being here with him was dangerous. If he were to get upset and threaten to turn me in, there would be no other choice left than to silence him.

"I didn't intentionally sleep with you. It's not like that. It's just that-"

Justin paced away from me, his hand stabbing through his hair as he scoured his thoughts for any possible reasons or excuses for why I'd jumped from one bed to another.

What he didn't understand is that I would always jump into another bed. He wasn't the type of man who could demand my loyalty. He wasn't the man who owned my heart.

"It's because I didn't get you off, isn't it?"

My eyes widened at the question. Did he really believe I would shove a guy away because I didn't orgasm? Had he listened to my story at all?

284

"It's not that-"

"I think it is."

Stilling in place, he turned to me, his eyes raking down my body with thoughts swirling behind them that weren't good for either of us. I knew that look, had seen it in the eyes of so many men that I could paint a picture of it from memory. Heat brightening the color of his iris while his eyelids became heavy and hooded, his lips parting so he could drag in a deeper breath.

It didn't matter how reasonable and calm the man was. Once they got a taste of a woman that made their bodies sing with lustful desire, all logic flew out the window until they were willing to do just about anything for another taste.

Sex was like a drug that way. It made people do ridiculous things on a daily basis. It was almost as potent a drug as hatred and love.

I didn't think Justin loved me, but from the looks of him, he was craving another kind of fix.

"You know what? Fuck this, I'll show you what I can do for your body."

He ate the distance between us with two long strides, his hands cupping the back of my head as his mouth slanted against mine. It was a habit for me to open up to the kiss, my heart picking up speed as my legs weakened.

Rowan had once told me that there are people out there who are addicted to sex. It was in the psychology books he'd studied, an actual bona fide condition that led them to behaving dangerously, to having multiple partners, to cheating on their spouses because no matter how much they had, it was never enough. Rowan had believed it was possible that was my problem, the reason why I was always spreading my legs so easily. I'd laughed at the thought because the truth for me was far more simple.

Sex was a tool, one I'd learned to wield in order to get by in life.

It wasn't that I always wanted it, dreamed about, craved it as much as I did a joint or a beer. No matter how many times I tried to explain it to him, he wasn't convinced. I guess it didn't help much that after I'd started sleeping with him, I was an addict – but only for him.

I don't think he understood that the way I loved him was not the way I slept with other people.

Justin apparently didn't understand that either, not with the desperate way his tongue danced across mine, not with the speed of his hands in their attempt to pull away my towel. He was playing with fire and even if I warned him, I highly doubted he would care.

He was in too deep, his body pressing against mine as his hand gripped the edge where my towel was tucked together, pulling it open to let the terry cloth fall to the floor.

This was dangerous, both for him and for me.

"God, you have no clue how good your body feels." He spoke against my cheek, his fingers exploring between my legs as he palmed the weight of my breast. The back of my head fell against the wall, my mouth opening to warn him to stop because he had no idea what he was doing.

He wasn't the first man who wanted me, wasn't the first one to hope I would be his alone.

"Justin-"

"Shhh. Please, Rainey, let me show you."

His mouth was on mine again, moans pouring from his throat as he slid two fingers inside me to discover I was wet. "God, you want me, I can feel it."

Fighting to undo the button of his pants and slide down the zipper, he shoved the material from his hips, his cock hard and ready to go. My hands wrapped over his shoulders, my head turning in an attempt to break his kiss and talk, but he was determined to prove to me that he was the man who would get me off. What he didn't understand was that making me come wouldn't matter. It wouldn't change anything in the end.

He wasn't the man for me.

I wasn't the girl for him.

And if he kept pushing to change the way things had to be, it would end in heartache, pain and blood.

"Justin, stop-"

He lifted my legs to wrap them around his waist, his mind so focused on what he intended to do that I don't think he heard me.

Notching the tip of his cock between my legs, he looked at me with adoration in his eyes.

I shook my head, one last plea to make him understand that this couldn't happen.

"Please," I said, "you have to stop."

His expression fell, rejection blending with the desire. "Tell me you don't want this."

Our eyes locked as I tried to warn him with just a look, but he couldn't understand – *wouldn't* understand – what I was trying to tell him.

It was too late regardless.

He'd pushed too far.

Had woken a beast that would destroy every person who threatened my ability to move on.

Opening my mouth, I released one last tremulous breath before cupping my hands around his face. "Justin, I'm sorry."

Blood splattered my chest as both our bodies fell to the floor, pain shooting up my tailbone and spine as a crimson puddle formed where he fell.

CHAPTER TWENTY-SIX

Justin - Present

The first sensation I had as my eyes cracked open was pain. Throbbing, expanding, a hammer knocking against the inside of my skull as a dull ache burned along my neck from the odd bent angle. Lips parting, a breath hissed over them as light seeped into my eyes, the room around me blurred at the edges, my body sitting prone in a chair.

A groan crawled up my throat, my head falling back as liquid trickled down my temple, cold and sticky.

Muffled, a husky voice I recognized caught my attention, but I couldn't focus my eyes enough to make out the dark mass sitting in front of me.

Blinking rapidly, I fought to remember where I was, fought to understand why every inch of my body was tingling and numb. I couldn't move my arms, understanding of how I was positioned slowly rising to the surface as I floated from the depths of nothing into consciousness.

Rainey and I had been pressed against her wall, flashes of memory coming to me. A white terry cloth towel. God, I was so angry. Hurt, my mind not accepting that she'd lied and used me.

Why couldn't I move my legs? Why were my arms pulled behind my back, tied at the wrists? Who was sitting in front of me?

"I tried to warn you, Justin. I asked you to leave."

Rainey.

I would recognize that voice anywhere.

"Wha-"

My throat burned with the attempt to speak, my head lolling back as I struggled to remain conscious. The palm of a hand cupped my head pulling it forward, my lips pressed against a glass rim.

"Drink this. You've been out for a while."

Choking on the cool liquid, I pushed back, the skin torn and burning at my wrists, my ankles secured to the legs of the chair. With bleary eyes, I stared ahead, attempting to bring her face into focus.

My immediate thought was that someone had broken into her home, panic setting in with the rapid beat of my heart, the labored inhalation of breath. "Are you okay?"

Voice gritty over the question, I blinked rapidly to bring the room into focus beyond the blue eyes that stared at me. I didn't recognize the plain white walls and sparse furniture covered in sheets. "Where are we?"

She didn't answer, her mouth tilting down at the corners. "I didn't want this to happen. Not to you. But you kept pushing me and you wouldn't listen."

Another wave of pain when I attempted to shake my head of the fog clouding my thoughts. "Rainey, what happened?"

"I tried to tell you," she hissed, her voice a mix of venom and regret. "Tried to warn you that you needed to go, but you wouldn't stop talking. Wouldn't stop trying to take something that didn't belong to you."

She was framed in on either side by bright windows at her back. The panes were dirty and broken, sunlight flooding the room with such strength that I could only see her silhouette. Shadows painted her face and body, hair long and messy at the sides of her head.

Smoke wafted up from where she sat watching me.

"I thought you quit."

She snorted, the laugh more bitter than funny. "I can quit whenever I want, Doc. The problem is you seem to have a problem doing the same."

"Where are we, Rainey? Why does my head hurt so bad?"

Silence enveloped us except for the deep drag of her lungs, the exhalation creating a cloud of smoke that danced and swirled around her.

"Why am I tied up, Rainey?"

Not answering immediately, Rainey shifted in her seat, one leg crossing over the other. Within the shadow, I could see the strap of her dress hanging down over her arm, the skirt flowing down at the sides of her seat, still waving from her movement. As my thoughts came into clear focus, my pulse picked up in speed until it was thunder in my head, the steady *woosh-woosh-woosh* a counterpoint to the sound of Rainey smoking.

A deep sigh as she brushed the hair from her face and shook her head. "I wanted to tell you the rest of the story. I think if you'd listened, you would have understood why coming back to my house was the worst decision you could make. Damn it, Justin, I warned you, and you wouldn't listen. You can only blame yourself."

It's hard to remain calm when hit over the head and tied to a chair, hard to think logically when the slow crawl of understanding settles in. Was it possible that the entire interview had only been a game? Had the murderer been staring me in the face intent on seducing me into playing her game?

Four days ago and I wouldn't have believed her capable of such long-running deceit, yet here I sat, bound and helpless, while she took her time to sit and watch me.

"I can leave now, Rainey. There's still time for you to let me go."

More laughter. "Ah, Doc. I wish it was that easy." Her toe slid against the floor, the sun setting just enough to balance the light and bring her body into view.

The sun was setting.

It had been dark when I arrived at her house.

"How long have we been here?"

Canting her head, she blinked her eyes, the color still concealed by shadow. "A few hours. I couldn't keep you at my house. Someone may have seen your car if they'd driven by. There's been cops in the area since you turned in your report. It's as if they're looking for somebody."

It took effort to keep my voice calm, effort to appear unaffected when I was screaming inside. "They're looking for the man who's stalking you."

"I'm not being stalked," she answered as smoke poured over her lips. "I told you that, but you didn't want to believe me."

Pausing, a bark of laughter burst from her lips. "You truly believed I was a victim didn't you? It didn't matter that I told you how wrong you were. Like a dog with a bone, you'd clamped down on that opinion and refused to let it go. What were you planning on doing? Save me? Take me away from my horrible life that you believed would destroy me after a while?" Another laugh.

"Fuck, Doc, and here I thought you were the smart one between us."

Despite what she was saying, there were still factors that didn't add up. "Are we being held against our will?"

"We?" She shook her head. "No. Not we. You."

"Why?"

She stood up from the seat, the chair legs scraping over the ground from the force of her sudden movement. The skirt danced around her thighs as she paced in front of me, the scent of lavender and smoke mixing in the air between us.

"I think I should tell you the rest of the story."

Control was slipping from me as she walked back and forth, her bare feet wearing a rut into the trash littered floor. Where the fuck were we?

With my head throbbing a steady pulse and my vision still fading at the corners, I tested my hands and feet on the ropes binding me in place, the legs of the chair tilting with my effort.

"Stop that, Justin. It won't help. All you'll do is tip over."

Reality was setting in, the need to rip these fucking ropes apart so I could escape whatever hell she'd dragged me into. "Get me out of this goddamned chair."

She stopped, her head snapping left to look at me. "I'm afraid I can't do that."

Another wave of adrenaline poured into my body, fight or flight taking hold until logic dissipated entirely and I was struggling like an animal trapped.

Her hands clamped down on my shoulders, her dark hair brushing across my face. "Please stop. You're not making this easier."

"Then let me the fuck go. I've done nothing to you. Not a fucking thing but listen."

Refusing to be reduced to unhelpful tears, I took a deep breath and reached for everything I knew about hostage situations. I had to speak to her on a level she could understand, break through to her somehow to get her to identify and regret my suffering. I had to calm down before I lost control entirely and only pissed her off more.

Still, there were questions, her ability to incapacitate me and drag me to this new place not making sense.

"How did you do this? There's no possible way you could have lifted my weight."

Wood creaked as she retook her seat, that damn strap of her dress still hanging over her shoulder.

"I'm going to finish the story, Justin. If you hear the rest of it, you'll know why it all had to come to this."

Uninterested in her story, I grit my teeth and allowed my head to fall back, a fresh burst of pain rolling down my spine and over my skull.

The wound was in the back of my head, that much I could tell, but whether I was still bleeding was up in the air. How could I be? Judging by the dying light, I'd been knocked unconscious for close to twenty-four hours.

"If I listen to the rest of your story, will you let me go?"

Silence. One beat, two…

Rainey glanced above my head, the sweetest smile I'd ever seen in her expression sliding over her lips. Eyes soft, she didn't speak as heavy footsteps approached me.

I stilled in place, my head turning as much as it could so I could see who was in the room with us. On my left, a man rounded my chair to stand at Rainey's side.

Her neck craned to look up at him, hand lifting to take his and allow him to pull her to her feet.

Staring straight ahead, I waited silently for him to slap her on the ass and whisper in her ear before taking the seat in her place.

It answered how she'd brought me here, how she'd managed to knock me out while naked and pressed against a wall.

I recognized his face immediately, my eyes unblinking as he hunched over in his seat to rest his elbows on his knees, the bill of his baseball cap shading the color of his eyes.

"We meet again," he said, hands dangling between his spread knees, lips kicking up into a grin at the corners.

Shaking his head slightly, he met my stare. "I tried to tell you, man. Rainey's taken. But you just wouldn't listen, would you?"

A burst of laughter. "Ah, hell, it's not like I can blame you. She's like a drug, my girl. Always calling you back into her orbit no matter what fucked up thing she does."

Shrugging a shoulder, he reached to scrub his knuckles across his jaw. "What's a man to do, you know?"

For the first time, true fear bled into my veins, my shoulders tense despite the pain, my lips parted on shallow breath.

"Who are you?"

Reaching toward me, he offered his hand, laughed again and pulled it back. "Forgot you're a bit tied up at the moment. The name's Graham Pike. I think you and I may have met a time or two by now. I'm not sure on the exact amount, to be honest."

My thoughts raced through my mind, a tempest storm brewing that short-circuited my ability to stay rational and not give in to panic.

"We have," I said, my throat too dry over the words.

Graham smiled, the wolfish expression reveling in the moment. Relaxing back against his seat, he reached up with both hands to curl the bill of his baseball cap, shove it up enough that the shadows no longer concealed his eyes.

"You know, I hate that it had to come to this."

His biceps flexed beneath the short sleeves of his white cotton shirt, hands resting atop his head as he studied me. "I'm not a bad man, I want you to understand that first. There were simply too many issues that had to be resolved, too many...I don't know...roadblocks. You weren't one of them. Well, not a few days ago, anyway. But now?"

Shaking his head, he whistled softly. "Now you are because you just couldn't take no for an answer. That kind of shit really pisses me off."

My body was doused in cold terror, but I refused to give in, refused to accept that this man would do to me what I now believed he'd done to four other people.

"You can let me go, Graham. I won't say a word. I won't-"

His laughter cut me off, blue eyes dancing with a glimmer of psychosis.

Rationalizing with a killer wasn't in my repertoire of skills, but without a better option, I had to hope that humanizing myself to him – meeting him on some level he could understand – would convince him to let me leave this place with my life intact.

"Don't play with me, Doc. You know I can't let you go."

The front legs of his chair lifted off the ground, the back legs scraping to balance as he leaned back. Long jean-clad legs stretched out in the space between us. My eyes darted to a bandage on his arm in the same place where Rainey's mark had been carved.

"Tell me why I'm here. Perhaps we can work something out."

The corner of his lip twitched, hard eyes boring down on me with condescension.

"You wouldn't listen. There's not much more to tell than that. Rainey had a story to tell, and you brushed it off because you couldn't wait to get into her pants. I think that's a problem with men these days, don't you? Too many of them are so interested in what's going on with their dicks that they refuse to take the time to hear a woman out. Makes me a little sick to think about it. And sadly, it doesn't even matter what walk of life the man comes from. They can live in the gutters or, like you, have come from a nice place in life. Doesn't make a lick of difference. A pretty girl walks by and all they can think about is what dirty things can be done with her body."

I shook my head, the pain from where my skull had been split flaring to life, a heavy, unbearable thud. "No. That wasn't my intention. Rainey came on to me-"

"That's what they all say."

Throwing up his hands, he brought them down on his thighs with a sharp slap.

"And maybe they're right. My girl has a tendency to believe that the only thing special about her is that tight fucking body, but still, it doesn't give a man the right to treat her like a cheap fuck. You went for the gold. And I can't blame you for that, but your lack of foresight will cost you. She played you the first time to get that report

297

submitted exactly as she wanted it, but then you came back."

He laughed, his eyes tracking over my shoulder, where I assumed Rainey was standing.

"She told you to leave. I told you to leave. But your dick was like a leash leading a dog. Back you came. And how did I find you? With your pants shoved down around your thighs and my girl naked as the day she was born pressed up against a wall."

A heavy breath poured over his lips, his gaze still locked on Rainey. "Hate to tell you this, brother, but that just won't do."

The cold permeated every cell inside me, a sense of foreboding causing my heart to beat with heavy, uncoordinated thumps, my lungs fighting to drag in every shaky inhale.

"There has to be some way we can work this out."

Nodding, he leaned forward in his seat, the front legs clapping down on the floor. "You already had that chance. Really, the only reason you're still alive is Rainey. For some damn reason, she wants to finish the story she was telling you. I tried to make her understand that none of it matters, but here we are."

On cue, Rainey moved around the side of me to stand next to Graham, her hand reaching to wrap over the back of his neck as he tilted his head to press his cheek against the inside of her arm.

"Let me tell him," she said. "He deserves to know."

Clearing my throat, I spoke past the knot clogging my throat. "Know what?"

Turning her head to look at me, she gave me a sad smile. "To know why everything had to happen like it did. To know why you're in that chair now tied up like

298

you are. I didn't want this, Justin, but you gave us no choice."

Holding her stare, I spoke with us much certainty as I could. "Rainey, he's a murderer. You need to leave this house now and get as far away as you can."

More than likely, my fate was sealed, but she could still escape. She could still turn this man in for everything I now understood he'd done.

Graham stood from the seat and stepped aside to let Rainey sit down. Her hair fell at the sides of her face, her blue eyes soft with sympathy.

"Will you just hear me out? Please?"

What the hell else was I going to do? I was tied in place, hostage and helpless to whatever they wanted to do to me.

"If I listen, will you convince him to let me go?"

She sucked her bottom lip between her teeth before answering, "I think you need to hear this first, and then you'll understand."

CHAPTER TWENTY-SEVEN

Rainey - Past

The neighborhood wasn't the same after Jacob and Paul died. The only Connor left in the house next door was Frankie and I had already learned my lesson about messing around with him.

It didn't take long for him to take up as the newest drug dealer, and without having to share customers with his dad or brothers, I assumed it did pretty well for him. There were always people coming and going, wild parties being thrown where the music would pump so loud it shook the windows of my house.

Several nights, I sat outside on my front porch to smoke a cigarette and would see women leaving, their hair a mess and their bodies moving with a funny limp.

Apparently, Frankie never changed, still as rough as I remembered him. I wasn't willing to go there, though. The pot wasn't worth it, the escape any drugs could give not enough to make me risk abusing my body in order to have it.

That doesn't mean I didn't crave the high. I just didn't know where to get it. Other than my neighbors, I'd never taken the time to get to know anybody else in the area.

Depression settled in pretty quickly when I thought about all that had happened and all that I'd lost. There wasn't a day that went by I didn't think of Rowan and regret losing him the most.

Every night, I glanced up at the sky and knew that the brightest star was the love of my life. I spent hours finding him, hours wishing that I could take back all the choices that led to the night he died.

Maybe if I'd listened to him, he would be sitting beside me.

Maybe if I'd hated everybody around us as much as he did, I would have waited long enough for him to take me away.

So many maybes.

So many regrets.

And there wasn't a damn thing I could do to make up for them.

If anybody carried the weight of his death on their shoulders, it was me – a weight that was far too heavy for me to hold my head up high and continue living like I hadn't had the world in the palm of my hands, only to toss it away for nothing.

I think I'd worn an imprint of my ass into the cement step of my porch for as many nights as I sat there thinking about Rowan. People would pass by and wave, men mostly, tossing me curious stares before deciding not to approach.

My reputation left me open to various offers. Mostly for sex, like I was some pathetic prostitute who didn't know any better.

Fuck them all.

It was on one such night that I was sitting in my ass worn imprint when a man walked by. Wearing a pair of jeans, a white t-shirt and a ball cap, he slowed when passing my house. As usual, I looked up at him wondering when he'd wave, whether he'd approached, if he'd get mad when I told him to take a hike. He stopped for several seconds staring across the weeds of my yard without lifting a hand or calling out to me.

I'd walked outside around midnight, thought maybe I'd been there for an hour judging by the amount of new cigarette butts at my feet. It made me nervous to think that some stranger was prowling around my house, staring at me like he was starving and I was his next meal.

He must have stood there for five minutes, unmoving, not giving a damn that I was staring straight at him. Figuring I should be the one to give ground, I pushed to my feet and walked inside, making sure to lock the door behind me.

Nothing usually scared me in Clayton Heights, but after Joel's death, not to mention Jacob's and Paul's, I made a feeble attempt at safety. Without any clue who had killed them and why, I wondered if, maybe, I was next on the list. I couldn't imagine what for, but people were crazy.

Glancing down at my arm, I touched the scar someone had carved into my flesh after carrying me home. Four tally marks lined side by side perfectly. I didn't understand what they meant or why someone would have cut them into my skin.

A shiver crawled up my spine to think I'd been so out of it that night that a stranger had been able to carry me and put me in my bed, so fucking numb that I hadn't woken screaming when a knife was being dragged down my arm.

Shaking my head, I moved into the living to look out the window and discover that the man had moved along.

Although it was getting late and we were moving into the early morning hours, I couldn't sleep. Thankfully, I didn't have work the next day, so I sat on my couch and turned on the television, something I didn't do very often.

With my feet kicked up and remote in hand, I flipped through the few free local channels I could find, nothing grabbing my attention.

At that hour, it was mostly infomercials selling unnecessary inventions to a group of people that couldn't figure out how to do the simplest things. In a way, these long running ads were funnier than most comedy shows, just because it was hard to believe people were so stupid.

A glare fell on the screen within the next few minutes, as bright as sunlight pouring through the small window behind me. Confused, I pushed up on my elbows to peer over the back of the couch, my eyes widening into saucers to see the source of that light.

"Holy shit..."

I was on my feet in seconds, racing across the living room to clutch my hands on the window ledge, not believing the amount of red hot flames shooting high into the sky. The Connor's house was ablaze, thick black smoke rolling across my yard like fog, a plume of it rising into the sky.

Immediately I wondered if Frankie was home, if he was trapped within the flames or had made it to safety.

Running outside, I choked on the thick fumes, waving my hand in front of my face. It did nothing to clear the air in front of me. Racing forward, a wave of heat singed my skin when I approached the chain link fence separating our properties.

"Frankie!"

Screaming as loud as I could, I had to retreat. God, I hoped he was okay. Frankie and I had never really been friends, but nobody deserved to die by burning. Just the thought of it brought tears to my eyes, only because I knew that Rowan had died the same way.

I was back on my porch when I turned to see neighbors outside their houses, their faces illuminated by the light of their phones, some of them holding them in the air to take pictures. In the distance, the first sirens blared through the night, racing down the highway toward our neighborhood.

Unable to breathe, I retreated farther, letting myself into the house before racing back to the window to see if I could find Frankie running from the house. A shadow darted in my peripheral vision, my head craning left as a man ran away at full speed.

Once the fire trucks were on scene, powerful streams of water sprayed the house. They must have battled the blaze for hours. Every so often, I'd walk back to the window in an attempt to look through the mix of smoke and steam, but the night was too dark, the smoke too thick for me to see anything.

There wasn't a damn thing I could do for Frankie. Still, my heart felt heavy, urgency coursing through me to do *something*.

I wouldn't know much until the daylight hours and I went to bed, curling under my blankets to cry myself to sleep.

The house would be gone in the morning. The family I'd known. Everything erased as if it had never existed in the first place.

For some reason the loss of the house hit me harder than the deaths of Joel, Jacob and Paul. Rowan's room was in that house. His things. All left there in the same place as the day he last walked through the door never to return again.

Even though I hadn't seen that room in several months, I took comfort knowing it was still there.

Head heavy on the pillow, I didn't sleep. Tears soaked the pillowcase, my body drifting into a half sleep that left me floating. The memories were coming on too strong, images of a beautiful boy with big blue eyes and a smile that lit me up from the inside as if I somehow swallowed the sun.

My brightest star. He was above my head, his twinkle concealed by smoke, his light erased by what remained of his home rising up into the cosmos as embers and dust.

Inside my house, the silence was deafening. The sirens long gone. The sizzle of water meeting fire absent.

But then, that same silence was broken by a scream.

Time caught up, a hand covered my mouth.

I was stripped from the ether and brought back to reality by the heavy weight holding me down.

"Hey, it's okay. Stop screaming."

Nothing was making sense to me. All I knew was that someone was in my room, the darkness too thick to reveal a face, his hand so big it was covering my mouth and nose.

"Rainey, stop, damn it."

My legs kicked and my arms came up in the attempt to shove the man away. Nothing I did could budge him. He was too big, too heavy, too strong.

My thoughts went to the stranger outside staring at me, my eyes blinking rapidly at the sound of my name.

"Stop. It's okay. I'm not here to hurt you."

That voice…

I knew it.

God, how I knew that voice.

Stilling in place, my breath was shallow beneath the heat of his hand, my cheeks wet from the tears that leaked from my eyes. Heart hammering in my throat, I stayed silent waiting for him to pull his palm away so I could breathe deeply again.

Body heavy against mine, he shifted his weight, the woodsy scent of a man's cologne colliding against my senses.

Fear and hope surged through me, my mind trying to make sense of the impossible.

Pulling his hand free, the man leaned his head down to run the tip of his nose along my jaw, his lips pressing against my ear to whisper, "I promised you I'd find you, Rainey. Promised you I'd take care of you. That I'd protect you. That I'd love you more than you could love yourself."

My head shook, disbelief assaulting me because there was no way in hell this could be happening. I refused to accept it. Refused to believe that -

Oh, God, is it possible?

"Rowan and Rainey forever. I wasn't lying when I told you that."

Five promises.

This man, this impossibility, somehow knew every single one.

My mind couldn't make sense of it, fresh tears leaking from my eyes as I closed them and stopped struggling to make sense of what was happening.

I think, in the end, even without knowing if it was true or not, I wanted a few minutes to lie there and pretend.

Reaching up, I cupped the man's cheeks between my palms, pulling his head down with undeniable desperation to see his face. It was too dark, the light of the moon concealed by the lingering smoke, an abyss where none of us were seen or existed.

It was possible to pretend, possible to spend time with a dream, with a ghost, a memory that couldn't be here no matter how much I missed him.

"Rowan?"

"Rainey," he whispered back, a smile written into the tone of his voice.

Breath shuddered in my chest, my hands gripping so tight to his face in an effort to keep him from disappearing.

Soft laughter shook his chest, his hands burrowing into my hair as his mouth brushed my lips, an invitation to forget that the moment was a figment of my imagination and become lost to the sensation of loving him again.

Our mouths pressed tighter together, his tongue sweeping out to tangle with mine. I lost the ability to breathe, but didn't give a damn because my heart was racing too fast, my head swimming in fog.

Writhing beneath him, I welcomed the feel of his hands on my body, his palm traveling down the side to tug up my shirt and take a possessive hold of my breast. Arching into the touch, I thought I'd died without knowing it, that despite all the horrible things I'd done, the universe had forgiven me and allowed me to be a star right beside him.

His kiss was my absolution.

His touch, a drug that I'd always understood I could never live without.

He was a part of me, this man, a phantom that had found me when I didn't know I was lost.

Too afraid that it would end, that Rowan would evaporate to be blown away like dust, I didn't ask questions, just allowed my body to be loved by him even if it would kill me when the sun next rose and I learned he had been a dream.

Breaking our kiss, Rowan pressed his forehead against mine, his breath hot against my face as his hands explored my body with the same desperation I had for him.

A soft whisper over my skin, a tremor rushing up my spine to hear it. "Can I touch you, Rainey?"

The tears wouldn't stop pouring from my eyes. Nodding my head, I could barely speak around the knot in my throat. "You can touch me, Rowan. You can touch me forever as long as you swear to me you'll never stop."

It didn't matter if I was crazy. If this is what it meant to snap, then I hoped when they tossed me in that padded room, when they locked my arms down with a straitjacket, that whatever drugs they pumped in my body would be useless to bring me back.

I thought of all the tragic love stories in the world where one person is gone while the other dies slowly. Your heart can beat on. Your lungs will continue to inflate, but when the person you love the most is gone, the truth is that you die right there beside them.

When people looked at me, they didn't see the hollow vacancy beneath my skin. Their eyes perceived the shell, but not the rot that formed in place. I had been dying from the inside out since the night that Rowan left this world, and if it took a hallucination to bring him back, then I was happy to be insane.

How many other people would give anything just to have one more hour with the love that they'd lost?

How many would gladly go back in time to die in their place?

It should have been me in that car because I deserved the pain of fire.

But then, I was never the star, was I?

Not me.

While I blended so perfectly within shadow, it was his light that had brightened the way, his light that had blinded my eyes until I could see only him.

Lips trailed soft kisses down my neck as I whispered into the darkness.

"Tell me this is real, Rowan. Lie to me if only for a little while. Let me believe that it's possible to feel your body against mine again."

Another laugh, his chest pushing up so he could pull my shirt off. I lifted my arms to let him strip it from me entirely and toss it away.

Mouth brushing against mine, he whispered, "This is real, beautiful. I've been watching over you since the day I died."

This is real…

It couldn't be.

But it was.

Insanity had never tasted so sweet.

His mouth closed over my nipple, tongue sweeping over the taut peak as his fingertips dragged down my hips to pull off my sleep shorts and panties. I was in too much of a rush to have him inside me, my legs falling apart as my nails dragged down to the ridges and dips of his muscular back.

Rowan teased me with playful fingers, slipping between my legs to roll over my clit, my hips bucking in need of more, his voice soft against my ear on a laugh.

"I'm taking my time, Rainey. Do you know how long I've waited to come back to you? Do you have any fucking idea how hard it has been to stay away?"

His finger slipped inside me and a moan crawled up my throat, my body stilling in place as heat expanded in radiant waves all through me.

Fuck, I couldn't breathe, emotions a maelstrom surging through me, my eyes burning from the amount of tears I'd shed.

"Please, Rowan, just this once. I need you inside me. I need-"

Silencing me with a kiss, he hovered over me, his body moving as he shoved down his jeans and settled his hips between my legs. Gripping my hips in his strong hands, he notched himself at my pussy, swept his tongue against mine and thrust his cock inside.

My chest arched forward, my head falling back as I lost all sense of time and place to feel him moving against me, his hands holding me in place while his hips danced a carnal rhythm of lust and love, desire and passion, that primal and powerful connection that was a gift of nature.

It didn't take long for pleasure to overtake me, his name a prayer on my lips, a climax that stole my breath away with such violence that all I could do was hold on so it wouldn't break me.

I didn't care if I'd wake in the morning to discover this moment was just a dream. Didn't give a damn about the horrors that life had always tossed at me and the consequences of the choices I'd made.

All that mattered as I held on to a sweet boy who had grown into the man I never knew I needed was that I could show him I loved him even if I knew he'd leave.

Any person would do the same in my position.

And if you try to claim I'm wrong, then you've never lost a person who was a part of your soul.

This moment...

This phantom...

This impossibility...

If it took being crazy to love him, then I hoped to God I would never regain sanity again.

CHAPTER TWENTY-EIGHT

Justin – Present

My first thought was that her level of insanity explained why she couldn't remember the night her friends died.

In a perpetual fugue state brought on by mental trauma, Rainey was obviously delusional, her mind so desperate to believe that the love of her life had somehow returned, she was oblivious to reality, to truth, to the events that occurred around her on a daily basis, making it impossible for her to separate what was real from what was a figment of her imagination.

I should have seen it. Should have picked up on the clues. Should have stopped being distracted by a body that spoke to me in the most primal of ways to take a second and diagnose her condition.

Clearing my throat, I attempted to speak, but my mouth was too dry and sticky to pronounce a single word.

Rainey sat across from me, her eyes widening with recognition as she stood up to fetch a glass of water to offer. Holding the rim to my lips, she was careful to tip it slowly, although I couldn't understand why.

As far as I saw it, she had no problem letting her boyfriend knock me out and tie me to a chair; what harm would a few drops of spilled water cause?

Pulling away to let her know when I was done, I took a few seconds to allow the liquid to ease the fire in my throat.

"Rainey..."

Fuck, how could I make her understand that the man standing beside her wasn't Rowan?

Retaking her seat, she asked, "Do you understand now, Doc? The universe brought him back to me. I don't understand it myself, not all the details, at least, but he's here, in the flesh. I can put my palm against his chest and feel his heart beat. I can lie awake at night and watch his eyelids move with dreams. He came back to me, and no matter what he's done - no matter what I had to do to prove my love to him - we're together now. Forever, just like he always said we would be. You have to understand. You have to admit that it's the perfect end to the tragedy of our story."

I understood a few things, actually. First and foremost was that the guy pretending to be someone he couldn't possibly be was taking advantage of a very sick woman.

Glancing at his face, I knew he would kill me for telling the truth, but then it was likely I was a dead man regardless. Perhaps I could plant a small seed in her brain that would make her question this impossible reality.

"Rainey, I'm not sure how much you know about the night Rowan died, but there is no possible way he's alive. They identified his body through DNA. That's not something that can be faked. I don't know who this man is, or why he's claiming he's Rowan, but you need to stop and think about what you're doing."

Graham, or fake Rowan, or whoever the fuck he was at the moment tapped Rainey on the shoulder and offered his hand to help her stand. "Babe, why don't you go in the other room and let Justin and I talk? I'm not sure he'll believe the truth of all this unless I'm the one to give it to him."

Slowly, Rainey padded barefoot from the room, casting me one last look before she was out of sight.

313

Graham took the seat facing me, his mouth pulled into a smirk as his blue eyes locked with mine.

"DNA, huh? Yeah, that's a hard one to work around, but if you're inventive enough, you find ways."

"Why are you doing this to her?" Adrenaline was rushing through me again, anger for what he was doing to a woman who wasn't in a state of mind to know any better. With no way to move, my arms shook under the force of it, the chair beneath me shaking.

He grinned at the noise, his eyes slipping down to glance at the legs scraping against the floor.

"Doc, listen. I hate to break it to you but you're the one who doesn't know better. I go by the name Graham now, but that's the part of the story Rainey wasn't there to witness."

His eyes returned to my face, so certain that what he had done was right he didn't so much as blink in response to my panic.

"Have you ever loved a woman, Doc?"

He scratched his chin before lifting his arms again to rest them on top of his head. Almost twice my size, it would be no problem for him to drag me down if I managed to escape.

"I mean, really loved her? Not the hearts and flowers crap that most men do, the meaningless, and quite frankly, lazy method of showing her what she means to you. Rainey is worth more than that. Always has been."

Smiling, he stretched back, returned his hands to his lap, and shook his head. "From the first day I met her, I knew. This girl is special, I thought. Like a ray of sunshine. She didn't belong in Clayton Heights, that was for damn sure. Yet, there she was, sitting on her porch waving back at me even though she didn't know my name, my age, the hell I lived in. Nothing. She

314

knew nothing. I thought I'd fallen in love when I first saw her face, but when she smiled I truly understood what the word meant."

This man certainly knew the story, but it was entirely possible Rainey had told him the same meandering, twisted tale she'd told me. There was no way to know. Not with what he'd said so far. Tugging at the ropes at my wrist, I realized they weren't budging, but that didn't mean I wouldn't try.

"Anyway," he continued, unconcerned that I would break free, "I fell in love, like I said. Not just love, hell...I looked at that woman and spent every day of my life learning exactly what she needed in life. The drugs were just an escape, the men she slept with a means to an end, and while she mistreated her body by giving it up, I watched and I waited. I am who I am because of her, and every promise I made, I meant. People are so quick to toss out promises. Nothing but empty words, really. Mine weren't. They're eternal, unbreakable."

Five promises, to be exact. The mark on her arm made sense.

"You meant them so much, you carved them on her body. How in the hell can you call that love?"

The corner of his lips quirked.

"She let me carve the last one the morning after Frankie died. Five deaths. Five promises. I'd fulfilled every one. To love her is a given, but to protect her, I needed to do the one thing she couldn't do herself. I broke her free of a nasty habit that was slowly destroying the woman I loved."

Canting his head, he smiled. "Come on, even you have to admit those assholes deserved it. What they did to her? The advantage they took? Over and over and over until she'd grown so used to it that she no longer considered it wrong. And her stepfather," another shake of his head, "he deserved worse than he got."

Okay, well, yeah. I could agree with him on that.

"I don't deserve this."

Holding up a finger, he said, "Give me a second. I'm working up to what brought us to this particular moment."

With his long legs stretched in front of him, he asked, "Now where was I? Oh. Right. My family deserved to die. The truth was they would continue using women, selling drugs, or in Frankie's case, beating the hell out of people for fun. Did you know Joel would get high school girls drunk just so he could fuck them? That's rape, Doc. Young girls who are too naïve to understand what's happening to them, and he kept getting away with it. Our legal system is seriously fucked up. But that's neither here nor there. The point is I didn't feel sorry for taking them out."

Behind him, full night had settled over the horizon. A single bulb above our heads the only light in the space. It cast shadows under his cheekbones, lent an eerie mask to the face of the man who had every intention of ending my life.

Sweat trickled down my temples, my vision still blurring from the head wound I'd suffered.

"You know, it's funny. My high school had elective programs for the kids who had decent grades. Had I stuck around long enough to graduate, I would have been at the top of my class. One of those electives was Introduction to Forensics. It was intended as a jumping block, an overview into a possible career path we could follow." He laughed.

"I mean, talk about dumb, the class gave me just enough knowledge to be dangerous. Seriously. They just hand that information to teenagers." A shake of his head.

"It took some time to set it all up, but the night I died, I invited some poor idiot to the house. The guy had no family and was new to the area. He asked to borrow a toothbrush, which we just happened to have extras. So, I saw it as an opportunity. I had money saved up, enough to get some new clothes and keep me going for a few months, so after he was finished brushing his teeth, I pocketed my toothbrush and replaced it with his. You're not wrong that the DNA was a match to the body in the car because the toothbrush my family handed over wasn't mine.

"After he died, I took over his identity, never returned to the shitty job he had, took his personal documents I found in his apartment to have a new driver's license made, and ta-da...The world now knows me as Graham Pike. Easy as that."

Jesus Christ...

"Why?"

Sure, his story was possible, but I couldn't understand his reasoning. "Why not just convince Rainey to leave?"

Rowan shrugged.

"She wouldn't go. And I had some promises to fulfill. I wanted every one of those bastards to pay for what they did to her, but I couldn't do it as Rowan. If I were caught and went to prison, Rainey would never forgive herself. She would carry that blame for the rest of her life, just like she carried the blame for my death. If I died trying to avenge her, it would have destroyed her more than a car accident. No. I wanted to make sure every one of them was in the ground before returning to her. So, I broke into the house, knocked Frankie the fuck out and then lit the place on fire."

His reasoning still wasn't adding up. "After everything she did to push you away, you kill for her? Without even knowing whether she loved you back or not?"

Smiling Rowan scratched his chin. "I knew she loved me. Rainey was simply caught up in too much stuff. But it's not about how much she loved me that mattered. It's about how much I loved her. How much she didn't love herself. I loved her enough for the both of us. And that love was enough for me to move Heaven and Earth to save Rainey from herself. If you've ever felt that way about another person, you would understand."

I didn't doubt the truth of what he was saying. Everything he felt for Rainey was there in his eyes, plain and obvious for all to see.

"You're the one who carried her out of the house the night Paul and Jacob died."

"Someone give this man a medal," he joked. "Did she tell you what she let them do to her? It's not that I don't hold Rainey for partial blame, but what man, what decent person, would do that to a woman?"

"You regret none of it," I observed.

"Nope. Not a single one. Not in my family, at least. I'd be a liar to claim the looks on their faces when they saw me weren't priceless. It was as if I'd risen from the dead. Too bad they didn't have enough time to welcome me home."

I didn't approve of anything he was telling me, but that didn't mean I couldn't understand. While Rainey had told me the story, I was all too pleased to know those men were dead.

"Why the other four? Your family was dead. You had Rainey. You could have just left and nobody would have known."

Glancing at the doorway to the room where Rainey had wandered off, Rowan answered, "That, well, that wasn't planned actually. As usual, Rainey had run off to do something stupid. She left me with no choice but to take Michael and Preston out. Angel and Megan weren't intentional, they just got in the way. I didn't want them to die."

My brows knit together. "Are you saying Rainey killed all four of those people?"

"No. She doesn't have the strength." Another shrug. "But it's like I said. A man will do anything for the woman he loves. She says jump and you better believe I'll ask how high just to see her smile."

Rainey entered the room, her eyes seeking mine with apology written into the blue depth. Her approach was a slow crawl, long hair partially masking her face. Stepping up beside me, she brought the glass of water to my lips, allowing me to drink deeply before pulling it away.

"Would you like some more? Your throat must hurt. It pains me to hear you talk."

Nodding my head, I hoped like hell that this meant she was reconsidering killing me. Rainey allowed me to drink the rest, the cool liquid extinguishing the fire in my throat.

Her sullen expression didn't last long. The instant she looked at Rowan, her lips pulled into a shy grin, her eyes widening in response to the way he turned, as if she were the only person in the room.

The moment didn't bode well for me, panic taking over as my traitorous chair scuffed the floor with my movement. *Scrape, scrape, scrape…* The legs refusing to budge while I watched a delusional couple eye each other with more love than I'd seen in normal married couples.

Finally crossing the room, she sat on Rowan's lap, reached to pull the ball cap from his head and kissed his forehead with such tenderness it would have been sweet if they weren't homicidal psychopaths.

His hand slid up her thigh, a light tap before he returned his attention to me, a sense of finality hovering between us.

The story was told, everything except for what happened the night four people died, all bludgeoned to death within the walls of a single two story house.

"The bandage on your arm," I said, interrupting their affectionate moment, "are those your promises as well? You carved them into her, so it only made sense to mirror the disfigurement?"

While Rainey leaned over to rest her forehead against the side of his head, Rowan answered, "No. These represent her promises to me."

I wasn't sure I wanted to know. But if you have to die, might as well do so well informed. "And those are?"

"I promise to respect my body." Rainey's husky voice was barely a whisper, her eyes for one man alone. "I promise to love him until the day I die. I promise to believe I'm worth more than what I've let people do to me. I promise to never let another man touch me. And of course, Rowan and Rainey forever."

"You kind of broke one already," he commented, slanting his head up at her.

She rolled her eyes. "I had to for the report."

"Yeah, but then I found you naked against a wall with another man between your legs."

A sigh blew over her lips. "He didn't give me much choice."

Rowan's gaze returned to me. "We should talk about that, actually. She told you to leave. I heard her tell you to stop. But damn if you weren't thinking with your dick."

It wasn't that I was calm when facing the unfortunate truth that my life was ending, it was that the fear had run so deep, my body reached an inertia of sorts, a moment where every muscle and bone had become numb. My life wasn't passing before my eyes, and I wasn't crying or begging to live. It was with calm certainty that I accepted my fate, but that didn't mean I agreed with their reasoning for what I knew they would do.

"A moment of weakness," I admitted, unable to deny what he was saying was incorrect.

"Understandable. Unfortunately, I had a moment of weakness as well. After hitting you, I couldn't exactly leave you there for Rainey to clean up. And here we are. I let you go now and you run to the police to tell them I'm alive and have killed a lot of people. That brings Rainey down along with me, and I will kill again if it means she walks free. I made a promise. I will protect her. I'm sure you can respect that."

In psycho logic, sure, it made sense. But to any rational person, these two were about as sick and demented as they come.

"What happened the night those four people died?"

"I'm not sure you want to know that, Doc."

"Why not."

Rowan grinned. "Because then the story ends with a happily ever after, which means Rainey and I need to ride off into the sunset. I only have two seats on the bike and we ditched your car a while ago. Unfortunately, we won't be able to bring you along for the ride."

A drop of sweat traced a slow trail down the side of my face, along my jaw, hanging on my chin before dropping into my lap. The throbbing in my head got worse. It was possible I had a brain bleed, the slow seeping blood gathering and pressing on my brain. It would explain the dizziness, the waves of nausea, the fogginess of my vision that was only getting worse. Shaking it away did no good. It only worsened the pain. Blinking didn't help either.

"What do you plan to do to me?"

"Don't worry, Justin," Rainey said, "It won't hurt. I wouldn't do that to you, not after the way you helped me."

I asked again. "What do you plan to do?"

Rowan answered. "How are you feeling, Doc? Is the room spinning around you yet? The lights dimming just a touch as everything gets all scrambled inside that head of yours?"

Every muscle in my body went rigid, but not for long. From one second to the next I was drowning in throbbing pain and then so relaxed that nothing seemed to matter.

"You've already done something," I speculated, the room dipping right as I realized what he meant. "The water…"

"Afraid so. But she's right. It won't hurt. She asked me to make sure of it. Soon, it will be nighty night time

322

and you'll wander off into the afterlife while Rainey and I stick around to love each other a little longer.

"Do you really want to know?" Rainey asked. "Before you can't listen any longer. Do you want to know what happened in the house that night?"

I wasn't sure I cared, not with the way the drugs were settling in, not with the way the walls of the room danced around my vision.

Maybe I nodded my head, I wasn't quite sure. Either way, Rowan opened his mouth to tell me.

CHAPTER TWENTY-NINE

Love is pain.

It doesn't matter who you are, where you come from, how you live or what you live for; to love another person is to become them. And I don't mean that in a figurative sense; it's literal.

To love another person is to slip beneath their skin. If they hurt, so do you. If someone attacks them, you've been attacked as well. If they are drowning, your head is being dragged under water right beside them. And if they die, you might as well start digging your own grave because a part of you belongs to the ground.

That is what love is.

That is how I loved Rainey.

For years, I watched her destroy herself. Sure, she'll make you believe she knows what she's doing, and in a way, she does. But she's oblivious in another sense, not quite understanding that she gives away a piece of herself every time she allows a person to use her, to hurt her, to treat her as if she weren't worth her weight in gold.

Because I loved her, because I crawled beneath that beautiful skin to take up residence and experience every heartache, every fear, every wound inflicted on her lovely soul, I couldn't sit around and watch her give us both away to people who didn't deserve us - couldn't sit back and watch those small pieces of her be flung to the dirt and crushed beneath a sick man's sole, not when they were pieces of me as well.

Two years is a long time to remain at a distance. Although I wasn't by her side in the days and months

324

after I supposedly died, I was still very much *there*, could still feel her living and breathing around me, pulsing and expanding, could still experience every pain, ever punishment, every moment she laid her body down to be abused.

Talk about torture, loving that woman up close is hard enough, but to be away from her is the true test of how much you can handle. To miss a smile, to not hear her laughter, to be absent when all I wanted was to be up close? Hell. That was a feat of absolute willpower to stay at a distance. But I did it...for her.

I wonder how many people out there can honestly say they know how it feels to be loved by another person. Judging by the skyrocketing divorce rates, the easy tales of infidelity, the neglect that deteriorates the bonds of so many couples, I would venture to say not many.

Rainey could say she was loved. It just took a while for her to know it.

I'd made that woman promises and she wore them on her skin, but still, I'd given in too soon, gone to her on the night Frankie died and loved her in a way I had never loved another.

It must have destroyed her to wake up and discover I was gone again. While she slept like a damn angel, I slipped away back to the shadows, a demon waiting in the wings, biding my time, giving the world a moment to catch up to what I'd done and move past it.

Still, I watched.

The police had swarmed the neighborhood the following morning, Frankie's body dragged out of that house as crispy and charred as the man I'd killed to start a new life, and I saw Rainey out on her front porch answering questions. Knowing it would happen was why I had to leave because how does one explain that the man who was a part of her had come back to life?

She must have believed I was a dream, and for a few weeks, I had to accept that. Not for long, though.

Not forever.

I should have known better, should have understood it wouldn't take long for men to come sniffing around, should have realized that to break her heart was to send her sliding down a deep ravine from which she would seek an escape.

Rainey had a lot of problems, but the monster she'd created wasn't one of them. I would love her. I would take care of her. I would protect her and I would always find her.

Forever doesn't mean until the end of our lives, it means until the end of eternity.

Off she went, with Megan of all people, a party held in another neighborhood in a house I didn't recognize. Keeping an eye out wasn't difficult. They were unconcerned that the night was dark, the house lights were on and the blinds were open. I was able to count every head inside that small party.

Angel. Michael. Preston. Megan.

None of them were good enough for Rainey.

Not for my girl.
Not for me.

I would have left them alone if Preston hadn't gone tearing out of there to buy some drugs. Fucker talks a lot of shit, his mouth too big for the pinprick of a cock everyone knew he had.

...Drug the bitch and she'll spread for anyone...three, you know? Not that Rainey needs the encouragement...

Smiling at the comment, I waited for him to part company with his friends, stalked off until I was a several feet ahead. Stepping out the shadows, I let him approach.

"Hey, Preston."

He turned, his red stained cheeks puffy beneath bloodshot eyes narrowed in an attempt to recognize me in the low light. "Who the fuck-"

One punch was all it took to flatten his ass over the concrete. I took the GHB he'd purchased in order for Michael and him to run their train on the girls, and walked off, my hands in my pocket without a care in the world.

The fat fuck fought about as good as he fucked. At least, if all the rumors were true.

He woke up eventually, made his way back to the house as pissed as they come. From my perch outside, I watched Angel take him upstairs. Losing Joel must have fucked her all up to sink low enough to spread her legs for Preston.

Joel...It was too bad he was so messed up when I killed him. It would have been nice for him to know that death was coming.

Leaning against a wall, I watched. Megan was hot for Michael, the shy girl she'd once been lost to the passage of time.

An hour passed. Two. Michael didn't look too pleased when his girl passed out, but then he turned to mine.

Dammit, Rainey...

She would never learn, not unless I showed her what it meant to love.

I pushed away from the wall, a ball cap shielding my eyes, the hood of my jacket pulled over that. The dumbasses had left the door open. Anybody could just walk on in, and I was happy to oblige.

Scanning my eyes right, I found Megan sleeping on the couch, her phone on the table beside her. Out like a light, she wasn't a problem, while above my head music pounded from where I assumed Angel and Preston had gone. They weren't too much of an issue in that moment, so I wound my way down a shadowed hall to listen to Rainey and Michael talking.

I don't know about this...

Just shut the fuck up and go along with it...

Nope. Not my girl. She wouldn't be going along with shit.

Backing away, I wandered the house in search of a little help. Eventually discovering a closet near the front door stocked full of sports equipment, I lifted the metal baseball bat, tested its weight, smiled and walked back through the hall.

With a toe against the door, I pushed it open, the hinges making enough noise to draw Michael's attention my way. He didn't see me, not in the shadows.

Shit...Megan's awake.

Untie me, Michael.

No. Just sit tight, I'll see if she wants to join in...

Michael!

The sound of his fist against her face brought Rainey's demon to life.

Feet silent over the floor, I crept back into the living room. Michael emerged from the hall, shirt off, eyes narrowed on Megan where she slept on the couch.

This ended tonight. The games. The drugs. The waiting.

"Hey, Mike."

328

He turned at the sound of my voice, eyes wide, refusing to believe what he was seeing. "Rowan?"

Lips tipping into a grin, I answered. "It's good to see you again. But too bad you're fucking with the wrong girl."

There was no time for him to scream before the bat caught him in the head. Blood splattered the walls, his body dropping before I gave him a few more whacks to remember me by.

Not that he would remember much. With his head cracked open, grey matter had spilled onto the floor.

I think I could have left it at that, could have walked away, but then I heard a familiar voice on the stairs behind me, turned to watch Angel running back upstairs.

"Fuck..."

It wasn't my intent to take them out, too, but a man in love is a feral creature, driven by a sultry grin, made hard by a tempting body, gone mad to know there were people still breathing who could threaten the woman that was his.

Not bothering to lighten my steps as I climbed those stairs, I listened to the frantic screaming, Angel trying to explain to Preston that his buddy was downstairs missing a head.

Rowan just killed Michael!

The dumb, fat fuck wouldn't believe her. Although, I couldn't blame him. To everybody in this house I was dead. They just didn't know I'd been reborn from the ashes. A monster. A shadow. An avenger.

Men.

How many times did I have to tell them to listen with their ears instead of thinking with their dicks?

Turning the corner I leaned against the doorframe, the bat in my hand dripping with blood and bits of skull, Preston's eyes rounding as big as fucking saucers in his pudgy, crimson cheeked head.

One glance down at his naked lap, and I'll be damned. The rumors were true. I wasn't sure you could even refer to that prick as a penis.

To my right, Angel was screaming, her back against a wall, fingers clutching over the towel she'd used to cover her naked body. Normally, it was a rule of mine to always respect a woman. But...she'd seen me.

Eating the distance on two long strides, I made her death quick, one swing like a pro hitting that ball right out of the park. *Pop...* Her skull was as thin as an eggshell.

You would think, based on the pitch of the screaming behind me, that another woman was in the room. Turning, I eyed the dumb fuck still frozen on the bed, a bark of laughter volleying from my throat because he hadn't thought to run.

"Please don't kill me! Please, man. No!"

He threw his arms up to shield his head, so I brought the bat down between his legs. Like a stuck pig, Preston squealed.

"Trust me, Buddy, with a dick like that, I'm doing you a favor. You and all the women in the world. Only dickless punks like to drug women so they can fuck them, Preston. It's about time someone teach you why it's wrong to take advantage of other people."

He tried to wiggle away, his hips not working quite right, and in my head I heard an old nursery rhyme. It's odd the things that come to you when you're in the middle of seriously fucking up someone's day.

"All around the..." Damn it. I always forgot that first part.

I stepped around the bed, lifted the bar above my head.

"The monkey chased the weasel..."

Preston wasn't a good enough sport to sing along. Just kept screaming and crying, as if that would do much good.

"The monkey thought it was all in good fun..."

Canting my head, I grinned. "Come on Preston, you know the last part."

The bat swung down against his head.

Pop!

Poor Preston. He was a really shitty weasel.

Oh well. My job here was finished. Every last asshole who thought he could lay a hand on my girl was now missing a few parts. It was time to let Rainey meet her demon.

Slowly, I lumbered down the stairs, made my way through the living room. Stepped over Michael's body and turned my head to see a pair of bleary eyes peering over at me.

"Rowan?"

Blinking a few times, Megan reached up to wipe the sleep from her eyes, her disbelief obvious. I sighed.

"I really wish you would have kept sleeping."

Like Angel, I made it quick. Alive one second, dead the next.

Her phone fell off the table next to my leg and I picked it up, thumbed the screen and clicked on the social media page that was left open.

Fuck, fuck, fuck, fuck, FUCK!

She'd posted several pictures of the party. Three had Rainey in the background. It looked like I wouldn't be taking Rainey away from this place. If the cops showed up and she was gone, they'd try to blame her for the murders. I could delete, but already, people had liked and commented. They knew Rainey was here.

I slipped the phone into my pocket and made my way down the hallway.

Only two sets of lungs remained breathing in the house, but if you remembered what I said about love, really there was one.

Every breath she took was mine.

Every beat of her heart a pulse in my chest.

Every thought in that beautiful head, a whisper against my ears.

Dropping the bat, I didn't bother to clean the blood from my skin before rounding the corner into the bedroom where she sat bound to the bed. Already a bruise was blooming over her cheek and jaw from where Michael had hit her. I felt the sting of it on my skin.

I took two steps into the room and she looked up.

"Hey, beautiful."

Rainey's blue eyes stared at me like a ghost floating within the ether. Lips parting, her head shook, a tear escaping one of those sapphire orbs. I wanted to kiss it from her skin, but with the blood on me, I couldn't touch her.

It was like fighting against a black hole. Everything about her reached out to pull me in, but to touch her would mean I couldn't let her go.

"Rowan."

One word. One name. A prayer, a song, a whisper.

"I've missed you," I said, my fingers clenching my palms because I couldn't touch her.

She laughed, the sound sad, so full of sorrow that it hurt my heart just to hear it. "I'm crazy, aren't I? Absolutely mad."

"No, Rainey. I'm the one who's mad. I just didn't realize how much until the day I left you."

She reached for me with the one hand she was able to free from the rope, her long fingers stretching forward. It was pure torture not to reach back.

"I have to go."

"No, Rowan, please don't-"

"Don't worry, Rainey. I'll find you again. Just go to sleep. I won't let you stay here for too long."

She sobbed when I walked from the room, not understanding that this parting wasn't forever.

Forever only applied to the promises I'd made.

Forever was the eternity I planned to give her.

CHAPTER THIRTY

Rainey - Present

Not all love stories begin with hearts and flowers. Mine didn't. Instead, mine started on a day when I'd been driven into the heart of another run down town, *a new start, a new day* that would end with ruined lives.

My love story began with a fifteen year old boy who'd looked across a chain link fence to see a girl sitting on her porch. The boy had waved, had smiled before stretching his long legs to walk on over, and introduce himself as the man I could never live without.

It was my fault for not believing him.

I wonder how many lives could have been saved if I'd only looked up into those big blue eyes and trusted they belonged to my savior.

"You ready to go?"

Tossing a few more large twigs and leaves over Justin's body, Rowan brushed his hands off on his jeans and turned to look at me. I stared down at the odd lump in the ground wondering how long it would take for someone to find him behind the abandoned house. He didn't deserve to die, but there wasn't much I could do about that. Not now. Not ever.

At least it hadn't been painful.

"Yeah, I'm ready."

Rowan stepped up to me, took my hand and pulled me against him. Eyes searching my face, he gripped my chin and tilted my head so he could inspect what was left of the bruise near my eye. Tenderly, he brushed his fingers over the skin, moving my hair aside to lean down and kiss it softly.

"I should raise Michael from the dead just to kill him all over again. Nobody touches my girl and gets away with it."

Remembering what I'd seen when the police led me from the house with a blanket wrapped over my body, I thought Rowan had done enough.

"I think we're done now, aren't we? We can finally leave?"

"In a couple weeks." Tilting his head toward the body, he said, "His absence will be noticed. They'll want to talk to you and find out what you know. Just play dumb, Rainey, and they'll go away eventually."

Hating that I'd just gotten him back and yet I was still trapped to a life that almost destroyed us both, I reached to cup my hands over his cheeks and bring his mouth to mine.

The way we kissed was poetry, a love forged in fire, two heartbeats pulsing as one, defying the odds we'd overcome to end up here. It was messy, our love, but anything worth having is never drawn within established boundaries and neat ordinary lines.

Not in the life we'd lived. Not with the foundation from which we'd sprung.

Rowan and I hadn't climbed mountains, scaled walls or jumped hurdles. No. We'd crawled on our bellies through brimstone and hellfire and had somehow survived the trauma. Our love story was a different beast, one filled with insanity, with heartache and misfortune.

Still, we survived, and that just goes to show that you should never look down on a person who the world will tell you is unworthy. You never know what that person is willing to do to survive.

Breaking the kiss, I wrapped my arms around him, my cheek pressed to his chest. "So, you're Graham Pike now. What's my name going to be?"

With his hand brushing down my hair, he laughed. "Whatever you want it to be. It'll be a hell of a lot better than Rainey Summer Day."

I grinned, the emotions hitting me all at once, a force so strong, I couldn't blink my eyes fast enough to keep the tears from falling.

"I love you, Rowan."

"Hey," he caught my face again, tilting it higher so he could search my eyes. "I'm tired of the crying." With the pad of his thumb, he wiped a tear away. "You're better than that."

Laughter shook my shoulders and I pressed my chest against his. "That's what you always say."

God, that smile. It always blinded me.

"You should have listened to me the first time."

"Live and learn, right?"

Shaking his head, Rowan led me by the hand around the house. Tucked inside the small garage, his motorcycle was propped up on the kickstand, a large machine of chrome, glass, and leather that reminded me of the one Paul used to ride.

Rowan lifted the garage door, climbed on the bike and backed it into the driveway with his feet. His eyes met mine as he reached out a hand to help me onto the seat behind him.

So warm, so strong, to feel his body against mine again was a miracle I could have never guessed would happen. This man was the beginning and end of my life. He was my shelter. My rock. The star that had swallowed me whole just to absorb me in its light.

Handing me a helmet, Rowan waited for me to put it on before starting the engine. It was a heavy rumble beneath me, my arms wrapping around his abdomen as he turned the front end and drove onto the street. Stopping suddenly, he glanced over his shoulder, tapped on my helmet and pointed up at a sky that was painted in shades of reds, orange and yellow.

I guess our love story wasn't that different from the rest after all.

The bike took off down the road and, together, we rode off into the sunset.

THE END

KEEP IN TOUCH

If you are interested in reading additional books by Lily White or would like to know when new books are being released, Lily White can be found on:
Facebook, Instagram and
Twitter

Join the Mailing List!

If you are interested in receiving email updates regarding additional books by Lily White or would like to know when new books are announced or being released, join the mailing list via this link.

http://eepurl.com/Onoeb

Join the Facebook Fan Group!

If you are interested in receiving exclusive previews for upcoming novels, or to participate in giveaways, join the fan group for Lily White Books.

FAN GROUP LINK

Follow Lily on BookBub!

https://www.bookbub.com/profile/lily-white

WEBSITE:
WWW.LILYWHITEBOOKS.COM

Made in United States
North Haven, CT
22 April 2024

51653892R00211